Taking   nd
looked down at the small child on the ground. Grotesque
didn't describe it properly. Bizarre? Maybe. Horrific—
definitely. Hanna Parker lay on her back with her arms
crossed in front, as if she were laid out for viewing at a
wake. Her body was by no means disfigured or in bad
shape. As a matter of fact, I couldn't see any signs of injury.
The first thing I noticed was the red ribbon tied in a bow
around her neck.

Hanna Parker was made up to look like a doll. Her face
had been painted white, with red circles on her cheeks
and a heavy amount of pink eye shadow over her closed
eyes. Black eyelashes had been drawn to give them a more
dramatic effect, and her lips were colored bright red. It
looked like her hair had even been curled. A red bow,
mirroring the one around her neck, sat prominently atop
her head. The killer had even brushed off and smoothed
out her clothes.

"Oh, dear God in heaven," I murmured, putting my
hands over my mouth.

Hanna's fingernails had also been painted bright red,
but that wasn't what drew my attention. It was the object
under her hand...

STACY DITTRICH

THE DEVIL'S CLOSET

LEISURE BOOKS NEW YORK CITY

A LEISURE BOOK®

October 2008

Published by

Dorchester Publishing Co., Inc.
200 Madison Avenue
New York, NY 10016

ISBN 10: 0-8439-6159-7
ISBN 13: 978-0-8439-6159-1

Printed in the United States of America.

10 9 8 7 6 5 4 3 2 1

Visit us on the web at www.dorchesterpub.com.

For Amy, Polly, and the others

ACKNOWLEDGMENTS

Launching CeeCee Gallagher and her adventurous co-workers couldn't have happened without some extremely special people. My agent, Claire Gerus, who became a long-lost sister, and my editor Don D'Auria—the two people who saw the authenticity of CeeCee and brought her to the pages. Olga Vezeris, my former editor, agent, and dear friend; *Mansfield News Journal* reporters Mark Caudill and Jamie Kinton, Richland County Coroner's Assistant Paul Jones, and former FBI Behavioral Specialist Roy Hazelwood. My personal fan club, book critics, and friends, Kim Shook, Kathy West, Michelle Alfrey, and Stacie Bailey for pawing through all the manuscripts, Mansfield Police Lieutenant Joseph Wendling—the greatest mentor and father, who led me through life with added gray hairs. Susan Staral, thanks for the encouragement, Mom. Candy Wendling and Larry Staral. To all of my "brothers and sisters" at the Richland County Sheriff's Department and Mansfield Police Department, your support meant the world; always stay safe. Mansfield Police Officer Brian Evans, we miss you—rest in peace. My beautiful daughters, Brooke and Jordyn, for the much-needed hugs. Lastly, my best friend and husband, Richard—it wouldn't have happened without you, most of all.

THE DEVIL'S
CLOSET

"I want to apologize to my family for putting them through this, for going against community standards."

—*The Doll Man*

"The last thing Polly saw before she died was Richard Allen Davis's eyes. The last thing Richard Allen Davis will see is my eyes, I hope."

—*Marc Klaas,*
father of murder victim Polly Klaas

PROLOGUE

September 12, 1985

Staring at the light invading from under the door, six-year-old Anna Kovinski wondered how long it would be until she could see her mommy and daddy again. The bad man told her earlier that if she was good and didn't make any noise, he would take her home. Anna pulled her knees close to her chest and hugged them tight. Wearing only her underwear, she wanted to get warm. The dark room was cold and damp. There were others in here with her. She could see the shapes of their heads, but they never moved. Regardless, Anna was comforted knowing she wasn't alone, and sometimes she talked to the others. Although they never answered her, it made the long hours go by easier. She couldn't remember how long she'd been here; it seemed like a long, long time. The day the bad man took her away from her family was a day she thought about a lot.

She was just walking her dog back and forth in front of the house, like she was supposed to. She wasn't allowed to go any farther. Mommy yelled at her to come inside because she was on the phone, but Anna didn't listen. She would've gone inside, but the bad man pulled up in his car with that cute puppy and asked Anna if she wanted to pet it. When she reached out to pet the puppy, the bad man grabbed her arm and pulled her into the car. It all happened so fast. By the time she thought to scream, she was already inside the car and the bad man was pulling away. She had instinctively let go of the leash that held her dog, Pepper, and he went running away. Now sitting here in the dark room, Anna wondered if Pepper was lost out there somewhere. She shouldn't have let go of him, but she couldn't help it. She needed both hands to try to free herself from the bad man. Anna wondered if she would ever see Pepper again, and she began to silently cry. She missed him. She also missed her parents, and she was scared. More scared than she'd ever been in her six years of life.

She must have cried herself to sleep but then something woke her up—it was footsteps. It seemed that it had been days since she had seen the bad man, and now it sounded like he was coming again. Anna expected he had food for her. She was hungry and thirsty. She'd wet her pants several times. She prayed this wouldn't make him angry.

As Anna heard the footsteps nearing the door, she scurried to the back of the small room, hiding so he wouldn't see her. The door opened, and the light flooded in, fully illuminating Anna at the back of the closet. The bad man saw her immediately.

"Hello, Anna. Are you ready to play dress up?"

CHAPTER ONE

Present Day

"We've got an Amber Alert!"

I looked up from my desk just in time to see Captain Naomi Kincaid poke her head in my office, inform me of the alert, then turn to rush down the hallway. Head of the major crimes division of the Richland Metropolitan Police Department, nestled within the hills of Mansfield, Ohio, she was my boss and had just given an order. I needed to get to the street immediately. A missing-child alert is one of the most serious situations any law-enforcement officer can, and most likely will, encounter.

Growing up in a family of police officers, I never thought to question any order from a commanding officer—something my father, a thirty-five-year veteran of the force, drilled into my head. But when it came to Naomi Kincaid, I had to bite my tongue. My uncles, Mike and Max, and my husband, Eric, were with the department. I've known nothing but the life of a police officer since I was a small child—it surrounded me and consumed the lives of my parents. I understood the risks of the life first-hand when my father's youngest brother, Matt, was shot on the job in the late 1970s. He survived, but he had to leave the force on disability.

I hope the kid is asleep in her basement, and this is all a mistake, I thought as I grabbed the keys to my unmarked detective car and headed out the door. I'm CeeCee Gallagher, a court-certified, expert detective in the areas of juvenile sex crimes and homicides. The few times I've responded to an Amber Alert, my adrenaline has gone into overdrive. Any crime involving a child as a victim always turns my stomach. Having two small daughters of my own, I could never imagine worse anguish than that of a parent who fears her child has been brutalized, molested—or worse, murdered.

Jumping into my car and turning on the police radio, I could hear a partial description of the missing child. I grabbed the radio mic and interrupted several other officers talking.

"Seven twenty-seven" (my unit number) "to seven hundred," (our communications center) "can you re-advise the description of the female?"

They relayed the information immediately. "Affirmative. Child is Hanna Parker, five years old. White female, approximately three feet, six inches tall, with blonde hair, wearing blue-jean shorts, a pink T-shirt with the words *Sesame Street* on the front, and yellow flip-flops."

"Seven hundred, where was the child last seen?"

"The child was last seen approximately thirty minutes ago playing in the front yard of her residence. Location is 1414 Royal Oak Drive. Mother advised she went inside to answer the phone. Child was gone when she returned. No suspects or vehicle descriptions. Do you copy, seven twenty-seven?"

"Copy direct," I answered. "Has the alert been issued in the media yet?"

"Negative."

I wasn't surprised. Although the Amber Alert was a good idea, it still had many glitches; specifically, the amount of time it takes to announce it to the public. We had to immediately determine it was an actual abduction, which was sometimes difficult and took time. Since there were no witnesses or suspects in the Hanna Parker disappearance, there was also the possibility that she simply wandered off. Regardless, we were to treat it as suspicious until we were proven wrong.

I tried not to panic over the current alert. The incident occurred on Royal Oak Drive in Royal Oak Estates. A wealthy, private allotment, their "major" crimes ordinarily consisted of arguments over property lines and cats in trees.

Turning into the allotment, I called our sex-offender registration clerk. I asked her to find the addresses of all the registered sex offenders living within a two-mile radius of the missing child's house. Captain Kincaid should have already taken care of this, but in circumstances like these you can't take anything for granted. Even though she had helped save my life a year ago, and got shot in the process, I still questioned her investigative skills. Naomi never had to work like the rest of us to get where she is. Bottom line is she's a good test taker, and she aces the promotional tests. Common sense, however, has never been her strong suit. I was pleasantly relieved to find that Kincaid had indeed already put in the request.

There were probably twenty to thirty sex offenders within the two-mile radius of the child's house, which would make the investigation extremely difficult.

Still not convinced this was an actual abduction and hoping for the best, I turned onto Royal Oak Drive. Uniformed officers and neighborhood residents were all over the place: in the front yards, backyards, sidewalks, garages, and on the street. They were searching houses, car trunks, and garage refrigerators and freezers. Police canines had their noses in the grass, sniffing around the house, attempting to find a track. Other officers were trying to find any witnesses in the neighborhood.

You couldn't miss the house. There were about ten marked police cruisers in the driveway and street. Before I parked my car and got out, I could see Captain James Norris, head of the uniformed road patrol, standing on the front porch talking to several citizens. He saw me walking up the driveway.

"I'm glad you're here, CeeCee. We've got nothing so far," he said.

"Is Coop here yet?" I asked, referring to Detective Jeff Cooper, my best friend in the bureau. Coop had also played an integral part in preventing my demise last year when he, along with Naomi and an FBI agent, shot my captors. There was something solid and comforting about Coop. His dark hair contrasted with his light complexion and blue eyes, and his stocky build was meant for the jeans and T-shirts he wore. The perfect class clown, he wore his emotions on his sleeve. There was never a question as to his opinions. His face said it all. You always knew where you stood.

"He's inside with the mother. As you can imagine, she's a wreck."

"Any custody problems? Where's the father?" I asked, scanning the front of the mammoth house before me.

"He's on his way from Cleveland. He's some bigwig eye surgeon at the Cleveland Clinic."

"Hopefully, we find her before he gets here. I'm assuming the house was thoroughly searched, kitchen cabinets, dryer, laundry baskets, and all?" I already knew the answer since Captain Norris was here, but had to ask anyway.

"Of course."

I watched as he got into his marked SUV and pulled away. I had to mentally prepare myself to go inside the house, knowing the mother was panic stricken. It took a conscious effort in situations like this to keep myself from appearing rattled.

Taking a deep breath, I opened the door and was barraged by screams and sobs emanating from the thirty-something attractive blonde sitting on the couch in the living room. Several neighbors or family members were seated around her, and Coop was standing in the middle of the room. Undeniably, she needed to calm down before we could accomplish anything. I hated to be the bad guy, knowing the mother had every right to be out of control, but something had to be done. We were losing valuable time.

I walked directly to Corrine Parker, the mother, and knelt in front of her. Out of the corner of my eye, I saw the dread on Coop's face, aware I was going to do something but not knowing what. The woman didn't seem to notice me until I grabbed her shoulders and gave them a slight shake.

"Mrs. Parker! Please. You need to try to calm down."

She looked at me and let out a walloping scream, her spit spraying me in the face. I hated the thought of having to slap her in front of all these people. Instead, I grabbed her chin and forced her to look at me.

"Mrs. Parker, you need to compose yourself and focus. If you want to help Hanna, take a deep breath and look at me. Now." My voice was soothing, but stern.

From the expressions on their faces, everyone near her was appalled at my actions, but I didn't care. They weren't my problem—finding Hanna Parker was.

Corrine Parker began to settle down, wiping her eyes, taking deep breaths, and using the tissue offered to blow her nose. It took several minutes before she finally looked at me and spoke.

"Do you want to tell me who the hell you are?"

She was agitated, but anger can be good sometimes. It takes one's mind off their other emotions.

"Mrs. Parker, I'm Detective CeeCee Gallagher with the Richland Metropolitan Police Department, major crimes division. I apologize for being somewhat harsh, but we need you focused and thinking as clearly as possible. There are a lot of questions you might be able to answer that could help us find Hanna."

She blew her nose again, grabbing another tissue to wipe off the black mascara that had run down her face.

"She just *vanished*!" Tears resurfaced, and it looked like she was going to lose it again, so I had to redirect her quickly.

"Mrs. Parker, tell me who you saw outside while you and Hanna were in the front yard before you went in to answer the phone."

"I already told that captain—*nobody*! Nobody was around! No one mowing their grass, getting their mail, nothing! Melissa Brewer lives across the street and took her son to preschool, but that was like, maybe ten minutes before my phone rang."

Coop was already on his way out the door to find Melissa Brewer. Next, I began to ask her about the days and weeks prior to today, and whether there were any suspicious cars, prank phone calls, or anything else unusual.

"No, nothing." She hiccuped. "My husband is a doctor, an ophthalmologist, and I stay at home with Hanna."

I moved on quickly. "Mrs. Parker, has your husband had any medical malpractice suits or denied worker's compensation claims recently? Does he discuss those types of things with you?"

"Yes, he would, but I haven't heard about anything. Nothing that would make someone so mad they would steal my child! He should be here soon, and you can ask him then."

"Mrs. Parker, try to think of anything you can that will help. And please, stay here. Whatever you do, don't leave. I'll be back shortly."

CHAPTER TWO

I met Coop in the front yard after he had finished talking to Melissa Brewer.

"Well?"

"Nothing. She left to take her son, Austin, to preschool, forgot his book bag, and came back. But she didn't see a single, living, breathing soul the entire time she was in the neighborhood. She said she was in such a hurry to get the book bag, she didn't pay attention to whether Hanna was still out in the yard. After Hanna turned up missing, she ran and got Austin out of school right away."

"You'll need to get the department shrink or victims' advocate here to prepare the Parkers for reunification at best, and death at worst. Also, don't forget to let all the family members know that every psychic and fruit loop from here to Cincinnati might be calling."

Coop nodded, and I suddenly had a thought.

"When Mrs. Brewer came back to get her son's bag, did she take him in the house with her or leave him in the car?"

"I didn't ask since I was trying to get her to nail down everything she could remember. You think the kid could have seen something? By the way, that kid is really cute, and Mom isn't too shabby looking either."

I was already heading toward Melissa Brewer's house, and Coop started to follow. A woman peered out the front window as we approached the door, which she opened before we knocked.

"Yes?"

"Ms. Brewer, I'm Detective Gallagher. Detective Cooper just informed me of the conversation he had with you, and I had a few more questions."

"This is the third time. There's nothing else I could possibly tell you—other than I'm terrified for my son and heartbroken for the Parkers!"

"When you came back to get your son's book bag, did you leave him in the car or take him inside with you?"

"I left him in the car." She quickly added, "I was only in the house a few seconds."

It was obvious she was lying—I could tell immediately. But why would she lie? There was no evidence pointing toward her or involving her in any way. She fidgeted for several minutes as I looked around at the house, at her, and at her car. Then, the reason she was lying came to me. I was a mother too, and I could've knocked myself in the head for being so stupid.

"Ms. Brewer, if you're worried about us looking at you for child endangerment for something as minor as leaving your son in the car when you ran into your house, please don't worry. I've left my four-year-old in the car for a few minutes to run inside my own house before. It's really nothing to stress over as long as he's secure in his car seat and you have the car keys. Now, let me ask again, how long were you inside the house?"

She put her hands on her face and let out a deep breath.

"When I came in, I grabbed his book bag and started for the door, but the phone rang. It was my mother asking me to schedule something, so I had to look at my calendar, coordinate with her, and pencil it in. It was five minutes tops. I swear."

It was the following answer that presented the first hope of the day. I asked if she parked in the driveway. She said she was in a hurry and had merely parked along the curb in front of the house before running inside. The direction her car was facing would have given her son a clear view of the Parkers' front yard.

"Where's your son now?"

"He's taking a nap. I just laid him down when the other detective left," she said apprehensively, the frown lines deepening in her face.

"Please, bring him down here. I need to talk to him."

Melissa initially looked like she wanted to argue, but apparently decided against it.

I was good at interviewing children. My years spent investigating juvenile sex crimes required me to interview hundreds of them. If Melissa's son, Austin, saw anything today while he was waiting in the car, I would find out what. Hearing the cries of a small child, I sympathized with Melissa for a brief moment, knowing what a horror it is to wake a four-year-old in the middle of a nap, an act that would leave the child crying and whining for the rest of the day.

Coop was right. Austin Brewer was adorable, with brown hair and large brown eyes, which he was rubbing furiously. His round, chubby face was scrunched up, and his fists were clenched, not happy that his dreams of teddy bears, candy, and puppies were interrupted. Melissa set Austin down in front of me, and I bent over so I could be at his eye level.

"Hi, Austin. My name is CeeCee, and I'm a police officer. I'm sorry I had to wake you up from your nap. You were pretty tired, weren't you?"

He nodded slightly, while grabbing on to Melissa's pant leg. I took my badge off my waistband and offered it to him.

"Here's my badge. Do you want to hold it?"

Austin stayed in the safety zone of his mother's legs for a few minutes before reaching out and taking the badge. He broke out into a smile while he looked at it.

"Now, Austin, I have a very important job for you, and, if you're okay with it, I'll pin my badge on your shirt and make you an honorary police officer. What you'll have to do is go into the other room with me and help us catch a bad guy. Would you like that?"

"What's oniwary?" he asked.

"Hon-or-ary. It means you would be a very special little policeman."

"Okay!" He nodded furiously.

He was thrilled. He threw my badge back at me, puffed out his chest, and pulled his shirt out, wanting his badge. After I pinned the badge on Austin's shirt, I made him hold up his hand while I swore him in as the youngest police officer in history.

With Melissa's permission, Austin and I headed into the family room and sat on the floor in front of his toy police cars and fire trucks. I began asking Austin all the familiar questions to make him comfortable with me: "What's your favorite television show? What's your favorite toy?" These were a few. I noticed a pack of crayons on a play picnic table near us, which I grabbed for my next series of questions. I held up each crayon and asked Austin to tell me the colors. Then I let him color on a blank piece of paper nearby. After that, I asked him to count to the highest number he could, which was twelve. Then I felt confident to start asking Austin about the disappearance of Hanna Parker.

"Austin, do you remember when Mommy forgot your book bag today before preschool?"

"Yup—she was drivin' fast!"

"When Mommy went inside to get your book bag and left you in the car, do you remember seeing anyone outside?"

"Jus' Hanna."

My heart began to beat a little faster as I crawled closer to Austin and took his right hand.

"Austin, do you remember what Hanna was doing when you saw her?"

"She was playin' with the mailman," he said, pulling his hand from mine and picking up a red crayon to color a picture of a fire truck.

The mailman? At first I was shocked until I realized what Austin was saying.

"Austin, do you mean he had a uniform on?"

"Yup, the mailman."

I grabbed the dark blue, light blue, and gray crayons from the pack and held them up.

"Do any of these crayons look like the color of the mailman's uniform?"

He looked up from his impending masterpiece, irritated that I had interrupted his creative streak. He quickly grabbed the light blue crayon from my hand and shoved it forward.

"What did you see Hanna do with the mailman?"

"She got into his car and they drived away."

That was it. Calmly, but with an extreme sense of urgency, I went through the crayons with Austin to find out the man's race, hair color, and the color of his car. Using Austin's play cars, I learned the man was driving a brown full-sized van. Satisfied that there wasn't anything more to get from Austin, I got up to leave, taking my badge back and replacing it with a junior deputy sticker badge. That made his day.

As I grabbed Coop on my way out the door, Captain Kincaid was in the front yard walking toward us. No matter how much she irritated me, I had to admit Naomi Kincaid was a striking presence: tall and blonde, her hair always in an elegant chignon or bun, her blue eyes sparkling. She might look severe sometimes in her classic matching slacks and shirts, but she managed to make an impact as a beautiful woman who looked like she meant business.

"I was just looking for you two. Corrine Parker said you guys came to Melissa's house. Did you find anything?"

"We've got a description of the suspect and need to get it out on the air immediately. He'll be a white male wearing a light blue uniform, maybe even coveralls from a local factory. He's got dark brown hair, tall, and drives a full-sized brown van. That's all I've got. This is unquestionably a stranger abduction."

"Damn it!" she said. "We're almost at two hours."

Kincaid started walking quickly, almost jogging, to her unmarked SUV to give the dispatcher and other listening officers the description of the suspect and his vehicle.

I was filling Coop in on my interview with Austin Brewer when Kincaid came back.

"They're getting it out. The juvenile detectives and uniformed officers have the sex-offender listings and are knocking on doors right now. But I don't anticipate this guy went home."

"I doubt it. Let's contact all the uniform shops and dry cleaners to see which businesses or factories wear a light blue, coverall kind of uniform."

"I'm on it," Coop said, heading toward his car.

"We also need to ask Mrs. Parker and her neighbors if anyone has had any plumbing, electrical, contracting, or landscaping work done. Maybe someone will recognize the van. The suspect has been watching Hanna and knew exactly when to take her," I suggested.

"Do you suppose he saw Austin Brewer?" Kincaid asked.

"I don't know, but just to be on the safe side, we need to have Melissa Brewer keep a tight leash on him. At least until we know more."

"Consider it done. By the way, as if you didn't know, you're the lead investigator on this case."

"I kind of assumed that. Right now, I need to figure out where to go from here." Kincaid was already walking back to the Brewer house.

There were rumblings coming from news helicopters making their way to the area. Something as serious as an abducted child was one of the few times I welcomed the local media. Although our department had its own helicopter in the air searching for Hanna, the news helicopters were extra eyes. The more help the better.

I walked to my car and called the dispatchers to ask them to find any reports of stolen brown vans in the last six months within the county. The dispatcher I spoke with was less than pleased. They already had enough going on with putting out the Amber Alert and monitoring all radio traffic. My request would take an enormous amount of time. Their resistance was anticipated, and I quickly thanked the dispatcher before hanging up.

I called my husband, Eric, and told him I was going to be late. He had already assumed this by watching the news. Eric is a uniformed officer with the department and usually works on the night shift. Currently, he's training a new officer on the afternoon shift, but today was his day off.

"How late do you think you'll be, hon?"

"No idea. Where are my two beautiful girls?"

"They're next door at Chloe's playing 'run from the bad guy.' They saw the news."

"Fabulous. I'll see you soon. Love you."

Over the next five to six hours I walked miles. Nothing else could be done until I got all the necessary information back. I assisted the uniforms, other detectives, and civilians, all out searching for Hanna. We looked in drainpipes, under fallen trees, in the woods, in the trees themselves, under parked cars, porches, garbage cans, Dumpsters, and everywhere else we could think of. By the time I got home, it was very late and I was exhausted. Kincaid gave me a maximum four-hour break to rest, during which she would take over. Cases like this don't stop. Not one person stops until the child is found.

CHAPTER THREE

The next day was spent going over the list of sex offenders with the other detectives in the office. We were targeting anyone whose former victims were girls between the ages of four and eight. Since we had over four hundred registered sex offenders in our county, this was not a quick task. Now that the rest of the country had the story, our parking lot was filling up with news vans, campers, reporters, cameramen, satellites, and the like. A lot of these people knew my name since my near-death shooting last year had made national news. At the time, I'd been deemed a hero for uncovering one of the largest drug operations ever, at a place referred to as Murder Mountain. This latest case couldn't have been more different, and we were under serious pressure, which didn't help. Dr. Nathan Parker was adding to that pressure by standing in front of the media. He was informing them that he didn't think we were doing enough, or were competent enough, to find his daughter.

Sheriff L. Richard Stephens and Chief Paul Raines, numbers one and two of the department, came into my office later that afternoon for a briefing. Naomi Kincaid was in tow. The sheriff was clearly under great stress, but his face never showed anything other than kindness, as did his voice. A pleasant-looking man in his fifties with thinning brown hair and a growing middle, the sheriff rarely showed concern. It was unsettling to see him so upset.

"What have we got, CeeCee?"

"Nothing. Zilch. Right now I'm just waiting for dispatch to get through the list of stolen cars to see if there were any vans matching the suspect's."

"There's nothing else we can do right now?" the chief chimed in, as frustrated as the rest of us.

"I don't think so," I answered. "We've got over one hundred uniforms and civilians searching through every sex offender's house in the county, and neighboring counties are doing the same. The Parkers' phone logs have come back, and there's nothing suspicious or helpful on those either. The kidnapper isn't stupid. It seems he's had this planned and taken every possibility into account."

"CeeCee," the sheriff began, "you're the one who knows how these sickos think. Can you come up with anything?"

"Not really. I don't know enough at this point. If it is a sex offender, which would be an easy assumption, most of them believe they're stronger and smarter than the cops. They get off on knowing we don't have a clue as to who they are, and that's an important part of their fantasy. But what I'm counting on is the grand finale of the whole fantasy. They want to actually sit across from a detective and tell him or her how smart he thinks he is and how much he got away with. Some of them want to get caught just for that reason—to tell the cops how smart he is. It may be one hell of a long shot, but hopefully, this animal thinks like that."

"But you're not sure," Kincaid added.

"Chances are very slim that's the case. There's never a guarantee with anything. Naomi, you know that."

Everyone remained silent. The sheriff leaned forward as he let out a deep breath. He began to speak when I noticed

Coop standing in my doorway. Everyone else followed my gaze to see Coop, who looked like he'd come down with the flu; his face was a light shade of green. I was a little concerned. Coop does not usually look unsettled.

"What's the matter?"

He put his hand on the door frame, as if he needed it to maintain his balance.

"We found Hanna Parker."

CHAPTER FOUR

He whistled quietly while he washed the floor in preparation for his new visitor. Vigorously, he wiped away the memory of the last one. It was only fair; he had done the same for her and the one before her. Only the best for his special guests: this was their temple, a tribute to them, and it needed to shine. He wanted to make them feel welcome. He wanted them to feel as one, a string of brightly lit lights, each attached to the other, lights that would shine for eternity. . . .

My stomach churned. I didn't need to be a law-enforcement genius to know that Hanna Parker was dead. Coop's face said it all. The sheriff was first to regain composure.

"Where did they find her?"

"An Amish family located her in their field, up in the northern part of the county. The crime lab and the coroner are already on their way, so we'd better get going."

"Do her parents or the media know yet?" I asked Coop.

"Not yet. Captain Norris and the department chaplain are on the way to tell the Parkers. As for the media, it's just a matter of time."

"And they're sure it's her?" Captain Kincaid asked, one of her more brilliant questions.

"I can't think of any other blonde five-year-olds wearing a pink *Sesame Street* T-shirt that would turn up dead in an Amish cornfield, can you?"

"Just asking," she said, a little embarrassed.

Well deserved, if you asked me. She was one of the few people who could be counted on to come up with the most dim-witted questions.

"Let's get going," the chief said, already heading toward the door.

"Damn it all to hell," the sheriff mumbled, expressing everyone's sentiments quite accurately.

I gathered my bag and notebooks before following the others. I wanted nothing more than to get into my car and drive straight home. I can't bear seeing a dead child, especially one that's been murdered. People weren't meant to see things like that—it wasn't in the grand plan. It doesn't matter who you are, a civilian or a cop, looking down on the body of a dead child ruins you mentally for years, if not for life. One can understand and accept the often fragile psychological stability of a police officer who has seen many such cases. Like I have. It's worse when the victims, like Hanna Parker, are female and close to the age of my two daughters. My youngest, Isabelle, is four years old. Selina, my oldest, is ten. Times like this, I need to flip the off switch in my head in order to do my job.

When I pulled into the driveway of the Amish farmhouse, the family was standing on the front porch. I would start with them, but first I needed to get a long-distance view of the body and crime scene. The rear of the house looked out over the cornfield. About two football fields away stood a group of people and several white vans. I guess it was a good thing the field had been recently harvested, or it could've been a while before she was found. Of course, there was also the awful thought of the combine cropping through the field and over Hanna Parker.

Notebook in hand, I went back to the Amish family to get a more detailed statement.

I introduced myself to Eli Zimmerman and asked him to tell me what happened. He began speaking in a thick German accent, one I could relate to since my husband is from Germany. Eric spent only his first year there, and you'd never know it by talking to him. His parents, on the other hand, sound like they're straight from the old country. Even after all these years, I have a hard time understanding their English. My mother's parents were from Germany, so I learned a few words growing up. Mainly obscenities from my grandfather.

Eli said they had been at another farm helping to build a barn since early that morning and had gotten home only about an hour and a half ago. It was while walking out to his barn that he saw something in the field and he went to investigate. When he discovered the body, he ran back to his house and had his son bicycle to the nearest Mennonite farm to call the police.

"I tell him, *Geh jepzt! Mach schnell!*"

Even with my very limited German vocabulary I knew that meant *Go now! Hurry!* Eli said he could see it was a body from ten feet away and didn't want to get any closer. It was dark when they had left in the morning, so he didn't know if the body was out there at that point or not. He answered "no" to the customary questions about any suspicious cars, people, and the like.

After my conversation with the Zimmermans, I was walking back to my car to confirm their account at the Mennonite farm when Coop yelled from the side of the house.

"CeeCee, get over here and look at this."

"It's really not necessary, Coop. You don't need me out there," I said, opening my car door. Coop promptly shut it before I had the chance to jump in.

"Yes, we do. I can't explain it, it's . . ." He paused. "It's grotesque. I've never seen anything like it, and you might be able to give a little insight. I know you don't like dead kids. None of us do, but whoever did this is sick, very sick, and he needs to be caught. Please, CeeCee?"

Coop always knew how to lay a guilt trip on me with nothing but a successful outcome. I took a deep breath and prepared myself.

"Fine, let's go," I groaned.

As we walked through the field, an impending sense of dread filled me the closer we got to the body. Oh, how I hated this. Nearing the small, pink and white lump that lay on the ground, I felt my stomach give a quick flip. I instinctively shut my eyes. Taking another deep breath, I opened my eyes, and looked down at the small child on the ground.

Grotesque didn't describe it properly. Bizarre? Maybe. Horrific—definitely. Hanna Parker lay on her back with her arms crossed in front, as if she were laid out for viewing at a wake. Her body was by no means disfigured or in bad shape. As a matter of fact, I couldn't see any signs of injury. The first thing I noticed was the red ribbon tied in a bow around her neck. Fighting back tears, I bent down and crossed myself: a subconscious act from my Catholic upbringing. I looked at the grotesqueness that Coop was referring to.

Hanna Parker was made up to look like a doll. Her face had been painted white, with red circles on her cheeks and a heavy amount of pink eyeshadow over her closed eyes. Black eyelashes had been drawn to give them a more dramatic effect, and her lips were colored bright red. It looked like her hair had even been curled. A red bow, mirroring the one around her neck, sat prominently atop her head. The killer had even brushed off and smoothed out her clothes.

"Oh, dear God in heaven," I murmured, putting my hands over my mouth.

Hanna's fingernails had also been painted bright red, but that wasn't what drew my attention. It was the object under her hand.

"What's she holding?" I asked Coop.

"I don't know. Let me grab a lab tech to lift her hand."

I watched silently as the crime lab technician held out a small, white plastic doll shoe that had been under Hanna's right hand. Coop looked confused. "Is that a baby shoe?"

"No, it's a doll shoe," I said, noticing that by now the sheriff, Kincaid, and others had joined us.

"It's a little big for a doll's shoe, don't you think?" Kincaid asked.

"I believe it comes from one of those My Size dolls. My girls have them. They're anywhere from two to three feet tall—I had one as a kid," I said, leaning in for a closer look.

The lab tech turned the shoe over, and sure enough, *My Size* was stamped on the bottom.

"Does anyone know if she had one of those or was playing with it when she disappeared?" Coop asked.

"I don't think so. Her mother probably would've said something, but we should double-check anyway. I strongly believe it's all connected, and the shoe has something to do with the way she's made up. If it doesn't belong to Hanna Parker, it is, under any circumstance, a key piece of evidence."

We watched as the lab technician carefully placed the shoe in an evidence bag before taking it to the crime lab van. Processing the scene was almost finished, so there was no reason to stick around. Kincaid had already confirmed the Zimmermans' story with the Mennonite family.

"CeeCee," the sheriff began as he stood by my car, "I just got off the phone with the chief. No surprise, but the media's gotten ahold of the story. Frankly, I figured it would be sooner than this the way those vultures are. I'd as soon kick a couple of them in the teeth the way they act, like this is a new, up-and-coming true-crime novel rather than a dead little girl." He paused. "You want to do it?"

"No, sir, that's why you get the big bucks." I got into my car to leave.

I was never good at dealing with the media, so I decided to take the back way into the station. I watched out my office window while the sheriff, who arrived just after I did, gave his statement to the mob of reporters and cameras.

"Ladies and gentlemen," he began loudly, "as most of you are aware, approximately four hours ago, this agency received a report of a body found in a cornfield north of the city. The body appears to be that of a small child. At this time, I am unable to confirm that the body is Hanna Parker's. Once the body has been positively identified and the family contacted, I will give you another statement. Until then, I would appreciate it if you would wind down a little. We need to be able to perform our duties efficiently and effectively. Thank you."

The sheriff promptly turned around and walked away, ignoring the media's pleas for more information. Since I'd heard enough, I closed my window to muffle the loud sounds of commotion.

After the media began to thin out, I called Captain Norris to see how the Parkers were doing. Understandably, not good. An ambulance team had to be called to their home to sedate Corrine Parker. Captain Norris was still at the scene, so I asked him how Dr. Parker was.

"He's angry, CeeCee—pissed off, bitter, slinging insults, the whole lot. Right now, he's saying it's our fault because we didn't handle it right and find her fast enough."

I wasn't feeling too peachy myself. I always wonder if

there's something I missed, something else I could've done. It's never hard to feel guilty.

"I'm sorry to hear that. Grief will bring out the worst of emotions. Since he probably won't want to hear any pertinent questions from you, would you try to find a family member who spends a lot of time there and ask them a question for me?"

"I'm all ears."

"Ask if Hanna had a My Size doll. It's like a life-size doll for kids, and they've been around for years. They're about three feet tall. If she had one, try to find out if she was playing with it when she was abducted."

"Will do." He sighed in the phone. "It was pretty bad up there, huh?"

"You can't even imagine, Captain. Let me know ASAP when you find out about the doll, please."

Just a brief image of Hanna's body in my head made my heart skip. I still felt an overwhelming urge to rush home, hug my kids, and never let them out of my sight.

CHAPTER FIVE

Looking as haggard as I felt, Coop walked in while I was hanging up the phone. He slumped into one of the chairs in front of my desk, let out a long breath, and rubbed his forehead.

"I need about ten shots of whiskey."

I smiled. There were many days when Coop and I ran to the nearest watering hole after work.

"Any word?" Not that I expected a yes, but I like to hope.

"Nope. What a sick freak! Man, if I catch this guy, I hope I don't end up snapping his neck."

"So now what?"

"I don't know. I need some time to think."

At that moment, I knew he was about to change topics by the wide smile that emerged on his face.

"Hey, off the subject, have you seen Eric's new cub?"

Coop was referring to the rookie Eric was training. I knew the officer was a female, but I hadn't given it much thought. At least until now, when I saw the smirk on Coop's expressive face. Bill Sinclair, another detective, was on his way into my office when he heard Coop's question.

"Whoooee! I sure have! Man, oh man, they didn't have rookies like that when I was in uniform. She is smokin' hot!"

"Is that right?" I felt my face turn red, and I started to shuffle papers on my desk.

Coop chimed in. "I don't know about her face, but she's got a hell of a rack on her and an ass that would stop a space shuttle. What's her name anyway?"

"Jordan Miller," Bill answered. "I think she's around twenty-five—just a pup."

"She may have a nice rack now," I said, unable to maintain my silence, "but I'm sure when she's my age, they'll be hanging to her knees." I said this, as if being in my early thirties put me in my golden years.

"What's this?" Coop's brow arched. "The famous Cee-Cee Gallagher getting jealous over a little rookie? That's not like you." He tried to keep a straight face.

"I'm hardly jealous," I lied. I'd be damned if I let them see me getting in an uproar over someone I don't even know. Pride is one of my strong suits. "Anyway, let's get back to business. You got anything for me, Bill?"

Bill, like everyone else so far, had nothing. Kincaid joined us for a while since she did have some positive news, so we were able to plan our next course of action. A stolen brown van had been located in the southern part of the county. It appeared to be our suspect's van, according to the uniforms that found it.

"The uniforms contacted the van's owner and talked to him briefly, but they said he didn't raise any red flags. He seemed legitimate," Naomi related.

"I'll still have to talk to him, which is fine. I need something to do right now anyway," I said.

"Dr. Parker is still raising hell over the murder, placing the blame on our incompetence. He's already called the FBI, and now they've called me *twice* to offer their valuable assistance." She sighed.

"This isn't their jurisdiction," I snapped. "This is local. I hope you didn't ask them to come down here."

"Relax, CeeCee," Kincaid answered. "I haven't decided yet, but if Dr. Parker keeps this up, the sheriff may be forced to bring them in. Remember, this is about finding a child's killer. Not feeding our egos."

"Thanks for the ethics lesson."

Kincaid started shaking her head and walked out, followed by Bill. She could still incense me like no one else—a talent I'm sure she was proud of since she knew how I felt about her.

"Nothing will ever change between you two," Coop said, putting his hands behind his head and stretching in his chair.

"It will if she wakes up one morning no longer a twit, which is highly unlikely."

Naomi Kincaid was a beautiful woman by most standards, but had the brain and common sense of an empty beer can. After Coop left, Captain Norris called. An aunt who frequently babysat Hanna Parker said she didn't have a My Size doll. She knew that specifically because every time Hanna watched a commercial for the dolls on television, she always commented on how she thought they were "scary looking." I took all the information on the aunt from Captain Norris, before leaning back in my chair. I didn't understand the relationship between the doll shoe and Hanna Parker, and it bothered me. I knew the shoe was the key.

When I looked at the clock, I realized Eric should be somewhere in the department getting ready for his shift, so I called his cell phone. No answer. While I tried to act like the comments about Jordan Miller didn't bother me, deep down they did. Surrendering to the disturbed mind-set of a jealous wife, I assumed Jordan would be in the female locker room gearing up for her shift with Eric. I had been meaning to take my bulletproof vest out of my locker and figured there was no better time than the present. A quick check in my compact mirror made sure all of my makeup was in place. I was anticipating a showdown and had to look my best. Onward, to face the enemy. I headed to the locker room.

Eric and I went through a pretty rocky time last year after I had been kidnapped and beaten. We were both trying to heal the wounds, so I needed to deal with Jordan to confirm to myself that my marriage was still solid.

The female locker room was in the basement, four floors down. When I stepped off the elevator, I could feel my nerves tighten up, which really angered me. I'm not one to be insecure around another woman, but I suppose Coop and Bill's comments got to me. I already had a plan as to how I would scope out my competition. When I got to the locker-room door, I took a deep breath, stood straight and confident, and walked in.

There was only one other woman in the locker room, and I immediately knew it had to be Jordan Miller. She was gorgeous. She was standing in front of the mirror in her locker, whipping her long dark hair into a bun. She wasn't very tall, maybe five feet four, and probably weighed 115 pounds at her heaviest. By the time she finished fussing with her hair, I was nearby with my locker open, fumbling around inside, pretending to look for something.

"Hi there!" I heard from behind me.

I turned halfway, looked her up and down, and gave a small, fake smile. I was always good at being condescending without saying a word, when it was needed. Like it was now. I muttered a quiet "hi" to her sparkling white teeth, violet-colored eyes, and deep dimples in her

cheeks before turning back to my locker. I couldn't believe I was trembling a little. This girl had me worried,
but there was no way I would let that show.

"Oh my gosh, are you Detective Gallagher?" She kept
talking before I could answer. "I read all about you in the
papers last year when you busted up that drug ring and stuff!
I know you won't believe this, but you're one of the reasons
I went to the police academy and became a cop. I admire
you a lot." She held out her hand. "By the way, I'm Jordan
Miller. I'm sure you know Eric is my training officer."

Maybe it was the fact that she said "Eric," instead of
"your husband" that bothered me, but something did. I
reached out and shook her hand, quickly.

"Thank you, Jordan. It's nice to meet you. I knew Eric
was training someone right now, but I never asked who.
We don't talk about work much at home."

"Well, I can only hope to be half the officer you are. I
think you're amazing, and everyone around here talks
about you like you're a celebrity. They say, 'She's beautiful, tough, and smart as hell.' Everyone agrees."

"I wouldn't go that far, but thank you again. How's your
training going?" I asked, opening up my locker wider, revealing a large picture of me and Eric with the girls; stak-
ing my claim. Just in case she had any thoughts . . .

Jordan looked at the family picture with particular
interest. One point for me.

"My training is great," she began, still eyeing the
photo. "There's so much to learn sometimes I don't know
if I'll ever be able to remember it all. It's overwhelming."
She paused. "But Eric makes it easier. He helps me right
along and makes me feel like I can really do this job. I
certainly couldn't ask for a better training officer."

And a point for her side. I grabbed my vest, slamming
my locker door shut.

"It was nice to meet you, Jordan. Good luck." I headed for the door.

The entire situation hadn't gone well, at least for me. I knew I wasn't very nice, but that was precisely the point. The ideal objective was to make her feel small and unimportant, which I did. But this pettiness didn't make me feel better. Any normal, living man who would have to ride around in a car for eight hours a day with a girl like Jordan Miller would be one happy, and horny, man. I don't care who they are or how happily married, men are only human. I'm realistic.

I desperately needed to get my head back in the Hanna Parker investigation and off Jordan Miller. I checked with the crime lab to see if they had any preliminary tests back. Luck was with me.

As suspected, Hanna Parker had been sexually assaulted. But there was no seminal fluid found anywhere on her body, inside her, or on any of her clothing, which was very strange. They did find traces of drywall on her dress, but before I asked, the lab technician told me there had been drywall in the back of the stolen van, so that was to be expected. An analysis for fibers or other microscopic material hadn't come back yet, and they would let me know as soon as it did.

After leaving the lab, I went back up to my office and found Coop waiting.

"I forgot to tell you earlier, we checked into the blue jumpsuit thing. There are four factories in the county whose employees wear blue jumpsuits: a total of twenty-six hundred people. We're going to start cross-referencing every one of them against the four hundred registered sex offenders, but as you can imagine, it's gonna take a hell of a long time."

"Fantastic," I said under my breath.

"CeeCee, can you come up with any type of profile at all on this guy? I know you're not a profiling expert, but you usually nail it regardless."

"I can't come up with anything but the obvious. A white male, anywhere from age forty to late fifties, very organized, and I believe obsessive compulsive. Look how meticulous he was in brushing the dirt off Hanna's clothes and making them neat. His house is probably spotless. There's also her hair and the makeup. Maybe the guy has gender issues? I don't know, Coop. Maybe Kincaid is right and we *should* ask the FBI for additional support."

Both Coop and I remained quiet for a few minutes, deep in thought. How I hated hitting a brick wall. Normally, there's always something to check out, but when it stops, that's when the case gets difficult. We had to be missing something.

"CeeCee," Coop said finally, "I was trying to figure out a way to tell you, but I don't know how other than to just spit it out. Kincaid just spoke with the FBI a few minutes ago. The sheriff had talked to them earlier and set it all up—they're coming. There is no other option."

"So? That's fine. I'm not *that* upset about it, for crying out loud."

"I have a feeling you will be after what I have to tell you." He paused before dropping the bomb. "Michael is one of the agents. He'll be here tomorrow."

Direct hit. I stopped breathing. And on top of that, my heart started beating so rapidly I thought I was having a heart attack that very minute. I don't know why it never crossed my mind that Michael could be one of the agents coming.

Special Agent Michael Hagerman, the man who helped the others save my life a year ago, was also the man who nearly cost me my marriage. And he was coming back.

Michael and I had worked on the infamous drug and homicide case together last year, and grew more than close during it. We kissed several times, but it never went any further physically. Unfortunately, our emotions did. Michael was deeply in love with me when he left, and though a part of me was equally in love with him, I chose to stay with Eric and my children. It was difficult when Michael left and I truly never thought I would see him again. But there wasn't a day I didn't think about him, even if only for a few seconds. When it was happening, Eric knew everything and handled it quite well. He even teamed up with Michael and the others to save me from my captors. But to tell Eric that Michael was coming and would again be very involved in my life was just asking too much of him. And me. Coop was very well aware of the situation.

"CeeCee? Did you hear what I said?"

"I heard you," I answered quietly, closing my eyes and sucking in as much air as I could. It felt like I had quit breathing for five minutes.

"I can't believe this. What am I going to tell Eric?"

"Tell him the truth."

"Oh, okay, and he'll have divorce papers filed by tomorrow morning," I quipped, amusing no one.

"What are your other options? After everything you guys went through last year, I genuinely think Eric will handle it just fine. He knows you love *him,* not Michael. Frankly, I don't think you're giving him enough credit, unless you're really worried about your own feelings when you see Michael." He looked at me accusingly. And the nerve he had found hurt. Badly.

"Don't be ridiculous. It's been a year, and I've been long over that," I said half-truthfully.

"Listen. Like I said, Eric will be fine with it. Just tell him the blunt truth."

I prayed Coop was right. I was terrified to go home and talk about Michael, but I had to. Eric and I always had a solid marriage, except for our shaky period last year, and we never kept secrets from each other. Not to mention, it would only be a matter of time before Eric saw Michael in the department. The icing on this entire fouled-up cake was that Coop was right. I was worried about *my* emotional reaction to Michael. Right this minute I felt I would be okay, but I wasn't so confident at the thought of standing face-to-face with him.

Not being able to get my active mind off the Michael situation, I called it a day and went home. Eric's shift didn't end until ten o'clock at night, a time when I was usually in bed since my day started early. His parents kept the girls while he was on the afternoon shift until I got home. When he returned to his normal shift on midnights, we'd go back to our regular routine of me standing at the door waiting to leave when he got home at six in the morning. Sometimes it's hard to have a marriage where you only see your spouse for less than an hour a week. You have to really put forth an effort—no doubt about it. Eric and I seem to have pulled it off. Or had we? My worry about Michael began to put some very serious doubts back in my mind.

After I put the girls to bed, I grabbed a glass of wine and sat in my living room. The wine didn't help. I was too nervous.

Hearing the garage door open an hour later, I jumped up and went into the kitchen just as Eric was walking through the door.

"Hey, baby." I walked over to kiss him on the cheek. "Bad night? You look tired."

"We were busy, and I *am* tired. Would you mind grabbing me a beer? I'll be down in a minute."

While Eric was upstairs getting undressed, I went into the living room and began chain-smoking. I usually don't smoke in the house. Eric hates it, but tonight was an exception. When he eventually came downstairs, I handed him his beer and, as expected, he sat next to me on the couch complaining about the smoke. The small talk continued while I figured out if there was a painless way to drop the bomb. As a counterpoint, I made sure to bring up Jordan first.

"I met your cub today. Certainly not what I expected." I was smiling as I said it so he wouldn't go on the defensive immediately.

"I wondered when you would bring that up. So *that's* why you're so edgy and smoking in the house." He grinned and gave me an affectionate hug. "Not to worry, my dear, there is no woman that will tear me away from my beautiful wife."

I loved him more than I realized. Or accepted. Supposedly, it's impossible to love more than one person deeply at the same time, or so I thought. But then I'd met Michael, and that's when it got screwed up. I knew Eric had a hard time getting over what happened between us, and he tried not to show his feelings. I respected him for that, and didn't want to hurt him any more. I could not let Michael come between Eric and me again, no matter how frightened I was of the possibility.

Now was as good of a time as any to bring up Michael's return, so I braced myself and hoped for the best.

"Eric, there's something I need to tell you." I put my wine down on the table, turned toward him, and took his hand. "Kincaid called the FBI in today over the Hanna Parker case. Sheriff's orders . . ."

"I figured she would," he said, setting his beer on the table and suddenly looking at me with suspicions. Eric was smart, he knew me, and knew something else was coming.

"That's not all." I paused. He was staring at me now, waiting. "One of the agents coming is Michael."

He yanked his hand from mine. He stood up and walked into the middle of the room, evidently trying to get as far from me as possible.

"I goddamn knew it!" He shook his head. "I *knew* that's what you were going to say!"

There were five very long minutes of silence as he stood in the middle of the room, just staring at the wall. I didn't know what to say, so I kept quiet. This wasn't exactly the reaction I expected, and I finally blurted it out.

"Eric, please, say something. When Coop told me today, I was just as dumbfounded as you are!"

He turned toward me, "I'll just bet!"

I was shocked at his response.

"Eric, it wasn't like I had a choice in the matter!"

He sat back down next to me and leaned forward, resting his elbows on his knees. He would not look directly at me and just stared at the ground.

"I don't know what to say. Of course I'm angry. Who wouldn't be? I know it's not your fault, but I *am* angry. I just don't think I can go through this shit again with the two of you! I don't want to talk about this anymore. Not tonight. I'm tired and I'm going to bed." His voice softened, but he still wore the same pained expression.

I watched him leave the room. It felt like there was a block of cement on my chest. That was it? I wanted to go after him, but knowing Eric, he needed time alone. After that, I was awake for hours—upset about Eric, anxious about seeing Michael again, and thinking briefly about the Hanna Parker case—before falling asleep on the couch.

When I woke up after a very fitful night, I saw that I was about to be late for work and had to scramble. Eric would get the girls up and ready for school. By the time I got to my office, I was breathless. Kincaid was a stickler for punctuality.

I began grabbing files and putting them in order before I left to interview the van owner. It was almost time to go when I heard a light knock. Looking up, I saw the face I had been dreading, and yearning for, in my doorway.

"Good morning, CeeCee."

Agent Michael Hagerman had returned.

CHAPTER SIX

He had prayed from the beginning that Agent Hagerman would be called in to assist the case, but he'd thought it was truly a long shot. Now, as the high-profile agent entered the Richland Metropolitan Police Department, he closed his eyes and mouthed a silent "thank you." Of course, there was always the chance that Hagerman was only stopping in to see his secret love, CeeCee Gallagher. But he didn't think so, not with her husband so close. He had done enough research on them that he knew better. Agent Hagerman's arrival was a sign, a sign from whatever god chose to bless him today, telling him things were going perfectly, telling him to continue because it was the only thing that could be done. There would be no stopping now. It would all be so breathtaking.

He looked the same. Though his hair was a little shorter, he was still so handsome he took my breath away. There was an awkward few seconds of us staring at each other before I walked over with the intent of shaking his hand. Instead, he pulled me into a tight embrace.

"It's good to see you, CeeCee. You're still as beautiful as ever."

Holding him and smelling his cologne opened a floodgate of memories, memories I didn't want to relive. My deepest fears were realized.

"And you're still quite the charmer. It's good to see

you too, Michael," I said quietly, pulling away as quickly as I could.

Standing there in my doorway, he was dressed casually in khaki pants and a light blue collared shirt. With those piercing green eyes, tan skin, and dazzling smile, his looks mirrored an Olympian ideal. It was very easy to remember how I found myself attracted to him in the first place. It wasn't just his tall-dark-and-handsome classic looks, but that smile always on his face, as if the world continually amused him. Forcing myself to focus on last night and Eric, I repeated the mantra: *Michael is here for business*. Summoning my hostess skills, I motioned for him to sit down.

We spent a little over an hour catching up on the previous year. He had not remarried after his divorce, another result of our relationship, and had only casually dated here and there. His prestigious career kept him from having any social life, which seemed to be fine. The free time he did have he spent with his son, Sean, who was now five.

"How are you and Eric doing?" He managed to summon a smile.

"We're doing well. A little rocky after last year, but we worked it out."

I saw a flash of disappointment come over his face, but it was gone before I could comment. I had, naively, assumed after this length of time and with no communication that Michael had long since given up on me. But now I wasn't so sure. He looked at me the same as he had a year ago. And that unnerved me greatly.

"Let me get this over with and ask. Were you upset when they made you come and help with the Parker case?"

Truthfully, I wasn't sure which answer I wanted. And I wasn't sure if he would tell me the whole truth.

His smile now seemed genuine. "CeeCee, I wasn't *made* to do anything. I volunteered to come here. You know I'm a sexual homicide expert and profiler, and this is about a dead child," he said, his smile fading. "Yes, they told me immediately you were the lead on the case. It wasn't difficult for the news about us to spread around the FBI too, but I know that on a professional level, you and I are a good team. Since you asked, how about you? How did you feel when you found out I was coming?"

I was quiet for a moment, mulling the best—and safest—answer to give him.

"Honestly, Michael, it caught me off guard. I really didn't think we would ever see each other again," I said. "Last night I had to tell Eric, and as you can imagine, it didn't go over too well. We've had a tough time the past year in many ways." I stopped and looked down at my desk, twirling a pencil between my fingers before continuing. "I don't know how I'm feeling right now about you being here, but you're right about one thing: we're a good team professionally, and we'll be fine." I tried to muster a genuine smile, but I knew Michael would see right through it.

He walked over to the window, and we stood together, looking out over the city.

"I'm not going to lie to you, CeeCee. I almost didn't volunteer because of you. But just the two of us standing here talking right now, it's as if this year never went by."

"But a year did go by, Michael."

"I know. I don't know how I feel about this right now either."

For someone who usually looks so self-possessed, my knees were shaking. I can easily deceive people into making them think I'm in control. Everyone says my expression is always serious, as if I'm concentrating fiercely on a secret only I know. Maybe that's what makes me seem so guarded and what can put people off. It's certainly not my looks, which, according to others, are above average. I'm tall and thin, with long blonde hair, a dark complexion, green eyes, and, as Coop puts it, a body that can stop a freight train. I take these opinions with a grain of salt. Like most other women, I have a significant amount of insecurities.

Michael walked back over to the chair and sat down. "We probably shouldn't be talking about this subject right now. It's too much to take in. I think for the moment we should just deal with the case. Why don't you tell me about this sicko you've got on your hands?"

A reprieve. I was more than happy to talk about the case, which took the better part of an hour and a half. There were two other agents assigned with him, but they were speaking with the sheriff, chief, and Kincaid about a timeline. All the agents were staying in a hotel by the interstate, paying by the week. No one knows how long an investigation like this might last, so they needed to be prepared for short- or long-term stays.

While Michael was studying the crime-scene photographs, homing in on Hanna Parker's painted face, it was easy to see how sickened he was at what was done to this poor child.

"Dear God, I've never seen anything like this. She was strangled and sexually assaulted, but no fluid found."

He put one hand over his mouth and strained his eyes, going into deep thought over the pictures. He then grabbed the close-up photo of the doll shoe and put the photos side by side on the floor. He looked closely at one, then the other, all the while saying nothing. There was an old *Adam-12* poster on my wall, which seemed to grab his attention while he studied the photos. Was there any connection? That was Michael; intense and mysterious, making people around him wonder what's going on in his head. I couldn't stand it anymore. I needed to know what he was thinking.

"What, Michael? What do you *see*?"

"You *do* realize the killer put the doll shoe in her hand to tell us she was painted to look like a doll, right? He didn't think we would have figured it out on our own—which concerns me. It's ritualistic, and it makes me wonder if he's done this before. I'm gonna say yes."

"What makes you think it's ritualistic?"

"Ritualistic killers remain constant, but are always improving their skills and testing law enforcement. Did you guys send out a national teletype to inquire if any other law-enforcement agency has had a similar homicide?"

"Of course, but it's only been a couple of days, so we haven't heard anything of substance yet. Why do you think he's killed before?"

"Because of the shoe. I think when he did it before, law enforcement didn't understand the message he was trying to get across. That made him angry, so he's decided to help us along. Regardless, even if I'm wrong, he's very smart, calculating, and the obvious—disturbed."

"The doll that the shoe came from has been around for twenty-plus years, sold in every retail and toy store across the country. This one particular shoe could never be tracked. So what do you suggest?"

"Let me think for a minute. I need to go catch up with the other agents. You said you're going to re-interview the owner of the stolen van? Let me know what you find out. I'll talk to you in a bit."

Michael left. I stared at the doorway and wondered what would happen from here. It was utterly clear that we were trying to fool ourselves and each other. Reality was that we both knew our feelings hadn't dissipated, but we also knew the unresolved complications they caused. I'd never made love to Michael, but we were dangerously close one night. It was Michael who stopped, mostly due to the consequence it would have for my marriage. Or so he said. I always wondered if he ever regretted his decision. A sizeable part of me did, but the other part—the intellectual part—was grateful. I genuinely believe that not sleeping with Michael was the only thing that kept Eric from leaving me. Had I done the deed, there is no doubt I would be divorced by now.

CHAPTER SEVEN

Carl Malone lived on the south side of town in a middle-class neighborhood. His house, a moderate two-story split-level with freshly mowed grass and trimmed bushes, was unassuming. I pulled in behind his older, rusted-out, gray pickup truck just in time to see him walk around the corner. It appeared he was doing some type of heavy-duty landscaping work in his backyard. Wearing gardening gloves and soiled jeans, he towered around six feet tall, slender, with thinning gray hair. Carl Malone smiled amiably at me.

"Well, hello there! May I help you with something?"

Carl took off his gloves and extended a hand, which I graciously shook, identifying myself and explaining my reasons for paying him an official visit.

"Sweetheart, I'll tell you what I told the other officers. I can't for the life of me understand why someone came into this neighborhood and stole my van, in particular. It's the safest neighborhood. We've never had that sort of thing happen here, and I've lived here for twenty-five years. I left the van parked in the driveway with the keys in it, like I have for the ten years I've had it. I know one thing: I don't want it back. Not after what happened to that poor child. Can I get you something to drink, Detective? Gallagher, right? Are you related to the other Gallaghers at the department?"

"Right. My father and uncles," I answered, declining the beverage. My visit didn't seem like it would add any new insight to the case.

"Hell, they've been in that department since Jesus was a boy. How many years?"

"Thirty-five and counting."

Enough with the small talk. I was anxious to get back to the interview. I got Carl back on track and started asking more personal questions. Initially, he seemed somewhat put off, but I explained they were standard questions and told him not to read into them. Carl had been married up until a year ago when his wife died of ovarian cancer. They had no children, and Carl spent his current life as a salesman for a local manufacturing plant, covering the Midwest. He retired when his wife got sick and began doing light drywall work on the side. Fifty-one years old, Carl had no enemies, was liked by his neighbors, and hadn't received so much as a speeding ticket, which I'd already learned when I first did a criminal history check. Carl Malone was as uneventful as his life, so I thanked him and left.

Back at the station, Kincaid, Coop, and the FBI agents were in the conference room waiting for me. A response to our inquiry into similar crimes had just come in from the Tampa Police Department. Jumping to it, Coop had already spoken to the detective on that case, which took place in 1983 and, by a miracle, the detective was still working there. Coop shared the case file the detective had faxed, along with a scanned photo sent through e-mail. Their case was unnerving, looking like a carbon copy of the Hanna Parker one—except for the shoe. Coop went on about how the detective said it was the case of his career that he forever wants to solve. He was stunned, and thrilled, to see our teletype. Simultaneously, our lab reports arrived, and they clearly showed Hanna had soil on her that differed from that of the cornfield where she was found.

"Did he bury her somewhere else first?" I asked.

"Not likely," Coop answered. "She had only been dead three hours or so before her body was discovered, but I'll get to that."

"It can't be possible. We're talking over twenty years ago," I said, referring to the Tampa killing. "Copycat maybe?"

"*That* would be impossible. It's got to be the same killer," Michael jumped in. "The body was found looking exactly the same, clear down to the red ribbon in the hair and around the neck—which, I might add, the Tampa Police never disclosed to the public."

"Could one of the original investigating officers be a suspect?" Kincaid asked.

"Possible, but highly unlikely," Michael said.

Tampa had no leads on a suspect, and the case had gone cold. I prayed we wouldn't suffer the same fate. No time for further ruminating—Kincaid wanted to begin the meeting. We all secured our seats at the conference table.

"Now that we may have a possible—and I say that loosely—serial murderer, we need to bust our asses. Agent Hagerman has prepared a profile on the suspect, which he'll give in a moment. It may come down to FBI jurisdiction due to the Florida case, but we are all going to help nonetheless. Before we get to Michael, CeeCee, what have you got? I want statistics and the whole enchilada put up on the dry-erase board to act as our guide."

Since I'm a certified expert, I'd anticipated the request. Nonetheless, Kincaid knew damn well the FBI agents had the same stats. Grabbing the marker, and feeling Michael's eyes on me, I started to write on the board.

"As most of you already know," I began, trying to alert Kincaid that everyone already knew what I was going to say (though the chances were she wouldn't catch on anyway), "we are dealing with a nonfamily abduction, specifically a stereotypical kidnapping. Stereotypical kidnapping being a child taken overnight, killed, or transported a distance of fifty miles or more. The perpetrator has evidenced intent to keep the child permanently." I took a deep breath. "There are approximately thirty-two hundred to forty-six hundred attempted nonfamily abductions every year with about fifty-two to a hundred and fifty-eight of those children being murdered."

Coop let out a low whistle. "I didn't realize there were that many."

"That's what the stats say," I said, taking my seat.

Coop was next in the hot seat with the autopsy report. Hanna Parker had rigor mortis in her small muscle groups only, indicating death had occurred three to six hours prior to discovery. Full rigor mortis sets in eight to twelve hours after death. The examiner indicated that the red ribbon around her neck had not been used as a ligature for strangulation, but that she had been strangled manually. This resulted in stimulation from the vagus nerve in the neck to cause immediate death from heart and breathing paralysis. Vagus-nerve stimulation gives the face a more normal appearance after death, avoiding the bloated face and tongue people assume come with strangulation.

That was the same method used in the Tampa murder. As for the sexual aspect, the report indicated there was severe sexual trauma, but no evidence of seminal fluid or DNA. Coop also put up a photo of the Tampa murder on the board. The victim, Cindy Lee Bowman, was also five years old when she died. Coop wrote their names next to their pictures.

Looking at both of the photographs, the similarities were remarkable. The faces were painted exactly the same, down to the lipstick color, and both had the same grotesque doll-like appearance.

The room remained quiet for several minutes after Coop finished. The other agents, Shoupman and Hurst, were scribbling furiously in their notepads, while Michael simply stared at me. We all agreed there was a distinct reason for painting the victims' faces, but for sane people like those of us in the room, it was hard to figure out why. This was where Michael came in. As he stepped to the front of the room, my heart gave a slight flip. Coop was looking directly at me in an attempt to read my reaction to Michael. I quickly looked away, but too late. Coop had already seen my face. I was sure of it. He damn well knew my thoughts.

Michael began with the intricate, detailed, and disturbing profile of the child murderer.

"At first, after reviewing the file, I believed the killer to fall under the category of sexual sadist, also known as an anger-excitation rapist. This is someone who is cunning and accomplished at deception and rationalizes their actions."

So far his description was clear enough. "Feeling no remorse or guilt, the sexual sadist considers himself superior to society and law enforcement in particular."

Both the Hanna Parker and Tampa murders displayed the three most important traits of a sexual sadist: ritualism, the killer's fantasies, and the crime itself, which is the least common and most violent.

He further went on to explain that a ritual murderer commits acts that are unnecessary to the commission of the crime. Examples in these cases being the makeup, ribbons, and doll shoe. What also pointed Michael toward a sexual-sadist definition is that ritualistic killers remain constant over time, but may add what they feel are enhancements—hence the doll shoe. The ritualistic aspect of the killer is a more powerful tool in finding him than his modus operandi, or MO. The killer's signature, a unique combination of behaviors across two or more crimes, would be the painted face and ribbons.

"I believe that the killer used a surprise approach in abducting Hanna, which is an immediate capture of the victim without injuries or force. I was convinced we were dealing with a sexual sadist until we saw how Hanna had been laid out, brushed off, and coiffed, as if a great amount of care had been taken. This contradicts a sexual sadist, but points somewhat toward a pseudo-unselfish offender, someone complimentary, apologetic, polite, verbally non-sexual, and reassuring to his victim."

Calm and stern faced, Michael walked to his seat and took a long drink from a bottle of water, while we all sat silent, trying to take in everything he said so far.

He began again, trying to explain how the sexual and ritual traits of our killer were contradictory and highly unusual for one killer to have.

"So you think there might be two killers, each putting their own flair into the murders?" Coop asked, reading my mind.

"I won't rule out anything right now. We could be dealing with a split personality, one man's imagination and fantasies. A combination that offers no sureties in any criminal case, no matter how experienced the profiler or law enforcement is"

He lightly coughed. "I believe our killer expresses the violence and urges of the sexual sadist, but later feels remorse. I also believe the killer realizes he is sick and that leaving the doll shoe is an indication that he wants to get caught, that he wants to be stopped. But the sadist part of him wants to find out if law enforcement is smarter than he is."

Coop interrupted. "Michael, from what you're saying, it sounds as if he's at the end of his rope and his behavior might be escalating."

"Absolutely. I think there will be another murder, if there hasn't been already. The killer may travel and not live here, and could already be in another state by now. Whatever, I think he's ready to explode."

Michael filled in more of the pieces. He felt the suspect was a white male in his late forties or fifties. His theory on the age was due to the time since the Florida killing.

"The suspect is very organized, educated, and knowledgeable in law enforcement, possibly from crime documentaries, books, or magazines. Sixty-one percent of serial killers collect violent-theme pornography, while nearly all pedophiles collect some type of child pornography and erotica." He also said that it was possible the killer held a job for many years and had no criminal record.

"The bottom line," Michael continued, "is he will continue to kill. Like all other pedophiles, asking them not to be attracted to children anymore is like asking a heterosexual to turn gay, or vice versa."

"How does he feel afterward, Michael?" Kincaid asked. "Elated, angry, remorseful?"

"I think his post-offense behavior would be that of remorse or guilt. He laid Hanna out with dignity because he felt bad. He may be feeling ill, losing or gaining weight, having bowel disturbances or sleep disruptions."

"So it's possible he shit his pants afterward?" Coop barked, laughing.

"This isn't a joke!" Kincaid snapped.

Coop put his head down like a schoolboy chastised by his teacher. For whatever reason, this produced a loud snickering from me. Now Kincaid just glowered at both of us. It was time for me to ask a question and get back on track.

"Michael, in this instance, what causes someone to be this way?"

I already knew the answer, but Kincaid looked like she was getting ready to bite my head off. The question was merely a diversionary tactic.

"It could be sexual abuse, physical abuse, drugs, alcohol, television, games, or music. No one really knows for sure."

"Any ideas about why he's doing the doll thing?"

"That I'm not sure of yet. It could be gender confusion, could be something else. Like I said, I've never seen something like this before, so I'm doing some extrapolating."

The information was what we needed to begin to put Hanna's murder into a general context, so it was time to start wrapping up the meeting. Kincaid told Coop to focus on finding a local sex offender who may have been in Florida around the time of the Tampa killing. She was right in checking it out. I agreed with Michael instinctively when he said the killer could travel. The downside of that theory was if it proved correct, our chances of catching him would be slim. He could be anywhere, and it's a very big country. If he still was in the country.

Michael and I were almost back to my office when my phone rang. It was Captain Norris from patrol.

"CeeCee, you need to know about this immediately. The Parkers got a package in their mail today. It was another doll shoe, possibly a match. They don't know anything about the shoe found with Hanna, but they called anyway because it was creepy. The box is small and covered in stamps, so there's no way to track it. The good news is that it was mailed locally."

"You've got to be kidding." I was stunned after strongly considering the possibility that the killer may have left the area. "I'm assuming the crime lab is already on scene to take the shoe and box for processing?"

"You betcha. I'll let you know if anything else turns up."

I hung up and told Michael about the other shoe. We'd have to go down to the lab to confirm the shoe was a My Size, but it was a good bet.

"He's playing with us. I was right in that he's doing all he can to get caught. He knows the family would turn the shoe over to us. He's saying, 'I'm sick and need to be put away, but let's see if you're smart and worthy enough to do it.'"

"Captain Norris told me the box was mailed locally. Do you genuinely believe he's still here?"

"Possibly." Michael ran a hand through his thick brown hair to relieve some of his tension. "Or he could've mailed it a couple of days ago and taken off."

Before leaving for the day, I needed to swing by the uniformed patrol squad room to see if Eric was out of roll call yet. I still hadn't been able to reach him on the phone, and wondering about the fallout from our little chat last night had been killing me.

Just outside of the squad room was a restroom that I desperately needed to use, my bladder feeling like it would explode after sitting in such a lengthy meeting. Washing up and cursing the extra five cups of coffee I'd had today, I heard the squad room door open. A group of officers walked into the hallway. It was impossible to miss their loud conversation, and I soon heard it concerned Eric and Jordan. Turning off the faucet, I pressed

my ear against the bathroom door, feeling like a com-·
plete ass in the process. Children eavesdrop like this, not
mature adults. But under the circumstances, a little pride
wasn't going to stand in my way. It wasn't clear which
officers were talking, and only bits and pieces of their
conversation came through.

"Hell, I'd do her if I was training her! Eric's got it
made. I'll give him a week before he hits that."

"A week? Shit. I heard he already has. She follows him
around like a puppy, and I'm sure he could do anything
he wants. The other night he told me she wanted him to
go home with her."

My heart raced, and now I was trembling uncontrollably. As their voices faded and their conversation switched
to another topic, I slumped down onto the bathroom floor
wondering if I should confront my husband. It would be
hard not to, but I wanted to give him the benefit of the
doubt. And how much did my own guilt about Michael
play into my tolerance? Guys in patrol assume things and
spread rumors. Uniformed police officers are the cattiest,
most gossipy group of individuals around. They put nosy
women to shame. The part that bothered me most was the
one officer said Eric told him directly that Jordan asked
him to go home with her. If it was all hearsay, like the
comment that he had slept with her, I might get over it.
Maybe. I knew Eric was upset over Michael, but the way
these guys talked, this had been going on for a while.

Keep driving! Keep driving and don't look at her. *The
voice of the other screamed so loud in his head, he felt his foot
press down on the accelerator even harder. The other, although
consistently fading over the last several months, still managed
to break into his reality with its undaunted demands.* But she
needs me! *He fought the other voice, looking at the girl who*

would become his beautiful new guest. She was skipping along, swinging her backpack, and singing. She needs me! *He kept repeating it over and over and over, holding his head with one hand while slamming his foot on the brake. He, decidedly, had enough. No more would he fall prey to the other voice, no more would he allow it to sway him, and no more would he ever listen to it again. Taking a deep breath, he looked at himself in the rearview mirror and smiled.* Good-bye to you, my friend— you don't exist anymore. Do you hear me? You are dead! You are DEAD! *Putting his car in reverse before driving back toward his guest, he never felt more alive.*

CHAPTER EIGHT

I rushed into the squad room to find that Eric and Jordan had just left and were probably getting into their patrol car. Outside, they were loading their bags into one of the cruisers. Jordan gave me a quick "hi," which I didn't return, and got into the car. She didn't seem as friendly today, something I tried to write off as my imagination. Eric seemed surprised to see me. Why?

"Hey . . . What are you doing out here? Everything all right?"

"I was looking for you, and no, everything is not all right." I tried to hide the anger on my face, but Eric couldn't help noticing it.

"Did something go wrong with your murder case?" He stood with his hand resting on the hood of the cruiser, and he looked slightly concerned.

"This isn't about the case. I just heard some gossip in the hall that was extremely disturbing."

By now Jordan had rolled her window down about an inch and was listening to our conversation.

"Look, CeeCee, I don't have time for games right now, so do you want to spit it out or not? We have to get going. There's calls for service pending in our zone."

I glanced at Jordan and back at Eric, hoping to give him a nonverbal, but very blatant hint. He got the idea, took his hand off the car, and just stood there.

"I know where you're going with this," he said, "and now is not the time or place. Please wait until I get home."

"I need to talk about it now if you don't mind, minus the audience, of course." I scowled directly at Jordan, which prompted her to roll up her window mighty fast.

"I said not now. We're late. We have to leave," he said, before walking to the other side of the car and getting in.

It was my turn to be shocked and angry. They drove away, and I remained where I was, completely dumb-founded. Eric said he knew what I was talking about? That scared me to death and also led me to believe the rumors might be true. I felt quite ill, but I pulled myself together so I could drive home without getting into an accident.

At home I could think of nothing else. By the time 10:00 rolled around, the end of Eric's shift, I was in a panic. By 10:47, I was almost psychotic when the phone rang. It was him.

"Sorry I didn't call earlier, but we had a late arrest. I'm gonna be tied up for a while. You might as well go to bed."

"No, I'll wait up. Like I said, we need to talk, and you obviously know what about. And, may I add, I didn't appreciate getting blown off in the parking lot today either. Or maybe that was just another way to impress your girlfriend?"

Eric was silent. Not a good sign. I can be haughty, sarcastic, and childish like the best of 'em, but it was out of character for me to act the way I was then: mean and spiteful toward the man I supposedly love. I think he was probably somewhat surprised, but more likely angry and even hurt.

"I will not have this conversation over the phone, and if you want to discuss it like a rational adult, I suggest you settle down," he whispered into his cell. "Good night, CeeCee. I love you," he said, and hung up.

I felt like a fool. I've been in law enforcement long enough to learn not to fall prey to the evil rumor mill, but this time I had.

I slept fitfully, waking around two in the morning to find Eric next to me sound asleep. I finally got up around five, tired of my nightlong tossing and turning. I wanted to shake him, wake him up, and tell him I was sorry, but I knew he needed to get some sleep. Before I headed to work, I left a note on the kitchen counter asking him to call as soon as he woke up.

Michael was already in my office when I arrived, complete with a box of doughnuts, scones, and bagels.

"You look tired."

"Thanks," I mumbled, grabbing a bagel.

"Is everything all right, CeeCee?"

"Just fucking fantastic."

"Okay. Never mind, I won't ask. Where should we start today?"

"I think we should go through the entire case file again to see if there's anything we missed before we re-interview anyone."

Two more weeks went by without a break in the case. Two weeks of Michael and me spending every day together. There was no denying it. Our emotions were out in full force and growing stronger than ever, while Eric and I barely spoke. Every time I tried to bring up the subject of Jordan, he put his hand up to signal he didn't want to discuss it, infuriating me further. One afternoon while Michael and I were contemplating where to eat lunch, a break in the case happened.

We were gathering up the case file when Coop came charging into my office looking like something was wrong. A very familiar scenario by now.

"What?" I snapped, anticipating the worst.

"Someone just tried to kidnap Austin Brewer."

CHAPTER NINE

"Where is he now? Is he hurt?" I asked, frantically grabbing my car keys.

"No, he's fine. He's at home. I'll follow you both over there."

Michael was barely in my car with the door closed before I peeled out of the parking lot. On our way I called Kincaid, specifically to chew her out about why no patrol car was keeping an eye on the Brewer house like I had requested.

"I had a patrol car there, CeeCee. The guys have to be able to break and eat lunch, for Christ's sake! I don't appreciate you questioning me about it either." Oh, she was snippy.

"If they left for lunch, then you should've assigned someone to replace them until they were finished." I was even snippier.

"I'm not going to debate this matter on the phone, especially since I don't answer to you. I'm the captain, remember?"

"I'm reminded every day," I said with my low, dry sarcasm.

"Melissa Brewer waited an hour before she called us," she said, ignoring my last remark. "She thought she was overreacting and being paranoid."

I relayed this information to Michael.

"She did what? What the hell is wrong with that woman?" Michael was taken aback.

Turning onto the Brewers' street, we saw Kincaid's SUV parked in their driveway. I was hoping to beat her there because, knowing Naomi, she probably started questioning Austin Brewer already, scaring him to death in the process. Coop pulled in behind us and as we started toward the front door, I heard a man yelling. Dr. Parker was standing in his front yard, waving for one of us to come and talk to him.

"I'll take care of him. You guys go ahead," Coop said, walking toward the doctor. Melissa Brewer was already waiting at the front door. When I walked into the living room, Kincaid was sitting on the couch with Austin. I hated being right. She was talking to him like he was a nine-month-old baby; directly in his face and loudly, like a toddler herself. Austin looked trapped and horrified until he saw me. He leaped off the couch and ran straight to me with his arms wide open. Being the wide receiver, I caught him immediately.

"Hey! Poweece lady! I almost catched the bad guy today!" Austin grabbed tightly around my leg, his chubby face gazing up at me eager to please.

"I heard, Austin! You did a very good job. You're going to get a special badge for the job you did today. You'll have to tell me all about it and how smart you were!"

"I will! I will!" he yelled. Then his voice dropped to a whisper and he pulled my shirt so I would bend down to him. "I don't like that other lady. She thinks I'm a baby and not a big boy with a badge!"

Austin's whisper was a small yell, loud enough for the entire room to hear, Kincaid included. Kincaid, red faced and going through her hourly ritual of being a world-class dumbass, walked toward the door.

"CeeCee, just fill me in on what he says. I'll be driving around the area looking for anything suspicious. Just call my cell."

"Okay, Cap."

I looked back down at Austin, who was now eyeing Michael with an air of suspicion. Throw a cap on his head and a pipe in his mouth, and Austin could be a regular junior Sherlock Holmes. Michael had remained quiet, though not resisting a smirk at Kincaid's ignorance and lack of finesse.

Melissa Brewer nervously asked if we would like anything to drink. She seemed as uneasy now as when I'd first interviewed her about Hanna Parker. I told Michael and Austin to get to know each other better while I talked to Melissa in the kitchen—where I let her have it with both barrels.

"You better have one hell of an explanation for why you waited one hour to call the police after someone just tried to kidnap your son."

She looked terrified and immediately started bawling, holding on to the countertop for support. I felt for her, but not all that much. Her passive responses to the last several incidents still had me steaming. The thought that we might have actually been able to catch the man who killed Hanna Parker infuriated me even more. I didn't want to hear sobs and cries; I wanted an explanation.

"You might as well get it out now, Melissa. Quite frankly, you could be facing felony charges, as well as an investigation by children's services."

"I-I know! I'm sorry!"

Austin led Michael into the kitchen. Upon seeing his mother a basket case, the child began crying and ran over to her. The hysteria was spreading and getting louder. Trying not to add to the confusion, Michael gave me a questioning look and I promptly waved my hand, sign language for *don't worry about it.* It would be useless to talk to Austin now that he was a blubbering mess. I signaled to Melissa that I needed to talk to Austin and would be out in the living room waiting. Michael brought up the rear.

"What was that all about?" he asked quietly once we were out of earshot from the kitchen.

"Not much, I just unloaded on her, essentially saying she's been a piss-poor mother and lucky if she doesn't go to jail."

"Knowing you, I'm sure that's exactly what was said. No sugar coating from you, right?" He put his hand on the small of my back and chuckled.

"Right." I turned out of his reach, feeling the familiar explosion of desire and need I experienced whenever he touched me.

Melissa and Austin walked in, both appearing to have settled down and now ready to talk. Melissa sat on the couch and motioned for Austin to sit next to her, which he ignored, climbing onto her lap instead. Melissa began telling us her version of what happened earlier.

Austin's preschool party was the following day, and Melissa had been in the kitchen making cookies while he was in the living room playing with his trucks. Austin was being his normal four-year-old self: loud, whistling, making siren noises and yelling "fire!" As with any parent who has a child that age or younger, silence brings about an immediate concern if the child is not directly in sight. Such was the case today.

"I didn't hear Austin making his fire sounds anymore. In fact there was no sound at all coming from the room."

Thinking he may have gotten into something he wasn't supposed to, Melissa left the kitchen, stopping dead in her tracks when she saw the front door of her house wide open. In a panic, she ran outside, fearing Austin had managed to open it and walk out, something he was able to do on two prior occasions. It was then she saw an older white station wagon backing out of her driveway and heading up the street at a high speed. The man driving was white and had blond hair.

"There was a temporary registration tag in the back, but I didn't get a close look at it."

Standing in the front yard, she began yelling Austin's name. He called out to her from inside the house, where she found him in the living room, playing with his trucks and once again making ordinary childish noises

"I asked him if he opened the front door, and he said it was the tall man that did it. I thought he might have been making things up and the wind blew it open, or he really did open it, then used his quite vivid imagination to come up with the story about the tall man. I guess I brushed off the car as someone just turning around in my driveway." She eyeballed me, waiting for a response. "I wasn't thinking, I guess. I mean, Austin does have an active imagination. There was one time our toilet got backed up with almost six cans of Play-Doh in it. When I asked Austin, he told me an old lady with a cane and a beard pushed him down, stole the Play-Doh, and tried to flush it down the toilet . . ."

Michael grunted, trying to suppress his laugh.

"There also isn't the slightest bit of wind today, Melissa," I interrupted.

"I know, but I thought maybe my husband or I hadn't latched it properly, so anything could have blown it open. Anyway, I went back to making the cookies, but the whole incident kept nagging me. I went back and talked to Austin a little more about it, and that's when he told me a man came in and asked him if he wanted to go play with Hanna. That's when I ran to call the police."

It was very, very quiet in the room. Michael was studying Melissa, analyzing her every word, something he is very good at. And he was clearly making her uncomfortable. Austin looked like he was on the verge of a deep sleep before I called out to him.

"Austin? Do you want to help me catch a bad guy again? You did such a good job the first time."

"Okay! I played with my fire twucks. The bad guy was standing wight there." He pointed toward the door.

"What color shirt did he have on, Austin?"

"White. He knew my name too! He asked me if I wanted to play with Hanna!"

"What did you say?"

"I wanted to play wif Hanna, but he runned away."

With my attention still on Austin, I explained to the child that he should never go with someone he doesn't know. In the middle of my little safety speech, my phone rang. Kincaid.

"CeeCee! Get out of there and start toward Bellville. A seven-year-old was just taken walking home from school. Keep an ear to your radio, we're getting a description now," she yelled before hanging up.

"This was a setup!" I announced to Michael and Coop (who had recently returned), rushing toward the door. "Another child was kidnapped. Melissa, do not take your eyes off Austin for a second, and lock all your doors and windows."

Speeding away from the Brewers', I filled Coop and Michael in on Naomi's call. Bellville was a small village about fifteen minutes south of the city. It was very obvious the suspect used Austin Brewer to distract us while he took another child. He was toying with us, luring us just close enough to think we got him and then disappearing yet again. This guy was brilliant. And fearless. Driving to the village, doing at least seventy-five mph, I radioed in the suspect description for the Austin Brewer case and told every listening officer to look for a white station wagon. As I was talking, I realized it wasn't much to go on, but it was a start. This guy changed cars, and evidently, his hair color. Right now he could be driving a yellow school bus and wearing a dreadlock wig for all I knew.

All we could gather on the radio was bits and pieces of what happened. Ashley Sanders had been walking home from school. A neighbor in the rear of her house heard the scream, went to her front window two minutes later or so, and noticed items from the child's backpack spilled out on the sidewalk. Again, no one saw anything more specific. Several uniforms on the scene were giving out the child's description, so I radioed for one of them to call my cell ASAP. We were almost at the scene when an officer called and told me what was found on the sidewalk. The child's backpack was fully open with the contents all spilled out. Papers, lunchbox, pencils, and candy were strewn in a very small area, maybe two by three feet. When the officer answered my question if anything else was there, I hung up, slowed the car, and looked at Michael.

"Shall I take a guess?" he asked.

"Of course you know the answer. They found a My Size shoe sitting on top of the child's backpack."

"Son of a bitch" were Michael's only words as we turned onto the street where Ashley Sanders was last heard from.

It was getting to be an all-too-familiar scene, and I hated to admit it, but the suspect had already started wearing us all down. No law-enforcement agency is ever prepared for multiple kidnappings no matter how well funded, trained, staffed, or anything else we are.

The crime lab processed what was on the sidewalk, and an Amber Alert was issued. I spoke with the woman who called, another imbecile who waited until her soap opera went to a commercial break before checking on what she thought was a child screaming. A few seconds after that, Ashley's mother had driven around the corner and seen the backpack and its contents on the sidewalk. She had finished her errands early and decided to pick Ashley up, knowing the route she took home. It was only when Ashley's mother was screaming hysterically that the woman called the police. Without a doubt, I believe the woman would never have called the police had Ashley's mother not shown up.

Ashley Sanders was beautiful. He'd known that when he'd taken her just a short time ago. After all, he had been watching her. He'd known the route she walked on her way home from school, he knew where she lived, and even in the darkest, deepest parts of his mind, had known she wouldn't fight much. He had been a little surprised when she'd screamed, but that only made it more interesting and exciting.

He relishes the dreams about each one; the watching, the waiting, and each second up until the moment. When it happens, when it's time, the frustration at the lack of excitement of the real kidnapping grows. It's never as exciting as when he dreams about it. Still, he can't complain too much. The sensations he experiences when he really took them were second to no other.

Today, when he watched her walking down the street, he felt the familiar quickening of his pulse, as he licked his parched lips. It was an emotion without a definition, an emotion no one could understand. They were already together in their minds; he knew that. He knew she dreamed of him each night when she went to bed. *Several days ago when she dropped her book bag and he handed it to her, he saw it in her eyes. Just as he had seen it in Hanna Parker's, and just as he'd seen it in all the others.*

Watching now as Ashley's mother fell to pieces on the street, he felt the sweet, high-pitched excitement in his body and the ache in his groin. Oh, how wonderful! The cop standing by Ashley's mother was CeeCee Gallagher, who had played right into his hands—just as he'd planned.

Hearing the stifled cries from the backseat, he knew Ashley was getting impatient and wanted to get home. Home to him. Smiling at the scene unfolding, he quietly drove away.

CHAPTER TEN

Michael and I drove and walked around the area for the next four hours, finding nothing. However, while we were walking the edge of a large area of woods with other uniformed officers, something interesting happened.

I hadn't been paying much attention to the time, so when I saw Eric and Jordan heading our way, I figured they had been called in early. Surprisingly, it was nearing seven o'clock in the evening and they had been at work for five hours already. I had been so focused on the case that I had totally forgotten about my problems with Eric. I looked around for a quick exit, hoping Michael hadn't seen them and vice versa, but it was too late. Eric came straight toward me, and I braced myself for the inevitable confrontation between Eric and Michael. It would be wishful thinking to hope the two of them might act like adults. It was hard to believe it took this long for them to run into each other. Eric was now only about twenty feet away when Michael saw him. Muttering obscenities, he sighed.

"Here we go."

Eric and Jordan, curiously, stopped about five feet away.

"Please, everyone, maintain," I whispered back.

No one said anything. It was one of the most awful, awkward, and uncomfortable moments I can ever remember. It was so bad and so obvious, it became comical.

The silence lasted about thirty seconds, but felt like twenty minutes. Eric broke first.

"Michael. How are you?" He nodded grimly toward Michael while speaking politely, though certainly without warmth or friendliness. That seemed as good as it was going to get, which I guess was OK.

Eric's face maintained the same uninviting look it had when he first saw us, and Michael merely nodded back, almost inaudibly muttering a sound that resembled "hello." After that, the two just stared at each other. Jordan kept looking at both men, waiting for one or the other to crack. She wore a contemptuous look that made me want to reach over and slap her into next week. It took all I had to keep my face expressionless and my mouth shut. I didn't even acknowledge she was there until I felt in control enough to speak.

"Have you been out long?" I asked Eric. "We're going on four hours now and coming up with nothing."

Jordan was the one to reply. "We've been at it for a good two hours now? Right, Eric?" Then, with an arrogant confidence I've rarely seen in another human being, she grabbed Eric's arm and started playfully patting it.

I felt like I would explode right there, but Eric slowly pulled his arm away from her. That did it. I had enough.

"I wasn't asking you, I was asking *my husband* the question, honey. If I were to . . ."

"All right," Eric interrupted sharply. "We're gonna keep walking. Let me know if anything turns up. By the way, CeeCee, my parents are keeping the girls overnight since I assume we'll both be late." He started walking quickly away from us, Jordan in tow.

I didn't move. I simply stared at an old rotted tree trunk and continued fuming. Not only was I berserk over Jordan's behavior, I didn't like how Eric seemed to come to her defense once I began to attack. He cut me off, walked away, and prevented me from causing her any kind of emotional pain or anxiety whatsoever. It also angered me that Jordan seemed to be aware of the tension between Eric and Michael. How much had he confided in her about the seriousness of our situation?

Now Michael saw it all laid out, impossible to miss. So much for keeping up the everything's-hunky-dory-at-CeeCee's-house front.

It took all I had to get myself in control. When I did, I was counting on moving along with our search and pretending nothing happened, but Michael wouldn't let me off that easy. I started to walk again, but he stepped in front of me, his eyes full of concern and knowledge of the truth.

"Got over the rocky patch, did you? Why do I get the impression the tension in our little meeting wasn't all about me for once? Who was the rookie?"

I sat down on a tree stump and let out a sigh. I couldn't hold it in. There was no reason to pretend or hide from Michael anymore. I told him about Jordan, the rumors, and the strain my relationship with Eric has been under since he, Michael, came back into the picture.

"Maybe Eric's trying to get back at me for what we did last year. Or maybe I was the one drumming up all the problems so I wouldn't have to acknowledge that my feelings for you haven't faded in the slightest over the past year. Not even a little. Never in my life did I ever think it was possible to be in love with two people," I said softly, picking up a stick and poking it around in the dirt.

Michael stood, looking down at me, listening intently. When I was finished, he knelt and took my stick away, tossing it into the woods, before grabbing my hands.

"Maybe I have the solution. I'll leave tomorrow, send another agent, and simply never come back. It hurts too much to see you so unhappy, and if I can fix it by leaving, that's the way it has to be."

I looked at Michael's eyes, his lips, his hair. I didn't want him to leave, not a second time. And certainly not forever.

"Unfortunately, whether you leave or not, it doesn't matter. Things will be the same. Eric will be training Jordan, or sleeping with her for all I know, and he'll still resent me for the relationship you and I had last year." I paused and put my hand up to Michael's cheek. "And most of all, I don't want you to leave."

Michael squeezed my hand tightly before standing up and looking at his watch.

"I'll stay. I can't tell you how happy it makes me to hear you say that, but it also scares the shit out of me. Who knows what's in the cards for any of us, but right now, let's just see what happens. We can talk more later. Right now, we've only got another hour of searching before it gets dark." He held out a strong, firm hand, pulling me up from my perch on the tree stump.

He wasn't careful anymore. It didn't matter. All the time he had taken to get the lips just right, no smudges or mistakes; the eyes dramatic with big, full lashes; cheeks a deep, glowing red was nothing but a distant memory. He still made the effect as best as he could with what time he had, but it was fine. They had gotten it. He didn't even curl her hair, just lazily tied the ribbon in, not caring when it slumped and fell to the side. There, there, my beautiful love, he thought, now we're as one. . . .

I didn't feel guilty, not one bit, for finally telling Michael how I felt. I was relieved that it was out in the open. Finally. What I did feel was anger at Eric. To be blunt, he might as well have picked me up bodily and thrown me into bed with Michael, as much as he was pushing me

away and letting me think something was going on with
Jordan. As childish as that sounds, it's the God's honest
truth. The best thing Eric could've done was be himself;
loving, attentive, honest, and most of all, faithful.

Michael didn't say much. He knew me well enough
to let me be. Kincaid had given us the first slot of the
four-hour rest breaks because we'd been at work since
early that morning. I was beyond exhausted. Four hours
didn't seem like much, but it was better than nothing.

Eric and I lived in the city only a short drive away, so
I told Michael I just wanted to go home and sleep. There
was disappointment and worry in his eyes; he knew Eric
got off work at ten. I felt like adding that it was highly
unlikely, after tonight's episode, that Eric and I would
roll around in bed like a couple of newlyweds, but I de-
clined. I didn't think Michael and I were quite at a level
where he needed to know that.

Naturally, my alarm seemed to go off right after I fell
asleep, but the clock showed that, indeed, four hours had
passed. I saw Eric sleeping peacefully by my side. It was a
good sign that at least he came home. Not that I expected
he wouldn't, but nothing was normal anymore, and I
wouldn't have been surprised at anything. I quietly took
a quick shower and put on fresh clothes before heading
back to the department.

Michael wasn't there yet, but he came strolling in
shortly. He didn't look like he slept much, if at all. Coop
was thrilled to see us, desperate as he was for his own
four-hour reprieve. He was halfway out the door, waiting
for us so he could leave.

Drinking our third cup of coffee to wake ourselves up
and clear our heads, Michael and I finally started in on
the case. Now both cases had become full-blown national news, and our parking lot had enough news vans

to cover the O. J. Simpson trial. A section of the road that runs alongside the department had actually been closed off to hold what media the parking lot couldn't. The department helicopters were still in the air, searching the county. Every poor soul who drove a white station wagon was pulled over and put on the ground at gunpoint. Most people understood. Unless you lived in a coal mine, it was impossible not to know what was going on. A few who were stopped threatened lawsuits, but nothing anyone took seriously.

For the next two days, Michael and I scoured every possible lead. The media was pressuring everyone, Michael and me the most.

The only good the media brought was that three other law-enforcement agencies contacted us with similar murders. They had missed our teletypes, but saw the news. Detectives from the Topeka PD, in Kansas, the Peoria PD in Illinois, and the Indianapolis PD were flying in first thing the next day with their files. The detective from Tampa was coming the day after. Each of their cases was over ten years old. The FBI officially took over the investigation on the second morning Ashley Sanders was missing, because, for now, it seemed the suspect was staying in this area. They formed a task force headquartered at Richland Metro with all the agency detectives, including me, and put Michael in charge of it all.

After doing everything humanly possible to try to find Ashley Sanders, we hit a dead end, and she'd only been missing for two days. There were uniform officers that had been awake for forty-eight hours straight, walking every square inch of the county. If Ashley Sanders was in Richland County, we would have found her.

The afternoon of the second day was spent arranging the room for the task force, a large conference room in the detective bureau. All the photographs of the victims with all their information had to be visibly posted on the wall and each investigator had to have a work space. Michael must've read my mind after we finished putting the room together.

"I really need a drink. We don't have to be back until five tomorrow morning, so how 'bout it?"

"Follow me, sir. I shall lead ye to the nearest watering hole," I said in a horrible, fake English accent, waving my arm toward the door.

Michael laughed out loud. I told him I would meet him out by my car, but needed to make a phone call first. I wanted to try to call Eric before we left since I hadn't spoken to him in two days. He was on a day off today, so I couldn't catch him at roll call. He'd been avoiding my calls and only left messages about the girls on my voice mail. My mother got the girls yesterday and took them back to Cleveland for a week—or two if needed—of fun and sun by the lake. Selina only had a couple days of school left anyway, so it didn't matter. My mom was used to helping out when a case consumed our lives, and the girls just looked at it as another vacation. Eric and I were very lucky. The girls adored both sets of grandparents and loved spending as much time with them as possible.

I didn't call Eric after all. I was tired of constantly trying to communicate with him when he was not making any attempt to contact me. Nothing. From now on, if he wanted to talk, he could find a way to get hold of me. The anxiety, pain, and fear of the situation notwithstanding, I'd had it.

We went to the quietest dive bar I knew, with maybe four local drunks in the entire place, and took seats at the bar. The bartender greeted me by name. (Coop and I have had many a drink there.)

"Old boyfriend?" Behind a straight face, Michael's eyes laughed.

"Cute, Michael."

For the next five hours, we did shot after shot, and drank beer after beer, hitting such an inebriated state that it was impossible not to talk openly. Neither of us could control what was coming out of our mouths. There was also the chance that we would get called back to work, so we were taking a huge risk drinking like we were. It was only when I asked Michael a question I've always wanted to know the answer to, that I thought, maybe, I went too far. I turned my stool to face him. The stools were so close together, our legs intertwined. Seeing two Michaels, I grabbed his face and pulled him as close to mine as possible, and tried to speak as clearly as I could, hoping my question didn't come out in one long unintelligible mush of words.

"Michael, come here."

"I'm as close as I'm gonna get." He was laughing and waving his arms loosely.

"Do you regret not making love to me when we were in West Virginia last year? I want the truth."

He stopped laughing, and in fact, didn't smile at all. I let go of his face, thinking I'd made him angry. His stare suddenly became so fixed, I thought for a brief second he wanted to haul off and hit me.

"Michael, I'm sor—"

"Stop, CeeCee. We went over this before. But now, a year later, do you really, I mean really, want me to answer that truthfully?"

"Michael, if you don't want to. I wasn't trying to upset—"

"Answer me. Do you want the truth?"

"Yes," I answered timidly, although now I wasn't so sure. But it was too late to back down.

He put his beer down on the bar before turning back to face me again. He sat looking at me for thirty seconds before taking a deep breath.

"Every day of every week of every month of the entire last year, I have done nothing but regret the decision I made that night. I have tried to will myself back in time so I can change the past, like a character in some dopey movie." He grabbed his beer and took a long drink. "My first day back, when I saw you, I felt like someone smacked me with a hammer. All I could think about was I had a chance to be with you, make love to you, and I blew it. I can't help but think that had I made a different decision, you would be with me now, and not Eric."

He took another drink and continued. "Every time I was in Cleveland seeing my son, all I could think about was how close you were. Just a short drive away. There was a time, about three months ago, when I couldn't take it anymore and drove down to talk to you. I sat in the department parking lot till you walked out and got in your car, but lost my nerve and drove right back. Seeing you for a few seconds like that did nothing but make it worse, plus I felt like a stalker."

I just stared at him and realized, like I had that night in West Virginia, that I wanted him more than anything right then, and I didn't believe the alcohol had anything to do with it. It simply made me more impatient. I was getting ready to suggest we could easily make up for lost time, but he wanted answers from me first.

"Now it's your turn. Something I want to ask you, and I want the truth."

I didn't know what was about to happen and I was very scared, actually. If I thought all Michael wanted to know was whether I would sleep with him now, we'd be out the door. Unfortunately, I was smart enough to know that wasn't all he wanted, and my nerves broke through, something Michael noticed immediately.

"CeeCee, stop being nervous, you don't even know what I'm going to say," he said, lightly putting his hand on my knee and leaning forward.

Sorry, but I had a pretty good idea. I was a decent investigator myself, and even being as drunk as I was, I braced for the question. I was scared because I knew I wouldn't be able to lie to him, this close, face to face. Or ever.

"Go ahead, Michael. Ask."

"I want to know . . . did you ever regret not choosing me over Eric, even once?"

I knew it, and as much as I wanted to lie for the sake of my marriage, I couldn't. Michael was as rattled as I was, nervously anticipating my answer, so I gave it to him, slowly and truthfully.

"Yes, Michael. I have had times where I have regretted it. Now, particularly, is one of those times."

Michael didn't answer; he merely pulled me to him and began kissing me slowly and passionately. I didn't feel guilty, I didn't pull away, and I wanted not part of him, but all of him.

He didn't think they would make it to the motel the way they were kissing and fondling each other in the parking lot of the seedy bar. How lovely. CeeCee Gallagher was nothing but an unfaithful, cheating whore. Maybe he could use this to his advantage. It wasn't necessary even to maintain a safe distance when he followed them back to Agent Hagerman's motel; they would never notice they were being followed. They were too drunk and too engulfed in their own sexual urges. He could relate to that, he thought as he began humming. Oh, the excitement he felt at his own brilliance! Fooling two smart, high-profile investigators almost compared to the feelings he felt when he was with Elsa—but not quite, for there was nothing in human consciousness that compared to that. He snapped the picture before they clumsily stumbled into the motel room. Then it was time to leave. They would be there all night, and he had other things to prepare for. . . .

CHAPTER ELEVEN

It seemed we couldn't get back to his hotel room fast enough, barely getting through the door before we were pulling each other's clothes off. An entire year of waiting and wanting exploded that very minute. He was everything I hoped for and someone I badly needed.

We fell onto the bed in a mad frenzy. Then he suddenly stopped. For a split second I thought he was going to back out again until I recognized he was just enjoying the moment and trying to believe it was truly happening. We hadn't even made love yet, and feeling his body on top of mine was too much; I didn't want to stop. I didn't think I could. It was clearly important to Michael, though. He gently brushed away the long, blonde hair that had fallen on my face and lightly touched my cheek. He was shaking a little, just as I remember he did that night in West Virginia.

"I have to say something," he whispered. "I know you're confused about how you feel right now, but I need you to know that I love you. I've never stopped loving you since the day we met, CeeCee."

"I do love you, Michael, don't ever doubt that."

And then we made love, over and over, falling asleep in each other's arms a little less than two hours before we had to be back at the department. In the middle of my slumber, I awoke to see Michael propped up on his elbow gazing down at me. I felt myself begin to smile. "Go back to sleep. We've only got a bit more time till we have to be back at work."

"I can't, CeeCee. I don't know if this will ever happen again, and I can't believe it's happening now. I want to enjoy every minute I have you to myself." I kept smiling until I fell back asleep.

I heard Michael whistling in the shower when our wake-up call came. I was exhausted and thoroughly hungover. Thankfully, I had a spare set of clothes in my car that I routinely kept in case I got caught at work. I can't even imagine explaining to Eric where I'd been all night. I have never slept with another man while I was married. The magnitude of what I had done quickly set in. But I pushed those demons away for the moment and climbed out of bed.

By the time I had gotten my clothes out of the car, Michael was out of the shower. We didn't have much time, so I took a quick shower, threw on some clothes and a dash of makeup, and, ready to go, grabbed my bag and car keys. Michael was already waiting at the door. We hadn't spoken much that morning, which Michael did not fail to point out on the way to the department.

"CeeCee, you really OK? You haven't said much since you got up."

"I'm fine." Michael probably saw through my fake smile instantly. "I'm just tired."

Michael remained quiet the rest of the ride to work. Now that our situation was out in the open, he knew I was in extreme turmoil, and it scared him. It scared me, too. All I could think about was my girls and how Eric was their father, and I may have just thrown it all away. The bad part was, I did love Michael, and that just made things more complicated and agonizing.

Coop and Kincaid were waiting. Coop looked at me as if the imaginary letter imprinted on my chest was bright pink neon instead of regulation scarlet. I remember back in college I had the standard couple of indiscretions. My roommate and I would always laugh that the walk back to our apartment the morning after was the walk of shame. That was exactly how I felt now, and Coop's accusing stare didn't help. He knew exactly what had happened.

My habit was to play my office voice mail on the speakerphone so I could do something else while I listened. The first message blaring out of the phone came in at two in the morning. It was Eric, trying to find out where I was. I hit the off button immediately. Too loud and too late. Michael, sensing the tension, excused himself to go get a coffee. Kincaid followed. Then Coop started in.

"Interesting message. Funny, Eric called my cell at three this morning looking for you. I didn't know what to say since the last time I saw you was four o'clock yesterday afternoon when you were leaving with Michael."

I glared at him, one of my best and closest friends. However, he needed to be careful about where his loyalties lay, or decide whether he should remain neutral. He was good friends with Eric and worked with me, was my friend as well. His best bet would be to stay out of it.

"Hmm. Jordan must've had something to do. I'm amazed he actually found time to call his wife," I barked, grabbing files and stuffing them in my bag.

"Stop it. CeeCee, do you know for a fact that something is going on with Eric and Jordan? Or are you just assuming?"

"I don't know, but I think you do! Why don't you tell me the truth since I can't seem to get it from Eric! Is he sleeping with her?" I was upset already and my day had barely started.

Coop sighed. "CeeCee, you know I'm in a bad spot, working and being friends with both of you," he said, quietly looking at the door to make sure no one was listening. "Eric's been asking the same thing. I told him I don't know anything. As for him and Jordan, I don't know for sure if they're sleeping together. Do I think *something* is going on? Yes, I do. I just don't know what. As for you, I didn't know what to tell Eric when he called. He put me in a very bad position."

"I stayed at my dad's, Coop. Eric and I haven't been getting along, so I went there and crashed a couple of hours," I lied. And I think he knew it.

As if I were being forever punished, my dad, who has probably seen the inside of my office twice, walked in. He was the lieutenant of the night shift and worked until six in the morning. Seeing my car already, he decided to take this rare opportunity to come up for a visit. How nice.

"Who crashed where?" he bellowed, making me and Coop jump in our seats.

"Hi, Pop. I was just telling Coop I crashed on your couch last night for a couple of hours."

"You did? Was Carly up?" He was referring to my stepmother.

"Nope. I snuck in, took a power nap, and snuck out," I continued to lie, making me feel even worse. Coop's look made me feel even more terrible, if that was possible.

We chatted for a few more minutes before Michael and Kincaid returned. My dad left, and the rest of us started in on business as if nothing had happened. I was glad there was something to take my mind off my disastrous personal life.

Kincaid gave us a quick briefing. All the detectives from the other agencies would be arriving in Cleveland within a couple of hours, and she and Coop were going up there to pick everyone up and take them to the hotel where the FBI was staying. After they got settled in, our first meeting would convene in the late afternoon.

Since it was my understanding that Michael was in charge, I gave him a raised brow, silently asking why Kincaid still seemed to be running the show. He pointed to the hallway and smiled. I understood. While they were out of my office earlier, Michael filled her in on everything and let her do the briefing so she could feel important. If she had things like briefings to occupy her time, she wouldn't screw up anything else. Smart man, my Michael.

Kincaid said the other two agents would continue interviewing sex offenders all day and that more agents would be here tomorrow. He and I were to be on standby, ready to go in case anything broke. In the meantime, we had to check, for the millionth time, to see if anyone missed anything. I was sick of going over the case files. We had gone over them with a microscope and couldn't possibly have missed anything. But, yes, we did.

When going over Hanna Parker's final lab report, I saw another sheet was stuck to the back of it. It had come fresh off the copier and was put into the file that way; the two sheets had not been separated and the static made it seem like one page. One would think we would've discovered it the previous hundred times we'd gone through the file, but, considering the file was now three inches thick, with papers jammed together, something like that was bound to happen. Pulling the pages apart revealed writing on the back of the lab report, a continuation of what was found on Hanna's dress. Traces of fiberglass.

"Michael!"

"What?" He jumped a little, startled by the excitement in my voice.

I handed him the report and explained the error. He looked at it and his face broke out into a smile when he handed the report back.

"Well?" I asked eagerly.

"You know what this means, don't you?" he said.

"Of course. it means Hanna was on, or around, insulation."

"Right, which means she was probably in an attic or unfinished room somewhere." He stood and began pacing. "This obviously doesn't solve the case, but it's a hell of a break."

Three more hours of concentrated work went by before Michael suggested we take a break for breakfast. Hearing the growls coming from my stomach, I leapt at the chance. As we pulled into the parking lot of a small downtown diner, my cell phone rang. Having caller ID, I usually didn't answer my phone if it didn't show a number. For whatever reason, this morning I did. Michael was driving. He found a parking spot, pulled in, turned the car off, and waited for me to take the call.

"Hello?"

No one answered.

"Helloooo?" I asked again, but still received no response. It sounded as if there was a bad connection, so I started to hang up.

"Detective Gallagher?" A deep, gruff male voice came out of my phone.

"Yes?" I asked uncertainty. Michael suddenly became very attentive, focusing on the perplexed look on my face.

The man started to chuckle quietly before getting louder again. He began laughing loud enough so I could hold the phone away from my ear so Michael could hear him. For a moment, I froze. This was my personal cell phone, and very few people had the number.

"Who the hell is this?" I barked. The laughing stopped.

"I have a poem for you, Detective. Pay attention: *Babies are dead, and CeeCee is blue, another one gone, find the other pink shoe!*"

"Oh my God!" I gasped, looking at Michael with sheer, blind terror.

"What? Give me the phone!" He reached out. I gently slapped his hand away.

"Oh, Detective? Are you there?"

"I'm still here. Who is this? Where is Ashley Sanders, and is she OK? Just tell me if she's OK." I tried to keep my voice even.

"Now, now, now! You know better than that, Cecelia. Tell me, how was the agent in bed last night, Cecelia? Did you leave that exquisite black blouse on when he fucked you?" He began to laugh once more, then quickly hung up the phone.

I was shaking as I put down my phone. Michael was ready to go through the roof waiting for an explanation of what just happened.

"What, CeeCee. What!"

"Michael, we're in trouble." I began to panic and worry about the safety of my family. "That was him, our murderer! He's been following us. He's knows about last night. He knows *me*! He recited a sick, deranged version of the 'Roses Are Red' poem." I got out of the car for some some air. Michael did the same.

"What do you mean last night? What about last night?"

"Michael, he asked if I left my black blouse on while you fucked me. He knew what I was wearing yesterday, and he saw us at the hotel. That's what! He even called me Cecelia, *and* he has my personal cell phone number!" By now, I was pacing back and forth like an animal alongside the car.

Michael got on his phone and called the main FBI office, giving them my cell number so they could try to
trace the last call by signal, if possible.

"That's a waste. If he's smart enough to do all this, he
sure as hell wouldn't call me from anything other than a
pay phone."

"At least we can determine that he's still in the county,
CeeCee, which is very important."

He was right.

*Ignorance must be a prerequisite for law enforcement these days,
he thought. Smiling, he watched as Detective Gallagher and
Agent Hagerman got into their car. The thought of how she
would explain her indiscretion to her coworkers brought forth a
mean-spirited burst of happiness as he carefully followed them
back to the police department.*

*This is what God must feel like. CeeCee Gallagher and
Michael Hagerman were nothing but characters in a plan of
which he had the ultimate control. That thought made him relish
his own brilliance. He had outwitted, and would continue to do
so, the top minds in law enforcement, just as he had for the last
thirty years.*

*The poem was simple enough. It came from a spontaneous
thought this morning, and he wrote it down quickly. He was
regularly amazed at his own cleverness for spur-of-the-moment
games; this one, the poem, stated everything to sheer perfection.
Elsa had been so proud of him she had given him a special gift,
a gift that made him feel glorious. His assumptions were correct.
Gallagher would have the poem figured out within minutes.*

*Thinking of her again, his smile faded. She was weak, this
famous detective. He'd heard it in her voice, seen it as she paced
back and forth by the car after he'd spoken with her on the
phone. Feeling a little disappointed, he wondered if he'd made
the right decision. Everything he'd read and seen until now, even*

the incident twenty-six years ago, led him to believe she was impossible to break. Now she was letting him down, and that made him angry. If only she knew. She really didn't want to make him angry.

He kept driving straight as they turned into the parking lot, looking ahead and chastising them for not paying attention to the fact that he was right behind them. Standard police work, you idiot. Always check your mirror to see if you're being followed.

He smiled again, knowing he could overlook their errors for today, but the low thud from the trunk of his car forced him to refocus. For today was only beginning . . .

CHAPTER TWELVE

Having lost our appetites, we went back to the department and alerted Kincaid, Coop, and the other agents about the phone call. I desperately wanted to omit the part where the suspect referred to Michael and me at the hotel, but that would be withholding evidence. Of course, when I got to that part, the other agents looked at each other and snickered. Coop glared. Kincaid was oblivious to it.

"What did he mean by that stuff at the hotel?" she asked, figuring something must be up but not knowing exactly what.

A large smile appeared on Coop's face, letting me know he was going to be very amused to see how I would get out of answering the question honestly.

"Just a guess from a lunatic pervert. I dropped Michael off at the hotel last night, and the guy just assumed something, or else he was just trying to push our buttons. I never even got out of the car." If I wasn't thirty-four years old, I would've stuck my tongue out at Coop and said, 'Smartass, what do you think about that!'"

"All right, then. Can you remember the poem?" Kincaid, mercifully, moved on. Michael stayed silent.

"I already wrote it down." I handed her the scrap of paper I grabbed off my desk.

"Okay. Michael, you take it from here," she said, handing him the note.

He had been leaning against my desk with his arms folded, observing Kincaid's briefing, worldless as usual. He looked at the poem again before passing it to the other agents.

"You guys pick this apart, see if there's any underlying message. Mostly, he's laughing at us because we haven't found Ashley or, should I say, Ashley's body yet. I think it's safe to assume she's probably dead." Reluctant nods of agreement followed. "One more thing, CeeCee. He's picked you out, so I don't think it's a good idea that you're by yourself at all right now. Are your kids still in Cleveland?" I nodded. "Good, keep them there. Let's get rolling."

Kincaid and Coop had to leave since they were already running late in picking up the detectives at the airport. I suggested to Michael we make an attempt to eat again and plan our next step. He agreed. We were leaving when I got a call from Captain Norris.

"CeeCee, Ashley Sanders's mom just got one of those little shoes in the mail, like the Parkers did."

"Let me take a guess, it was pink and matched the one found on her book bag."

"Yup. Crime lab is here now. I'll call you if anything comes up."

I told Michael, who promptly called the other agents. I guess finding the other pink shoe was no longer an option. What I didn't understand was why the killer called me with the poem the same morning Mrs. Sanders got the shoe in the mail. Wouldn't it have been better to make us sweat it out for a couple of days?

We went back to the same diner for the second time in one day, this time even more tired and hungry. And for the second time, when we pulled into the parking lot, my phone rang.

"You've got to be kidding me!" barked Michael as he looked at the phone. "Is the guy on the fucking roof of the diner watching us or what? How does he do it? No one appears to be following us." Just to prove his point, he craned his neck all around, looking for suspicious cars and upward to see if anyone was on a roof.

I couldn't believe it either, and now I was so nervous that I wasn't sure I would be able to talk to the killer again. My caller ID showed it was Eric. Maybe it would have been easier if it had been the killer. I asked Michael to wait inside the diner, reluctantly telling him why I needed to take the call. To say the least, he did not look pleased as he got out of the car and headed for the diner.

"Hello." My voice was shaking.

"It's me. Can you talk?"

"Yes, but I don't know what there is to talk about. You haven't wanted to speak to me in days."

"Do you want to tell me where you were last night?"

Eric was good, I'll give him that. He threw the question out right in the beginning, throwing me off guard; his intention, I'm sure. I was flooded with guilt and on the verge of tears, but I'd be damned if I'd tell him the truth. And damned I just might be.

A 911 page beeped in my ear, cutting into our call. It meant a major emergency, most likely with the Ashley Sanders case. I assumed that her body was found.

"Eric, I have to go. Now. I just got a 911. Can we talk later?" With no response, he simply hung up.

My stomach knotted, but I couldn't worry about Eric right now. While I was starting to call the office, I was motioning for Michael, who was sitting by a window in the diner, to quickly come outside. I was on hold and still waiting when Michael came out.

"What's the matter?" he asked breathlessly.

"I just got a 911 page. I bet they found Ashley's body, and I'm still on hold."

It seemed like eons before someone picked up the line. After explaining that I had just been paged, it was a matter of seconds before I was told why. And I didn't need a mirror to know my face went pale. I hung up the phone and looked at Michael, feeling like I was going to vomit.

"Good Lord, CeeCee! What's wrong?" Michael was impatient.

"Michael, it's not about Ashley. There's another Amber Alert, a five-year-old Amish girl walking home from school."

"He told us."

"He told us what?" I hated riddles.

"The poem—'another one gone.' We assumed it was Ashley Sanders. The pink shoe was found first, then '*another one gone*.' He went in reverse. He told us he was going to take another child *today*, and we missed it!"

After it sunk in what Michael was saying, I still thought that as far as prevention goes, he was wrong.

"Even if we *had* known and figured out the poem earlier, it wouldn't have made a difference. He never referred to a place or any timetable. We can't have officers surrounding every child in the county, for crying out loud!"

"I realize that, CeeCee," he snapped. "I'm just angry at how this is playing out. The killer still has the fucking upper hand."

Recriminations and further analysis were useless. We needed to get to the kidnapping scene as quickly as possible, so I got in the car without replying. He drove while I made calls, the first being to Kincaid, who was already aware of the alert. It was about a twenty-minute drive, fifteen if Michael drove faster. Planktown Road, where the child was taken from, was one of the northernmost roads in the county. Admonishing myself for not driving since I knew the area better, I was yelling out directions to Michael.

The officers gave a suspect vehicle description; a newer, red passenger car. No suspect description. The child, five-year-old Emma Yoder, was wearing a light blue floor-length dress with long sleeves, a white bonnet, and black shoes. A helicopter flew over us as we neared the scene.

"The perfect victim," I mumbled, looking out the window.

"What did you say? Do I turn here?"

"No, turn left at the next road. I said she's the perfect victim. With all the media attention right now, the suspect needs to be careful. A brilliant stroke to choose an Amish child. No one pays attention to the Amish, they don't read or watch news, they're not overly cooperative with law enforcement, and they're isolated. The perfect victim. He has long thought this out ahead of time."

"I do believe you're right, Detective," Michael muttered, pulling onto Planktown Road.

The sheriff was already on scene and saw us coming down the road. He waved us over.

"How's the family doing?" I asked the sheriff, nodding in the direction of the farm.

"You know them, CeeCee. When the officers first got here, the father insisted on discussing the matter with the Amish elders first, before talking with us. I guess it was the wife who spoke up, surprisingly, and started prodding her son to tell the officers what he saw." He took his eyeglasses off and peered through the lens before putting them back on.

"I don't know what to do." He sighed. "We've got to figure something out. I know it's the FBI's party right now, but this is still my county and these children live in it. I feel responsible for them. CeeCee, please." He lowered his voice as if there were a million people around; there wasn't one, "I don't care what you have to do to find this asshole, but do it. And I don't care how. I'm a parent, too. Do you hear what I'm telling you? I'll take the fall."

I heard him loud and clear. The Sheriff of Richland County had just ordered me to forgo all laws, ethics, and morals, if necessary, to catch a child murderer. And when it was all said and done, let the chips fall where they may, he would take responsibility. If the life of one child was saved, it would be worth taking the risk.

Frankly, what the sheriff just asked me to do was nothing compared to what I've done in the past. I'm by no means some rogue, dirty, or corrupt cop, but I've had my share of sins. The worst were trotted out last year in West Virginia when I almost died. I'd shot an unarmed man in the head on Murder Mountain and would do it again in a heartbeat, no questions asked. Eric, Michael, and Coop watched me do it, but none of them have ever brought it up, not once. And it will remain unspoken.

I told the sheriff I understood very clearly what he meant. He patted me on the back as we walked toward the farm. I went to see what Michael was doing. He was still standing by the car and had just hung up from call. He looked upset.

"That was my boss—the bigwig from Quantico himself. He's sending forty-five agents down here in the next twenty-four hours to scour every inch of this county. This is a nightmare, and he's keeping me in charge of it. He said I'm doing a good job. Can you believe it? Three kidnappings, one attempted, and one body found—oh, yeah—I'm doing a hell of a job!" he said with an amount of sarcasm unusual for him.

I gently touched his arm. "Michael, you're the best they've got. You *are* doing a hell of a job."

He just shook his head while leaning back against the car, arms folded. The Amber Alert had been put out on the radio five minutes ago, sixty-five minutes after the kidnapping—a world record. We were getting good at this.

"CeeCee, I'll tell you first before I tell the sheriff. My boss specifically wants local law enforcement involved only in the search. Not the investigation itself."

Hardly a surprise. The FBI can be a real group of assholes when it comes to local law enforcement. They waltz in, take all the information you've worked hard to get, and then leave, barely taking your phone calls afterward.

"Frankly, I've never agreed with the concept. Two heads are always better than one." Slowly, he stood. "I'm going to be busy working with the other agents when they get here. That means I won't get to see you as much. That makes it even worse and really bothers me."

He looked it, and I knew he felt it. I tried to make him feel a little better without leading him on too much, hoping he would be accepting enough to focus on the case instead of me.

"Michael, once the others arrive, we can all put our heads together." I put my hand on his cheek. "As for us, of course I'll see you and when this is all over—we'll sit down and really figure out about us."

"So I hear what sounds like a promise?"

I nodded before driving away. Looking in my rearview mirror at him, I realized we hadn't really been apart since he got here, and I was starting to feel more than a bit bothered that we were now going to be.

Instinctively, my police training kicked back in and my brain shifted to what the sheriff had told me to do.

Within thirty seconds, I knew where I was headed: back to the city to further investigate the one part of this case that made no sense at all. No sense as to why a person would venture into an almost hidden, modest-income, low-crime neighborhood to steal. No sense as to how quickly the car theft had run cold. I needed to go back and look deeper into the stolen brown van.

CHAPTER THIRTEEN

I hadn't been in my car for more than ten minutes when I heard from Michael, wanting to fill me in on the particulars of the kidnapping. Emily Yoder and her eight-year-old brother had been walking home from school when they started to argue about whose turn it was to clean the horse stalls when they got home.

"The brother was angry enough that he ran about fifty feet ahead of his sister, to scare her."

He went over the crest of a hill and was going to hide behind a tree to jump out at her, but she never came. Walking back up to the crest, he saw the back end of a red car and his sister getting into it. He yelled to her, but the car sped away.

"No cars had passed him, so the only logical explanation is the suspect turned around in the road."

All the brother could see in the driver's seat was the back of someone's head, but couldn't get more detailed than that. It then took him another twenty-five minutes to run home and tell his parents, who took another fifteen minutes getting to the nearest phone to call the police. That gave the suspect forty minutes to get out of the area.

"Forty minutes! He could've been almost to Cleveland by then!" I exclaimed.

"I know," Michael said hurriedly. "You were definitely right about how he picked this victim, and anticipating the lack of urgency and time it would take in calling the police. Listen, I have to get going, but I still don't think it's a good idea that you're alone. I just heard from the boss again and he said the first of the agents should be arriving within the hour. Just let me assign one to you?"

"Not a chance. Trust me, I'll be just fine."

Through the phone, I heard the helicopters arriving, signaling that Michael had to go. Yet again, a promise to talk later, though I didn't plan on speaking with him for the rest of the day and who knows how long after that.

I raced to my office, grabbed every case file pertaining to all the kidnappings and murders, called Kincaid to check in, then shut my door. My office is at the end of the hallway and the standard rule is if the door is closed, chances are the detective is gone. My car was parked deliberately on the other side of the building where I knew no one would see it. With any luck, I'd have some useful time alone.

I lost track of time going over every word on every page, focusing on the report of the stolen van, its owner, and the circumstances surrounding it. Who knows what time it was when I laid my head on my desk and fell asleep; I only knew it was very late.

It couldn't have been long afterward that someone lightly shook my shoulder. I sat up to find Eric, though hardly surprised he had found me. He was in uniform, and it dawned on me that he had gone back to night shift the day before and was still training Jordan. I was trying to get my eyes to focus when he pulled a chair over and sat down next to me.

"You know everyone's been looking for you," he said softly. "How come you didn't answer your phone?"

"I'm swamped," I said through a wide yawn, stretching my arms and back. "How'd you know I was here?"

"Your car was on the other side of the building, and as

logic would have it, I assumed you would be in here. Are you hiding from me?" He spoke quietly and carefully, the pain showing on his face.

"I'm hiding from everyone, not just you. The FBI took the entire case over. I think there's something important we missed, and . . ."

"And you think you'll find it before they do," he interrupted, and shook his head. He knew me inside and out.

Suddenly, seeing Eric there, I became conscious of how much I missed him and loved him. My anger about what happened over the last several days had flooded every other emotion I had. Now all the indescribable fragments of my feelings came tumbling back.

"So where's Jordan?" I asked defensively.

"Downstairs submitting evidence. CeeCee, we need to talk."

This time I interrupted. "I've tried that numerous times, but you chose to shut me out."

"I wasn't trying to ignore you. I just . . . I needed some time to sort things out. I didn't want to say anything I'd regret."

It was the ideal time for a cigarette, which I lit. Then I began to twirl the tip around in the ceramic pig ashtray on my desk. Selina had made it in art class; it was supposed to be a bowl, but turned out a little too small. Our daughter together. Our life together. I could not understand how Eric and I ever got to this point in our marriage.

"What exactly *are* you regretting now, Eric? Is there something I need to know?" The tears were starting to surface.

"CeeCee, do you love me?"

"Of course I do, Eric You don't need to ever worry about that."

He looked down at the floor and asked quietly, "Are you also in love with Michael?"

I hesitated before I answered, my tears now flowing freely. "I don't know" was my very simple, but telling, reply.

Eric's face openly showed the depth of his misery, and tears were brimming in his eyes as well.

"That's what I thought." He paused. "CeeCee, I love you. I'm not ready for this to be over."

I grabbed him and held on tight, crying into his shoulder like a small child. It was all my fault. I had betrayed him, our marriage, and myself. And through it all, with my love for Eric overwhelming me, my feelings for Michael had not faded away like I'd hoped. When I finally felt composed enough to let go of Eric to grab a huge wad of tissues, I was a mess. He kissed my forehead, the only dry area of my face, before wiping his eyes and standing up.

"I think you should go home and get a good night's sleep. You're exhausted. The rest of this we can talk about later."

I started sobbing again after he left, and this time I couldn't stop. I cried so much I was sick to my stomach and had a headache that seemed to take over my entire body. Eventually, though much later, I stopped crying and did exactly what Eric said. I haltingly grabbed my things and went home.

On the way, I turned my cell phone back on and checked voice mail. There were eleven messages. I guess Eric was right when he said everyone was looking for me. Two were from Kincaid, one from Coop, two from Eric, and exactly six from Michael, who sounded downright frantic by the fifth one. I knew I should probably call him. I knew he was awake in his room right now worrying about me, but I just couldn't deal with any more tonight. It felt good to be going to my own home to sleep in my own bed.

Once there, I quickly peeled my clothes off and slept for precisely two hours and fifteen minutes before I got out of bed to get ready to start another day.

I checked my voice mail again on the way to the department and, just as I suspected, there was a message from Michael, left at three A.M. Eric wasn't even finished with his shift yet when I pulled into the parking lot. As I was deleting Michael's message, the phone rang again. I looked at the number and saw it was Kincaid. I had no choice but to answer.

"CeeCee! Where the hell have you been? Everyone's been very worried about you!" She breathed hard into the phone. "A jogger just found Ashley Sanders's body by one of the trails along the Clearfork Reservoir. I know it's the FBI's show, but I'd like you to be there in case they have questions since you know the case the best. They should be down there by now. I told them you're coming."

I didn't know how much more of this I could take, but I told Naomi I'd leave immediately. The Clearfork Reservoir is a large lake used often for boating and fishing. Jogging trails run around the entire perimeter. The lake is just outside Lexington, a small suburb of Mansfield in the southern part of the county, far from where Emily Yoder was taken, but not that far from where Ashley lived.

There are several pull-offs around the lake, and the crime scene was by one on the north side. Our department had uniformed officers blocking off the scene and guarding it so the FBI could go in and work its magic. It was still mostly dark, and my first thought was how could anyone get up and go jogging at this hour of the morning. There was probably twenty minutes before daybreak, so I grabbed a flashlight.

The opening in the woods leading to the trail looked pitch black. Eric and Jordan were standing nearby. When Eric noticed me approaching, he headed right for me. He immediately pulled me into an embrace and kissed my cheek. Jordan, on the other hand, walked in the opposite direction.

"Did you get any sleep?" he asked.

"Not much. I just can't believe this is all happening."

Eric started brushing my hair back from my face, his arm still around me when I happened to look directly at the opening in the woods. Michael was standing there, looking at Eric and me with unreserved, complete devastation. Eric turned to see what I was looking at and let go of me the minute he saw Michael.

And as if this quaint scenario couldn't get any better, Eric shocked me into next week by what he did next. Seeing Michael watching, Eric smiled at him, turned around, grabbed me again, and gave me a tongue-exchanging lip-lock that could go in the record books. It was impossible for me to break away. I was simply too stunned. Before I was aware of why he was doing it, he stopped, and Michael was gone. Now I was seething.

"Why did you do that?"

"You're my wife. I was just giving you a kiss. Is there something wrong with that?" He smiled innocently.

"That was pretty childish, don't you think?" I was getting angrier and angrier.

He stopped smiling. "Kissing my wife is childish?" He was yelling now, and other uniforms started looking at us.

"You don't have to make a scene." I looked around me. "You not only proved your point, but drove it home with a vengeance."

I stomped away. I was furious, and he was getting there, but we didn't need a domestic dispute in the middle of a murder scene. I knew Eric hated Michael, but I obviously underestimated how far he would go. Eric had most likely planned this. He clearly saw Michael arrive at the scene and assumed I was coming. That's why when he saw me, he wanted to get to me before Michael did. The entire incident was so ridiculous it didn't deserve much thought, but lately the emotional stakes were very high. Every contact meant something. How much longer was this going to continue?

The crime scene was approximately fifty feet from the opening of the trail. The FBI was using our crime lab, which had already erected several lights to use until daybreak. I gave my name to the agent blocking the trail and keeping the crime-scene log. He had to write down the name of everyone who went in and out of the scene, and the time they did both. Kincaid was right: they were expecting me. He pointed to Michael, who was standing about twenty feet away along the edge of the woods, and said I needed to contact Agent Hagerman.

Walking through the all-too-familiar scene of white vans, flashbulbs, and men wearing white gloves, I came up behind Michael, who was with two other agents. They were taking photographs of the small body that lay along the edge of the woods.

"Agent Hagerman?" I said quietly.

"Yes?" He turned around, saw me, gave me a look of contempt, and began writing on his clipboard.

"I was directed to you. You're expecting me?"

"That's right, Detective," he said, not looking up from the clipboard. "If you would like to take a look at the body, we can start there."

My heart sank. If not for the task at hand, I feared right

then and there he would have nothing to do with me ever again. I would have to deal with this later, but for now I had to help catch a murderer.

I stepped to the edge and saw Ashley Sanders's body laid out perfectly on her back, makeup on, and a ribbon in her hair. She, like Hanna, had her fingernails painted. The difference was Ashley wasn't holding a shoe; the killer had already mailed the other one to her mother. I was bent over, closely looking for all similarities and any differences.

"Do you see anything, Detective?"

If he referred to me as *detective* again, I thought I would scream. Or hit him. Or both.

"Actually, *Agent* Hagerman," I began, emphasizing his title, "I do see a discrepancy from the last murder. Hanna Parker was brushed off, clean per se, as if a lot of care was taken to lay her out." I pointed at Ashley's dress. "That's not the case here. Her dress is wrinkled and dirty, and her hair is a mess, the ribbon just thrown on top. He's getting sloppy and trying to get caught, or he's frustrated."

"Right, Detective, we already figured that out. Do you have anything new to add?" He sounded so condescending I wanted to slap him.

"I don't remember figuring that out," I heard one of the agents whisper to another.

By now everyone at the crime scene was watching us. I reacted by laughing, even though I was far from amused.

"No, Agent, I do not. Furthermore, it is very clear you have everything here quite under control and are no longer in need of my services. On that note, I'm leaving." I turned and began quickly walking down the trail, feeling the tears once again well up in my eyes. I would not cry in front of these people.

"CeeCee, wait!" It was Michael.

"That's *detective*, asshole!" I kept walking, but he grabbed my arm, pulling me up short.

"Please, I'm sorry. Give me one minute," he begged, out of breath. "You have to forgive me, I should've never treated you like that." He wiped the sweat off his forehead with his arm. "I was up all night, thinking something might have happened to you. You never called back. And then I got to watch that charming production with Eric. You were with him last night, weren't you?"

I was so exhausted by now that I couldn't believe I was still functioning. Michael reached over and gently wiped the tears that yet again had begun to flow down my cheeks.

"Michael, he is my husband. We're married. I saw Eric last night briefly, and we talked, but if you're wondering if we slept together, no. As for what happened between us just now, that was some type of juvenile jab at you on Eric's part. You didn't stick around for the hostility after-ward." I gazed down the trail toward the crime scene.

"Yes, I did. I heard *a little* bit of what you said. I wasn't that far down the trail yet. I'm not stupid. I knew what Eric was doing. He was already here when I arrived and was determined to make me notice him. But, when I saw him kiss you and play with your hair, I couldn't help it. I freaked."

"That was no reason to stand there and belittle me in front of thirty agents."

"I know, I know. One of the agents actually called me an asshole, though not quite with the flair that you had. CeeCee, I'm sorry. Enough."

Michael leaned over and lightly kissed my forehead, past caring that twenty of the thirty FBI agents were watching. I knew we had been the golden rumor of the FBI, but I didn't realize so many agents knew. It was time for me to leave.

It was still too early to go over and talk to the van owner, but that was fine since I wanted to do it in uniform and so needed time to change. I headed back home. Not that I expected wearing a uniform would do all that much, but I always want to appear intimidating even if the person I'm talking to is innocent. I certainly don't intimidate anyone when in plain clothes, so my uniform is the only option. It makes people less likely to lie, or at least makes it harder for them.

After changing, I realized my gun belt was in my locker at work. In my exhaustion, I also forgot I'd need a marked police car, so I resigned myself to going back to the department. Coop came into my office while I was putting on my gun belt.

He let out a low whistle. "Wow! It's been a long time since I've seen you in uniform—you're kinda turning me on," he wisecracked. "What the hell are you doing?"

"I'd like to hear that, too," Michael said, standing in my doorway.

He was the last person I expected to show up here. I assumed the crime scene would keep him until at least late morning. I didn't know what to tell him. I wasn't supposed to be investigating now that the FBI had taken over. Obviously, I had to improvise a way out. He was looking me up and down, smiling. It never occurred to me that he hadn't seen me in full uniform before. I didn't quite understand what the big deal was.

"I have an interview to do, but it won't take long." I was putting the final belt attachment on.

"Who?" Coop and Michael asked in unison.

"You know, Coop." I gave him a look, begging him to

play along, which he didn't, considering the clueless look on his face. "That rape suspect I never got to from three weeks ago. I'm not doing anything this morning, so I thought I'd take care of it first thing."

"What's his name? And why, exactly, are you going in uniform?" Michael asked, suspicious, while leaning against the doorframe.

"Keith Edward Parsons, and he's a rapist. When I talk to him, he needs to look at me as a police officer, not a woman. Hence, the uniform."

I grabbed keys to the marked police car I needed and headed for the door, trying to avoid further conversation. Michael blocked me. All I could see was the smirk on his face.

"I think I'll go with you. You shouldn't face a rapist alone." He knew damn well I wasn't doing what I said; he just wanted me to admit it.

"No, you're not going. You have a case to work, and I've done this job for twelve years without an escort. I'll be fine, thank you."

"CeeCee, let's not go any further. Just tell me what you're up to."

I pushed him to the side to get through the doorway. "Nothing, Michael! I have to get going. I'll call you."

I looked back to see if he was following me down the hall. He wasn't, but he *was* watching. He knew I was doing something that involved the kidnappings; he just didn't know what.

I found the spare police car I needed and checked the lights, sirens, bells and whistles before pulling out of the parking lot like a bat out of hell. I didn't look to see if Michael was following me, but if he was, he'd never keep up.

Pulling onto Carl Malone's street, I had a clear view of his driveway. His empty driveway. He didn't have a full-time job, so I expected him to be here this morning. Disappointed, I pulled into the driveway, went up to the front door, and knocked loudly. No answer. I walked around the house to get a good look while it was daylight since I didn't want to be fumbling around tonight when I returned.

Coop called while I was on my way home to change into street clothes before heading back to the department.

"Hold your breath, CeeCee. The FBI just announced they have a suspect."

CHAPTER FOURTEEN

Coop continued, "The guys going through the sex-offender lists called Michael about five minutes ago. I guess we're having a big powwow in one hour, downstairs in the community room."

"Did they say who it is?" I was euphoric. Please, let this case be solved.

"Nope, not yet. They're announcing it at the meeting. Everyone will be there. See you then."

I was genuinely thrilled the FBI had found a suspect. In a case such as this, it doesn't matter who does what, as long as a child killer is caught before he takes another life. I found myself actually whistling a little as I went into my office. I called my mother and told her it wouldn't be much longer for her to keep the girls. I talked to them, like I did twice daily since they'd been gone, and couldn't wait to have them back home.

The community room was filled wall to wall. Every FBI agent, out-of-town and local detective, plus the sheriff, chief, and Kincaid were there. Standing in front of the room, waiting to begin, were the two agents who had found the suspect. There were seven rows of ten chairs each, and I, of course, chose one in the very back. I could see Michael notice me. He started the meeting and introduced the two agents, telling us that once they were done speaking, we would all try to decide the next course of action. The media didn't have this current information, nor would they until the suspect was caught.

The agents began explaining how they cross-referenced the area sex offenders with every case, out-of-state and local. One name in particular kept coming up in both. The man had lived as a vagrant in Tampa at the same time the old murder took place there, leaving the area immediately after the child's body was found. He had also been living in Indianapolis one month prior to the murder there. Six years ago, he'd been arrested in Cincinnati for raping and molesting four teenage boys at a nearby camp for troubled youths where he had been an assistant counselor. After being convicted and sentenced to fifteen years, he did five and was let out on parole. He was classified as a violent sexual predator at his sentencing, the worst of all sex-offender classifications.

"His name is Albert Edward Whitfield. He is forty-nine years old and has been living in Mansfield for eleven months now with his older sister," they announced.

The audience broke out in applause. I didn't clap because they were wrong. They had fingered the wrong suspect.

I shot a glance over at Michael, who saw my face and started walking toward me. I grabbed my briefcase, excused myself, and headed for the door quickly. He caught up to me in the hallway.

"CeeCee, wait! What are you doing? We're going to serve a warrant at this guy's house in a couple of hours, and you need to be there."

"Sorry." I looked down at my watch. "I have some things to do, and then I have to go to Cleveland to pick up the girls. Congratulations, you guys did a great job," I lied as I began to walk away again.

"You think they're wrong, don't you?" He refused to

break eye contact. "I know why you think they're wrong, too. But, CeeCee, think! It has to be him. These aren't merely coincidences, you know. But I admit there's no guarantee in the profiles."

I shook my head and looked innocent. "I don't know what you're talking about, and you guys are right on the money. If it's that important to you, I'll try to be at the search warrant."

My phone rang while I was walking to my car in the parking lot. It was the sheriff.

"CeeCee! Why'd you run out of here so quick? Isn't this great! I wanted—"

"It's not him, Sheriff. They've got the wrong guy."

"What? Why?" He began whispering.

"I can't get into it right now. Just play along like you're thrilled with everything, and I'll get back to you."

My personal investigation back on track, I had some things I needed to get before the FBI served the search warrant on Albert Whitfield. I decided it was best for me to show up so Michael wouldn't be overly concerned with what I was doing later.

Once the warrant was served and everyone was happy, I would wait until dark before I committed the crime of burglary.

CHAPTER FIFTEEN

Albert Whitfield lived with his sister in a run-down neighborhood on the east side, about five minutes away from the department. Everyone was meeting in the parking lot behind an elementary school down the road from Albert's house. Now was not the time for the media to catch on.

The FBI was using our department's SWAT team, which was one of the best in the state. Eric was on SWAT. In this setup, I had no role other than bystander.

After I pulled into the parking lot, I just stayed in my car and watched everyone run around like the end of the world was coming. I made a conscious effort to abstain from shaking my head at all of them, and from yelling out the window that they were all acting ridiculous.

After leaving the meeting today, I checked in to Albert Whitfield. He stood only five feet eight inches tall and weighed 155 pounds. This did not match the *tall* suspect Austin described. Albert Whitfield also had no history of violence. The rape charges he was convicted of stemmed from the fact his teenage victims were sixteen years old or less, and were under his temporary control, meaning they were directly under his thumb, their legal guardian, while at camp. In the court testimony, which I had Cincinnati Common Pleas court fax me, none of the boys ever claimed he was forced. One even said he loved Albert.

Plus, most sex offenders are consistent in staying with a

preferred age or sex. Albert liked teenage boys, not little girls, and, again, Albert's relationships with these boys, outside the scope of the law, were consensual. He didn't rape, brutally murder, and toss them in the woods.

It was impossible to believe the FBI didn't see any of this. I knew they did. And I certainly knew Michael did. He knew I would key in on those facts, which was why he'd reminded me no profiles were a guarantee. Most of all, I was disappointed in Michael. I knew he was smart, but I guess he had bosses to answer to like all of us, and had to do what he's told if he wanted to keep his job.

The bottom line, from what I've learned about Albert Whitfield, which hasn't been a lot since I didn't have much time, is this entire beat-the-door-down-and-flash-bang-him-right-out-of-there tactic was pointless. Most likely, if I went to his front door and showed him my badge, he would've probably urinated in his pants before sticking his arms out to be handcuffed. It was my assumption that he was a timid little weasel of a man who would never try to fight or resist.

This was nothing but a show for the media, as several agents would be videotaping the raid and the arrest. I was startled away from my disgust by Eric tapping on my car window.

"I tried to call you." He put his hand on my shoulder, and I promptly brushed it off.

"CeeCee, what's the matter?"

"Nothing. I notice you seem to feel affectionate right now—even though Michael's not watching," I said bitterly.

"Don't be like that. I know I should tell you I'm sorry about this morning, but I'm not. You are my wife. *My* wife! I shouldn't have to feel sorry or guilty for kissing you." He was getting angry again. I spotted Michael, who hadn't seen us yet, but it didn't matter. Eric stood by my window, looking around the parking lot. I was still ripping angry about that morning and really didn't have much to say at the moment.

"CeeCee." Eric sighed. "It's time we sat down and really laid out what's been going on. It's been long enough. We should both be able to think clearly by now."

I agreed. "How about tonight?" My detective work for the sheriff could wait until later; it didn't matter the exact time, as long as it was dark.

"I can't. I'm working."

"Take the night off." I laid down the challenge.

"I can't do that. You know I'm training someone right now. Let me get hold of you first thing in the morning when I get off work." To my surprise, Eric suddenly appeared uncomfortable.

I just nodded, waved him off, and didn't say anything. After he left, I tried to convince myself that Coop was wrong, that nothing was going on between Eric and Jordan. Eric told me there wasn't, and he had never lied to me before. Why was I now having a hard time believing that? I usually trust my instincts, but this time the results could be very destructive.

Did it really matter? Had I not been having an affair with Michael for over a year? Granted, we hadn't slept together until a couple of days ago, but we'd been emotionally attached since the first day we met. *It's the same thing, isn't it?* Then I saw Michael standing at my window. He'd been there a while.

"Where were you just now?"

"Nowhere, just thinking."

"Do you want to tell me about what? What did Eric want?" He'd obviously seen Eric by my car, and he looked a little concerned.

"He needed to know when we could sit down and talk about us, and said he'd talk to me in the morning after work," I said bluntly.

"Oh."

I stared straight ahead and was acting pissed off, which I was. The conversation with Eric and this entire botched investigation was mainly to blame for my feelings. I didn't want to take it out on Michael, but I also didn't feel like going into a ten-minute dissertation on what I was feeling and why. I knew he was a little hurt, but at the moment I didn't care.

"I just came over to tell you we're going to be heading to the house in a few minutes. SWAT will clear it first, and then the agents will go in for the search. I'd like you to go in with us to see if you pick up on anything."

"Fine."

He touched my arm lightly before walking away. I had time to regain composure since it was another ten minutes before the parade was on its way. I waited until everyone pulled out so I could be the last car. After we arrived at the house and SWAT did their thing, Michael waved from the front porch, signaling me to come inside. Albert Whitfield, or his sister, was nowhere to be found. It wasn't like they were avoiding us; obviously, they didn't know we were coming.

I tried to talk to Coop in the front yard, but he seemed distracted and didn't have an answer for anything. Michael pointed through the front door.

"Have a look around, and see if you find anything. But hold your nose."

I nodded and entered. It was a filthy house, like most in this part of town. The odor of cat urine was so strong it made my eyes water. I hate the smell of cats in a home, whether it's their litter box or urine, more than any other smell. My girls had wanted a kitten a few years back, but I forbid it. I know thousands of people have cats and don't let them urinate or defecate all over the floor, but I just happen to be in a profession where the majority of households I go into do. There were dirty dishes all over the countertops and garbage strewn all over the floor. Magazines piled three and four feet high were stacked against random walls of the house. I didn't dare go into the bathroom.

The only room I wanted to see was Albert's bedroom. It was up a small, carpeted staircase, the only room on the top floor. There were several agents in there already, so I stood outside and just poked my head in the doorway, looking around. It was small, filthy, and covered with cigarette butts and empty beer bottles. One of the agents pointed to the wall on the far side of the room. He apparently thought I was blind.

On the wall were two posters: an old Leif Garrett poster from when he was about fifteen, and a fourteen- or fifteen-year-old actor or singer who I'd never seen before. The agent looked like he'd struck gold. Other agents were pulling plastic sex toys and other items I couldn't quite identify out of one of the drawers in a bureau. Naturally, one of them could not resist a snide remark.

"Hey, Detective." He was holding up some type of sexual contraption. "If you want, I'll let you keep this. You and Agent Hagerman can play with it later." The others broke out in laughter.

I smiled politely. "Thank you, Agent. After you're done playing with it and pulling it out of your ass, I'll certainly take your offer under advisement. Just tell me how it works."

They quit laughing, and I had to admit I was somewhat proud of my response. It was when I saw them looking past me that I realized they quit laughing only because Michael was standing there. He looked furious.

"Agent Goldsmith, I *will* talk to you about this later."

"Oh, come on, Michael, I was just screwing around. She gave it right back to me, didn't you, CeeCee?"

I smiled again and remained silent. I know how cops are, and obviously, federal agents are no different. If these were the local cops I worked with, I would've heard much worse. There was no reason for Michael to come unglued, so I redirected his attention.

"You guys find anything downstairs?"

"Nothing but garbage and cat shit. What a hellhole this place is."

"Welcome to Mansfield."

We watched as agents bagged their finds to log as evidence. They were taking the posters off the wall so carefully, I wanted to laugh. An agent held out a picture they'd found in the closet of a naked boy about thirteen to fourteen years old, to show Michael. The agent had real excitement on his face.

"Child pornography!"

I was amused yet disgusted at the same time, and interceded before Michael could get a word out.

"This is a fucking joke!" I grumbled, then walked away and left the house.

The entire scene was unbelievable. These agents wouldn't know a child killer if he walked up to them and said he did it. Albert Whitfield was nothing more than a slob, certainly not the man who took care in making the bodies of the children neat and clean. The man who went to bed each night dreaming of Leif Garrett was not the man who took little girls and painted them like dolls; I was more positive of that than ever. Outside, the sheriff walked me back to my car so I could fill him in on my thoughts about the FBI's suspect.

"CeeCee, the FBI isn't going to give out Whitfield's name until he's found and interviewed. They're telling the media they have a person of interest. I've always hated that phrase—such a bullshit cover-your-ass term."

"Sheriff, there's absolutely nothing in that house that will tie Albert Whitfield to these murders. Unless they find him and get a signed confession, they don't have a hope in hell. And if they do, they'll bask in their glory until the real killer takes another child and utterly humiliates them."

"What's the next step, CeeCee?"

"I don't know."

"You ignorant, blind, fucking bitch!" Watching the SWAT team banter, while moving in and out of the residence, he was enraged. He had no idea whose house they were in, but he definitely knew why. They thought they had found the killer and it was all because of her. Short of sending in his driver's license and Social Security card, he could not possibly have given them any more clues to his identity.

Careful not to squeal his tires because of the heightened fury he felt, he slowly pulled away. Things were going to change, and they were going to change very soon. CeeCee Gallagher had just upped the ante with her stupidity. He had planned this for a very long time, and he would be damned if it he allowed her to fuck it up.

The familiar flash of blinding pain shot through his head, as it usually did when his mind was whipped into a frenzy. Far enough away from the house, he pulled off into a small clearing just to the right of the road. Leaving the car running, he opened the door and got out, both hands holding his head before falling to his knees.

"Noooooo!" he yelled.

He thought his head would explode right there, the pain unbearable.

"Little Jack Horner sat in a corner, little Jack Horner sat in a corner," he began to sing, relief flooding through him as the pain subsided. "LITTLE JACK HORNER SAT IN A CORNER!"

He sang the familiar rhyme that his father used to sing several more times before the pain went away completely. Soaked with sweat and trembling, he got back into his car and shoved his face close to the air-conditioning vents. He intentionally kept his mind blank until he calmed down. The pains were getting worse, he knew that, and it was all because of Gallagher.

He needed to see Elsa. She was the only one who could comfort him when the pain came. She knew just what to say, her voice calm and soothing while she gently ran her fingers through his hair as his head lay on her lap. Throwing the car into gear, he pulled back onto the road and headed for home.

CHAPTER SIXTEEN

Back at the department, I grabbed the keys to one of the junk cars at our impound lot. These were cars seized by the police because of drugs, DUIs, or other crimes. I left my detective car in the lot. I was just outside my office door when I heard a noise coming from Naomi Kincaid's office. The door was slightly ajar, so I tapped on it hard enough to open it all the way. Kincaid was in her office with her head on her desk. She was sobbing. Normally, I would've quietly closed the door and left, but she seemed so upset I actually felt bad for her and wondered what could be so terribly wrong.

"Naomi?"

"Yes?" She raised her head and looked embarrassed, while grabbing a handful of tissues off of her desk.

I shut the door. "Naomi, are you okay?"

"I'm fine, CeeCee, just having a bad day. Don't worry about it." She sobbed again and blew her nose.

I was a little concerned. "Do you want to talk about it?"

"No, I'll be fine, really, thanks," she said before continuing to cry, putting her hands over her face.

I didn't know much about her personal life except she'd been married twice and that she didn't have kids. Last I knew, she had been dating one of our county prosecutors, but I didn't think it was that serious. Somehow, I didn't think this episode was work related.

"Naomi, really, you're a mess. Why don't you let me take you home. There's nothing for any of us to do here today anyway," I suggested quietly. "Do you want me to call someone for you? Any friends?"

She looked at me through swollen eyes and with undisguised contempt. "I don't have any friends, CeeCee. I'm not like you!"

Waves of guilt and sympathy hit. I always knew she looked up to me, but I never paid attention to how lonely she might have been because I was always too busy criticizing her for everything she did. I could change that right now, and I would. Besides, I had plenty of time before committing my own crime, and it was good to have something to distract me from the whole Michael and Eric fiasco.

"Come on. I'm taking you home, whether you like it or not. You don't want these guys to see you like this."

She looked up, knowing full well I was right. Though she was a captain, she got little respect from her subordinates as it was, and having people see her now would only make things worse. Later, I could come back and get the car from the impound lot. I grabbed Naomi's purse, briefcase, and box of tissues for the ride home, and helped lock up her office.

She continued to cry in the car and I couldn't help asking if someone she knew died. All she did was shake her head. She remained quiet until we got to her apartment.

Once inside, I sat her down in her living room, got a bottle of wine out of her refrigerator, and poured both of us a glass. It was a few more minutes before she got herself together, and I waited patiently before I spoke. I wanted to be very careful of what I said.

"Naomi." I paused, thinking of how I was going to phrase what I meant. "I know we've had our problems, but

I think you need to talk to someone right now. I'm a good listener, and trust is something you never have to worry about with me."

She waited a while before finally unloading, and unload she did. It was, as I suspected, personal. She was no longer seeing the prosecutor, hadn't been for a while. In fact, she had gotten involved with someone else, never coming out with a name, who she thought was the love of her life. Their love was something she'd never experienced before, even during her marriages. Earlier today, he broke it off and she was clearly devastated. For a brief moment I felt a surge of anxiety, thinking she was talking about Michael. That is, until she told me this next useful piece of information.

"CeeCee, I know you won't think much of me for this, but," she paused, "he, he's married, and has decided to stay with his wife. She never knew." Naomi downed her glass of wine. "He swore he loved me and was leaving her."

The crying began again and all I could do was hand her a tissue. "Naomi, I am the *last* person in the world to judge anybody. I'm certainly no angel either. You know Eric and I were both married to other people when we met, and Mi—" I caught myself before I said Michael's name.

She quit crying and looked at me intently. "You're in love with him, aren't you?"

"Yes, I am," I said, knowing full well she meant Michael.

She nodded, and we sat there quietly drinking more wine, deep in our own thoughts. She never told me her boyfriend's name, and I didn't tell her everything about Eric and Michael, but it felt good to have someone to confide in. She had been seeing her boyfriend for almost a year, hanging on to the hope he would be with her in the end. Now, on top of feeling like her heart was broken in half, she felt like a fool.

We talked a little longer and when I was confident she wouldn't eat the end of her gun, I got up to leave. We promised to make every effort to get together more off duty. I felt like a breakthrough had been accomplished with Naomi, and it truly made me happy.

By the time I started driving, it was getting dark. I headed home to gather the things I needed for tonight, checking any missed calls on the way.

I had left my cell phone in the car so I could give my undivided attention to Naomi. Michael had left two messages, so I immediately called him back. He answered on the first ring.

When I told him I'd been with Naomi, he was quite surprised. Before he asked what she and I talked about, I beat him to it and asked him why he called. It seemed the agents had talked to a neighbor of Albert Whitfield's who gave them information along with the names of boys they should talk to. To make a long story short, it appeared that Albert was molesting neighborhood boys as young as ten.

"That still doesn't make him a child killer, Michael. Besides, these are boys, not girls, we're talking about."

"There's a small chance that Emily Yoder could still be alive, CeeCee. Her family hasn't gotten a shoe in the mail like the others."

"She's dead, Michael. You know that, and you also know Albert Whitfield isn't the one who did it."

He tried to convince me they were right, but it sounded more to me that he was trying to convince himself. He knew the FBI was wrong, but just wouldn't admit it. When Michael asked me where I was going now, I told him the truth—I was going home. I heard him sigh into the phone.

"Stay with me tonight, CeeCee, please? I miss you. I feel like I haven't seen you in days."

"I can't, Michael. There's something important I need to take care of. I'm sorry."

If I didn't have a burglary to commit tonight, I probably would've run to Michael's room. I missed him that much, too. I knew soon I would be faced with the same decision I had to make last year—if he or Eric didn't make it for me. My avoidance, and not necessarily my feelings, was going to determine my fate. When I got home, Eric was sleeping. Since he had the SWAT call-out today, he didn't have a chance to sleep much before work tonight. I grabbed the black utility pants and shirt, called BDUs, we wore for riots, along with some other things. It was similar to a SWAT outfit. Out of the biohazard emergency kit that I kept at home, I grabbed a pair of cloth foot covers and nylon gloves. I grabbed the black head cover Eric sometimes wore when he rode his motorcycle, then left to go back to the department to get a car from the impound lot.

The inconspicuous dark blue four-door sedan was perfect. I put a lock-picking set and a flashlight in the trunk, along with a crowbar that I hoped I wouldn't have to use. A crowbar left evidence.

Once I was on Carl Malone's street, I turned the headlights off, continued driving past his house, and parked four houses down. Like before, there was still was no car in the driveway. There weren't any house lights on either. I had already decided that if Carl was there, I would wait and break in after he went to bed. It looked like I was in luck.

Grabbing my equipment from the trunk and shoving it

into a black bag, I headed for the backyards so I could come up on the house from the rear. First I tried the doors and windows, all of which were locked. I knew he had no alarm system because I'd looked for one when I went by earlier today. I chose the back aluminum door to pick the lock on. It took less than thirty seconds.

Perfect, he thought. She was playing right into his hands. He gave her a high mark for intelligence, and even wondered why she had decided to break the law. "Tsk-tsk-tsk, Detective!" he said aloud. Now, what kind of upstanding law-enforcement officer would break into the home of a nice man like Carl Malone? He smiled. There was no doubt that she would find the item he had so carefully snuck in and left for her. He no longer had to worry about Carl Malone coming home. He had taken care of him for good. . . .

I checked the house first, just to make sure no one was there. Satisfied the place was empty, I was able to relax and look around. Carl's house was neat as a pin, decorated nicely, but not overly done. I spent an hour going through drawers, rooms, cupboards, closets, and every place I could think of, neatly so he would never know I was there. I found nothing of interest.

It was while I was standing in the kitchen going over my mental checklist that I saw a row of keys hanging by the door where I came in. That wasn't all. The keys were hanging on a large corkboard attached to the wall. Under each key was a small strip of paper with an address written on it. One key had an entire lease agreement underneath, secured with a red pushpin.

Carl Malone owned properties and rented them out. There were five properties total, and I wrote down each address, along with the name on the lease. I looked for something I could use to imprint each key so I could get copies made, but there was nothing. A bar of soap would work, but all Carl had on hand was liquid soap.

Back in my car, I felt let down. The trip had been wasted. I now believed that had I asked, Carl would've probably let me into his house and openly volunteered information about his properties. But it was just as well. I didn't have time to be wrong right now. Tomorrow I would call the city utilities department to see which names were on the bill at each address.

I was about ten minutes from the department, eager to switch cars, get home, and sleep until next month when luck fell upon me. I was rammed so hard from behind that it felt like I was going to go through the front windshield. All I could see in my rearview mirror was bright headlights. Getting rammed a second time, I almost went off the road.

I didn't have any choice but to call for help, even though I would have to come up with one hell of an explanation as to what I was doing. I grabbed my portable radio, which was nestled between the driver's and passenger's seat. I wanted to monitor where the patrol cars were when I broke into Carl's house, and also to see if anyone saw me and called it in. I never imagined I would need it to put out an officer-in-trouble call, but that's what I did.

I gave my location, car description, and direction of travel, telling the other officers I was being rammed by a vehicle that I couldn't describe. An officer said he was less than thirty seconds from my location, a piece of information I was thrilled to hear. If I was able to keep my car on the road that long.

I spoke too soon. I was rammed yet again, this time hard enough to send me spiraling into a tree along the side of the road. Just before I was hit, I got a quick glimpse of a large dark pickup truck speeding past. Thankfully, I wasn't going fast enough that any real damage was done. I wasn't hurt at all. But I was very rattled and quite shaky.

By the time I got out of the car, there were probably twenty cruisers surrounding me. It was time for the shifts to switch over, and it looked as if the entire night shift ran out of roll call to get here, Eric and my dad included.

The best lie I could tell was that the sheriff had personally asked me to stake out a public official, someone I could not name due to the sensitive nature of the investigation, which explained my clothing and the impound car. No one even questioned it. I gave the truck description as best I could so the patrol cars could drive around and try to find it, though I knew they wouldn't. I was waiting for the tow truck to take the car back to the impound lot when I realized Jordan wasn't with Eric.

"Where's your rookie?"

"She called in sick tonight."

"Oh." As much as I tried to keep my mouth shut, I just couldn't do it. "Herpes flare up again, did they?"

This angered Eric. "That's nice, CeeCee. Very adult. I'll see you in the morning." He stormed away.

I knew I shouldn't have said something like that. I've long since given up hope that tact would be at the top of my behavioral priority list.

It didn't take long before Michael heard what happened. I had already gotten into my own car back at the department and was driving home when he called. It wasn't worth bothering to ask how he found out.

"Do you want to tell me what the hell you were doing tonight?"

I gave him my stakeout-of-a-politician story which, of course, he didn't believe, but I stuck to it. I hung up just as I pulled into my driveway. It was very clear that the person who ran me off the road tonight was the same one who'd been murdering small children. It all had to be connected to Carl Malone or his renters, most likely the latter. I didn't take any chances. I had my gun in hand when I walked to my front door.

After a quick shower, I finally went to bed and slept for six hours, the most sleep I'd had in days. I woke when Eric got home and got into bed with me.

I had been in such a deep sleep that I didn't realize what he was doing until we were already making love. I certainly couldn't stop in the middle and profess my love for Michael; this was my husband, whom I also loved. Or so I thought. Eric and I didn't say a word to each other afterward.

The minute Michael laid eyes on me when I got to work, he would know. I tried everything I could to avoid him, but he tracked me down in the crime lab while I was going over old test results.

"Good morning." His voice was flat.

"Michael." I evaded his gaze. "I'll be a little while if you want to go on up to my office."

"That's not necessary. I was just there. I wanted to let you know that a lovely little bouquet of flowers your husband sent is sitting on your desk. Oh, how silly. I almost forgot—the note was quite sweet. He wanted to thank you for this morning." His voice raised three octaves at the end of the sentence.

Stunned, I looked up at him. His nostrils were flared and his face was a deep scarlet.

Eric had set me up once more, and as always, I never saw it coming. Frankly, I was crushed. He'd only made love to me for one reason: so he could let Michael know about it.

"Michael, you don't understand. . . ."

Michael wasn't hurt, he was downright livid. He grabbed my arm and pulled me out in the hallway.

"Tell me the truth! Did you sleep with Eric this morning?"

"Michael, I was asleep and—"

"Yes or no, goddamn it! I don't want your fucking excuses, just tell me the truth."

"Yes," I whispered.

"Fine." He looked at me with pure hatred. "I'm done." He began to walk away.

"Michael!" I screamed at the top of my lungs, loud enough that he stopped, turned around, and looked at me with surprise.

"You are *not* done until you let me explain!" I was still yelling. "Don't do this!" On the verge of sheer panic, I started shaking.

I was terrified he was going to walk away again, but he approached me, his face still red and angry.

"Michael, please . . ." I pleaded, my eyes beginning to water. "I was sound asleep when Eric got home this morning. I wasn't even quite sure what was going on when he started to, well, you know, but I didn't say anything. I thought maybe he was trying to smooth things over between us. I was confused but, again, I didn't say anything. Michael, please, now I realize he did this just to hurt you, and me!"

He didn't seem too impressed by anything I had to say at this point, though he was beginning to calm down. It had hit me like a lightning bolt and I knew, from that very moment on, I didn't want to lose Michael, no matter what. I gave him a promise that I had no idea if I would be able to keep, but I wasn't in any condition to think clearly.

I grabbed the front of his shirt and found myself crying. "Michael, I love you. I've never been so scared in my life of losing someone and I didn't know for sure until now. I'm telling Eric I want a divorce. I need to be with you."

Strangely, he appeared somewhat stunned. I don't think he ever imagined it truly was possible we would be together. And I couldn't believe I just promised him something like that either. I know I blurted it out in the heat of the moment, but how irrational was it? He took a step back and looked at me like I just sprouted horns.

"You don't mean that, you're upset."

"Yes, I do mean it. I'll tell him tonight."

He didn't say a word, but just stared at me. I thought he was getting ready to tell me it was too late, so I beat him to the punch. I started to walk away, still sobbing, before he came from behind and wrapped his arms around me. I felt him push his face into the back of my hair. He was breathing hard and holding me tightly. When he turned me around, I saw his own eyes were watery.

"CeeCee, I don't know what to say. I saw those flowers and it was like someone lit a fuse. Every day I think about you with Eric and all at once, I'd just had enough. But now I can't take it all in, that you truly want to be with me. Is that final? You need to really think about a decision this important."

"Yes, it's all very true."

Michael actually picked me up off the ground while he kissed me, then a huge smile broke out on his face.

"You have no idea how happy I am right now."

"Oh, I think I have a pretty good idea."

After returning to my office, even though I knew I was committed to Michael, I realized I wasn't 100 percent positive that a divorce was what I wanted. I was pretty sure Eric and I were headed in that direction, but

I didn't expect it this quickly. Perhaps all of us needed time to understand that a divorce was going to happen. No doubt he had gone too far with the flowers. This wasn't the Eric I married, nor was he the one I wanted to stay married to.

For some inexplicable reason, I needed to get Eric back at his own game and take out my anger at him in some idiotic, juvenile way. With the note still attached, I took the elevator down to the female locker room, and set the flowers in front of Jordan Miller's locker.

CHAPTER SEVENTEEN

Eric called shortly after I returned from my delivery to the locker room, wanting to know if I received the flowers.

"Yes, thank you, they were lovely."

"Did everybody else like them?" he asked, a transparent question that confirmed his not-so-sincere intent.

"Well, no one has actually seen them. Everyone is out of the office right now."

"Oh," he said, his disappointment showing. "Well, I'm gonna get to bed. I'll see you tonight. I love you."

"Hmm. Bye."

I stared at the phone, half expecting him to call back, but he didn't. I forced myself to get back to work, and remembered to call the utilities company with the addresses of Carl Malone's rental properties. I obtained all five tenants' names, but none had any type of criminal record. There was one name for which no information could be found. That name was Jim Carlson.

I would have to wait until tonight to check the apartments. Perhaps I wouldn't break in tonight, but I would watch them for a while and get a good idea of when the occupants went to bed, when they worked, and when they were home the most. It would take a couple of days to lay it all out.

I had been at it a while when Michael, who had been out tracking Albert Whitfield all morning, walked in and announced that he was ready for lunch. We were in the parking lot when Michael's cell phone rang with the call we were dreading. Emily Yoder's body had been found. Michael insisted that I accompany him to the scene. Any thoughts I'd had of a quiet lunch and some time alone were gone.

They had found her in a Dumpster behind a chain restaurant in the city. It wasn't close to looking like the other murders. Emily had the makeup on, but in a sloppy, clown-like fashion. Her fingernails were unpainted, she was dirty, and the red ribbon was nowhere to be found. She was also covered with garbage, which made it a difficult crime scene to process. Any trace evidence found could easily be argued to have come from the Dumpster itself.

The important constant between Emily's murder and that of the others was that she had been strangled and sexually assaulted. Throwing away the trappings of the perfect makeup and grooming, our suspect was beginning to come unglued.

A national search for Albert Whitfield ensued. The FBI gave his name and picture to the media, an act of stupidity, as I stated loudly. Albert only knew that the police were looking for him, which he probably assumed was due to the neighborhood boys he was molesting.

However, if he saw he was being fingered for mass murder of children, we would never find him. The supervising agent, Michael's boss, who was standing by the Dumpster, didn't see it my way, as I expected. He was looking at public relations for the FBI and nothing else. I was looking for the killer.

I walked away from the scene before I said something to him that would likely end my career. Michael was smart not to follow. I must admit he'd caught on quickly as to how to deal with me.

Kincaid was standing by her SUV, so I thought I'd get her thoughts on the matter. Her eyes looked as bad as they had the night before, and I figured she had continued to cry all night long.

"How are you feeling, Naomi?"

"Like I was drugged for the last twenty-four hours, but holding up."

She didn't have much makeup on, and her dark blonde hair was thrown back into a ponytail. Anyone meeting her would say she was strikingly pretty, and I actually thought she looked better now than usual. Except for her red, swollen eyes, of course.

"CeeCee, thanks again for yesterday. It meant a lot to have someone to talk to. By the way, have you had a chance to get together with Eric yet?"

"That's something we'll have to discuss over several bottles of wine," I groaned. "I'll tell you later."

Her phone rang. When she answered it, she went completely pale.

I walked away when I heard, "Why are you calling me?"

Ah, her "man of the hour." I watched to see if she was on the verge of another breakdown, so I could shovel her out of here. Miraculously, she was OK. The next time I looked, she was finishing the call with a smile on her face.

She actually waved at me before driving away. I was happy for her. Obviously, something positive happened during that phone call, but, at the same time, I also didn't want her to get her hopes up. If I knew who the guy was, I would be half inclined to give him a piece of my mind. Shortly after Naomi left, Michael walked over to brief me on the crime scene.

"Did you tell the crime lab to check for traces of fiber-glass on Emily?"

"Of course."

It was almost dark by the time we left, and I had surveillance to do. Michael wanted to know if I was going to
go home and finally talk it out with Eric. Despite all that
was said between us, I think Michael assumed I would
back out of my precipitous promise in some way.

"CeeCee, are you staying with me tonight?"

"Not until I tell Eric. Which I promise will be first
thing tomorrow when he gets home. Plus, I really have
work to do that I've been putting off."

Michael simply gave up, dropping me off at the department so I could get my car. Eric's cruiser was in the lot.
Only when I heard a loud fuss coming from behind did I
figure out Michael and Eric had run into each other. Michael had unknowingly pulled around and parked next to
Eric's cruiser. Eric was walking toward the door when he
saw Michael drop me off and pull around, so he waited.
I got to them just as they started squaring off. Eric was
ranting.

"Are you glued to her fucking hip? When are you
gonna learn she doesn't want you? Really, it's pathetic
the way you chase her around."

"Eric, enough!" I yelled over two parked cars.

They both turned to look at me briefly before going at
it again. This time it was Michael who had his say.

"Are you done? Because it seems to me your insecurities are all over the place and you're getting paranoid,"
Michael said, suddenly quite calm.

"Is that right? I don't suppose CeeCee told you she was
late this morning because she was home with me. Did
she tell you we were—"

It happened very fast. Michael coldcocked Eric right
in the jaw, and sent him flying backward. But not back

far enough that Eric wasn't able to retaliate and slug Michael. The fight was on, and they started falling over the cruisers, even breaking a window out of one.

The parking lot has security cameras monitored by the communication center. Seeing the fight, they dispatched patrol cars to the lot to stop the ruckus. I was in the middle, trying to pull the guys apart when I was bombarded by about ten uniformed officers who quickly got Eric and Michael separated. Michael was the first to take it further. Neither was going to stop, physically or verbally.

"You know what, Eric? You showed a hell of a lack of class and disrespect talking about your wife like that. I'm sure she appreciated it!"

Eric was being held by three officers and Michael by three. A tie, at least in my book. They both had faces and noses dripping with blood, and their arms were cut from having gone through the window of the cruiser.

It was only when the afternoon shift lieutenant, who unfortunately happened to be my uncle Max, arrived that the crowd began to disperse.

"CeeCee, what the hell is going on?" He looked bewildered.

"Nothing, Max. Just some full-fledged marital problems, as you can see." I couldn't believe it had come to this.

Max, always one for practical jokes and lightening up a bad situation, pulled me off to the side of the melee. "Well, your last name *is* Gallagher. Had you not kept your maiden name when you married Eric and gone with his name—Schroeder—like you were supposed to, this may not have happened. Gallagher is the definition of multiple marriages."

I didn't laugh. It was true. Everyone in the Gallagher family, father and uncles included, had been married at least three times, a couple of us more than that. The

Catholic Church had seen more annulments come from our family than confessions to the pope.

Since the fight was over, Max kicked it under the carpet and told Eric to go get cleaned up and ready for his shift, but first Eric had to see the nurse in the jail, who would take care of the cuts on his arm. Michael was already on his way back to his car. It was best to deal with him first.

"Are you okay? Let me see your arm." I tried to look at it, but he pulled away.

"I'm fine, CeeCee!" He was still pretty keyed up. "I'm going to my room to get cleaned up. This is unbelievable. I haven't gotten into a fight like that since college. I'll call you."

He was in his car, driving away before I could say anything more. Now it was time to see Eric. He was at the nurse's station putting bandages on his own arm. The nurse was nowhere to be found.

"Where's Donna? Don't you think she should look at that?"

"I'm fine. She's downstairs with a sick inmate."

"Eric, what is the matter with you? Why did you do that?"

He blew up. "He sucker punched me, or didn't you see that part? What the fuck do you expect? You can't imagine the shit I've been hearing at this department since he came back. There's only so much I can be expected to take."

"I'll wait for you in the morning when you get home. It's time we finally got the rest of this out in the open." No matter how apprehensive I was, I was also somewhat angry since Eric had, essentially, provoked the fight.

"Wait. I'm sorry I reacted out there. That was wrong, and I didn't mean to disrespect you. It's just that I'm grabbing at anything I can to keep our marriage together, and every straw I clutch keeps breaking." He sat down on the small cot against the wall. "Let's go away. Your mom already has the kids, so let's just leave tomorrow. We'll go to the condo in North Carolina to get away from everyone and everything. It's quiet there, and we can focus on working it all out."

Of course it sounded nice, but it also broke my heart. Eric was desperate and no matter what we were going through, I felt sorry for him. It was getting hard to believe I would ever have the guts to ask him for a divorce. We agreed to talk about it in the morning and parted.

I had no idea what I was going to do. The seesaw was back. Now I truly believed I couldn't keep my promise to Michael. But I couldn't lose him either. For the first time I wished he had never returned and that everything between Eric and me was normal. None of this garbage would have happened if Michael hadn't come back. I was to learn later it wouldn't have made a difference.

CHAPTER EIGHTEEN

At home, I grabbed an old large beach bag out of the hall closet and filled it with a couple of magazines, some fruit, and crackers. I filled a thermos to the brim with coffee and added it to the bag. After tossing in a couple bottles of water, I was ready to go. Who knew how long I would be sitting in my car tonight, so I needed to be prepared.

I made my way to the first house on the list and parked directly in front of it. The house was separated into two apartments. It was on the south side of Elmwood Street, a quiet neighborhood. When I saw an elderly couple come out of the top apartment cone and a woman with a small child come out of the bottom one, I knew this house was a dead end in terms of clues.

On my way to the second house, Michael called. I let the phone take a message, needing to focus my full attention on this case without any distractions. I was back in business, and it was a welcome mental shift. The second, third, and fourth houses had lights on the entire time I watched them, and the fifth house, Jim Carlson's, was dark. There weren't any cars in the drive, so I walked around and peered through windows. The house looked empty. I couldn't see one piece of furniture. Maybe it was free to rent and that's why the lease was attached to the board.

If Jim Carlson had moved recently, it could indicate he was trying to get away from something, or maybe not. It was late when I decided to give up for the night. But before pulling away, I saw a full bag of garbage in the can in front of the house. I grabbed it and threw it in my trunk.

Garbage is a fantastic tool in investigations, for it can show someone's entire lifestyle in microcosm. There is also no expectation of privacy regarding garbage as far as the law is concerned. Garbage set on a curb requires no consent, search warrant, or any paperwork at all, and it has set the foundation for many cases to acquire a warrant.

If this guy had just moved out, he probably threw away a lot of things. Possibly important things, but I didn't want to get my hopes up just yet. I was going to go through the bag the next day, but curiosity got the better of me. I pulled into an old factory parking lot and parked next to a Dumpster on the building's west side. I could go through the bag here, and if I found anything I'd keep it; if not it would go right into the Dumpster.

I was lifting the bag out of my trunk when I heard a woman yell from behind the building. It sounded like she was crying. I quietly put the bag back in the trunk, grabbed my gun, and slid along the wall of the building until I came to the corner. It would be just my luck to pull up to the one building where a rapist had dragged his victim.

My luck these days was downright extraordinary. I peeked around the corner and saw Eric and Jordan standing in front of Eric's cruiser.

Arms crossed, Eric was leaning against the hood, looking at the ground, while Jordan stood in front of him, alternately screaming and crying. She was waving around the note that came with the flowers. (I guess she found them.) I could hear every juicy word.

"You promised! How could you do this to me?" She shook the note at him. "I'm done, Eric! I can't take this anymore. Your precious wife is fucking around on you, and you're *still* chasing after her! I thought you had it up to here with her and you loved me?"

I don't know about Jordan, but I felt like howling myself. I had to hold my hand over my mouth to keep from reacting. All I seemed to do lately was cry uncontrollably, probably because this situation showed no sign of being resolved. For some reason, I never deep down believed that Eric was being unfaithful. But here it was, slapping me right in the face.

Eric approached Jordan. He held her in his arms while she cried into his shoulder. I couldn't take my eyes off them. That was even before I heard what he said, which made it worse.

"Listen, please don't cry." He tilted her face up to look at him. "You know I love you. What's it been, three months now? I haven't quit yet. I was ready to leave until Michael came back, but I'm not going to lie to you. I got scared. Just give me a little more time, would you? We have two little girls who'll be crushed if we split up, and I'm having a hard time dealing with that."

"So you had to sleep with her this morning?"

I had to hold on to the wall to keep from charging out there and confronting them. Since my arms and legs felt like Jell-O, that didn't seem to be the best idea. Three months! Three months was long before Michael showed up. And Eric said he planned on leaving me.

I thought back to how Eric reacted when I told him Michael was back, and it made me furious. I no longer felt guilty. He had already been seeing Jordan at that time. All the late calls and late nights I never paid attention to, he was with her. The nights I lay awake feeling guilty about Michael, before we slept together, and now I find out Eric was the unfaithful one. After Jordan began to calm down, Eric finally was able to speak again.

"You know what that was about this morning. I'm sorry, Jordan. If I could take it back, I would. Ego got the better of me, and it won't ever happen again. I love you." And then he began kissing her. I couldn't watch it anymore. I'd finally had enough.

Forgetting about the garbage in my trunk, I ran to my car and pulled away. I was so hysterical I didn't believe I would be able to drive. I was not only upset, but also flabbergasted. I never, ever, thought Eric would do this to me.

It was more than clear that he'd never gotten over Michael last year. Our current problems didn't have anything to do with Michael reappearing. If anything, Michael's arrival prevented Eric from leaving sooner. What hurt even more was that there was no question that our marriage was finished.

If I had been confused and unable to ask Eric for a divorce, I wasn't anymore. It was so utterly clear.

For a long time I had convinced myself all that had gone on in the past year was entirely my fault. The hard reality was that even if Michael didn't exist, Eric still would've fallen for Jordan. I saw problems in our marriage now that I had never seen before, years of them. This entire fiasco had opened my eyes, and we were both to blame. Equally.

I couldn't bear the thought of going home and sleeping in our bed, so I bought a bottle of whiskey at the nearest liquor store and drove to a park close to home.

For the next hour, I alternately cried and shook, drinking half the bottle before I acknowledged that I was entirely too drunk, not to mention too upset, to drive home. I didn't know what else to do but call Michael. He answered immediately, and I was so drunk and teary I could barely talk. I did my best to explain where I was and soon ended up putting the phone down and letting my head fall on the steering wheel. I was barely conscious by the time Michael arrived and put me in his car.

When we got back to Michael's room, he carried me in and laid me on the bed, kneeling down beside me. I opened my eyes and saw three of him. From all three views, I could see his face had bruised quite nicely from the fight with Eric. He tried to ask what had put me in such a state, but I was simply too distraught, and drunk, to answer.

"I think I'm gonna get sick." I tried to get up, but needed Michael's assistance to the bathroom. I begged him to leave, but he wouldn't.

For at least the next hour, between crying jags, I threw up. Michael kept holding my hair back, taking a cold washcloth and wiping my forehead off while my head hung lifeless in the toilet. When he wasn't tending to me from the neck up, he sat on the bathroom floor and rubbed my back, all the time not saying a word. The last thing I remember was the inside view of the toilet bowl.

When I woke up, I was in bed and dressed in one of his T-shirts. I felt like I had been run over by a truck, but even that wasn't enough to cover my embarrassment. The room was bright, and I could see Michael sitting on the edge of the bed looking down at me. I grabbed a pillow to cover my eyes. And my pounding head.

"Michael," I said hoarsely, "I'm sorry."

He actually laughed a little. "There's nothing to be sorry for, CeeCee. I just want to make sure you're okay."

"Why do I have your T-shirt on?" If we slept together last night, I'd missed it entirely.

"You threw up all over yourself, clothes included."

Still under the pillow, I groaned. How humiliating. There's nothing like breaking in a new relationship with an all-night throw-up marathon.

I asked how badly soiled my jeans were, and he said they were still wet because he had rinsed them out. Since they were all I had to wear, my options were limited.

"Honestly, just take it easy for a while and get some sleep."

I insisted that he take me back to the park to pick up my car. I really needed to get home. Michael winced at that.

"Michael, I need to go home to get some things. Eric should still be awake. I'm planning to leave there today, at least until he can make other arrangements," I said defiantly.

I finally had to tell him what happened last night and that what upset me most was all the guilt I had been feeling, mainly because Eric was making me feel guilty. Michael simply held me. No questions, no judgments. When we were ready to leave, he handed me his room card.

"You are coming back here, right?"

"Do you want me to?"

"I'm not even gonna answer that. I'll tell Kincaid you won't be in today, and I insist you come back and get some sleep. I'll check in on you later."

Michael dropped me off at my car in the park. When I got into the driver's seat, my stomach wanted to heave again. The entire inside of the vehicle smelled like stale whiskey. Somehow, I held it in (not that I imagined there was much left to throw up), before I headed home to face off with Eric.

He was sitting in the living room, waiting for me, his face looking as bad as Michael's. Seeing him, I was reminded of last night's scene between him and Jordan. As bad as I felt, I was more than ready to have it out at long last. The endless waiting would finally end.

I walked in and sat down in a chair that faced the couch. For a few moments, we just stared at each other silently. All I could see was his anger.

"Want to tell me where you've been?"

"Yes, actually I do. I was with Michael." There it was, out in the open.

He was surprised to get such a bold response, and somehow found the words to throw the doors wide open.

"Did you sleep with him?"

"Not last night, no. Ask me about the other night I didn't come home and you might get a different answer." I was pushing it, painfully and deliberately, but not without a strong sense of relief.

He stood up. "What the hell is the matter with you!"

I unloaded. I told him everything I had seen and heard last night between him and Jordan. It was now hard to stop talking. I spewed about how this entire time I had been confused about things, but no more.

"I saw the light last night, Eric. It was in the form of a short brunette. All this time you tried to blame Michael for our problems when you were just as much, if not more, to blame. . . ." I paused before dropping the bomb. Even after the scene I witnessed last night, I felt my heart thud and my stomach flip at what I was about to say. "Eric . . . I'm filing for divorce. I've had enough and I want out."

To my surprise, he sat down heavily. It was as if someone had just driven a knife in his chest. Tears were beginning to roll down his cheeks.

"CeeCee, no, we can fix this. . . ."

"It's over, Eric. You're just as guilty as I am."

I expected some combination of protest, silence, and

hostility, but surprisingly, Eric began simply to talk and confess his relationship with Jordan. To an extent, I was right. He had never gotten over what happened last year and it permanently affected our relationship. Even though Michael and I hadn't slept together, Eric was wounded just the same. So when he met Jordan and she thought the sun rose and set with him, not only did she make him feel good but also his self-respect returned.

"With you, I always wondered if you were thinking about Michael. Every time you were quiet, or staring into space, or asleep and dreaming, I wondered."

He didn't have to do that with Jordan; the slate was clean. By the time he was finished, we were both drained. Now wasn't the best time to figure things out, as far as the house and kids went, so we agreed to talk about those details later. I already knew we would be sharing custody of the girls. Neither of us would ever want to keep them away from the other. No matter what the relationship was between Eric and me, the four of us would always remain a family.

We would have to take things one day at a time. Eric came right out and told me to keep the house since it was the girls' home, but that he did need some time to find a place. This was not a problem. I told him I had already made arrangements to stay somewhere until he did. Despite knowing the obvious answer, he never asked where. As I went upstairs to shower and pack a couple of bags, Eric grabbed me and held me tight. Even after seeing him with Jordan last night, we both hurt terribly. We never imagined ever being at this point.

He remained downstairs while I showered and got some clothes together. I composed myself enough to call my mother, explaining the situation as briefly as possible. I asked her to keep the girls another week until we sorted out arrangements here. Eric and I agreed we would tell the girls together. My mother was reduced to tears and wanted to know more, but I wasn't in the mood to get into it. Actually, I wasn't sure I was capable of talking about it any further.

Eric was gone when I came back downstairs. I assumed it was too hard for him to watch me leave. I wasn't exactly thrilled at the prospect of saying good-bye to him forever either.

When I got back to the hotel, I called Michael, who answered his phone before I could even hear it ring. It hadn't occurred to me that he toyed with the notion that I might back out once I was face-to-face with Eric. Hearing the relief in his voice when I told him I was in his room said it all. I spelled out the entire conversation with Eric and when I was done he remained quiet for a while.

"CeeCee, please make sure this is what you truly want, and that it's best for you. I didn't pressure you, did I? I don't want you to resent me later." It was a bit late if that was so, but thankfully it wasn't the case.

"Michael, don't be ridiculous. This is what I've always wanted. It just took me this long to admit it.

"What do you mean?"

"We never really *communicated*, Michael. Have you ever heard the saying how someone can talk for an hour and say nothing? That was Eric and me. I can't remember ever sitting down and *really* talking. It was always about work, the girls, and saying I love you. If I had a problem, he'd say 'I'm sorry, I love you' and walk away. You know how I was after Murder Mountain, desperately needing someone to talk to and understand what was happening to me. Eric was always apprehensive about discussing it because Murder Mountain reminded him of you and me. I felt very alone—more than I ever have in my entire life—although

I've never admitted it to myself until now. We neglected each other emotionally. It was like we were together the last three or four years of our marriage for comfort reasons." I sighed. "It's hard to explain. And maybe the most painful of it all is that I'd heard rumors over the years, but never gave them any thought. Now, I question whether this is the only affair Eric has ever had."

"Don't do that to yourself, Cee. Maybe you'll find out, maybe you won't, but don't drive yourself crazy with what happened in the past. Right now, I am here for you, and I'll do whatever it takes, or wait for however long it takes, to help you through this . . . I love you, kiddo."

We said good-bye with his promise to check on me still good. I was physically and emotionally exhausted. I must have slept for ten hours at least, because when I woke up to Michael shaking me, it was dark out.

"CeeCee, you need to get up and come with me. There's a problem."

CHAPTER NINETEEN

I was disoriented. I had slept so soundly I wasn't quite sure where I was, let alone what time and day it was.

Michael didn't help. He was digging through my suit-case, grabbing clothes and tossing them at me. I looked at the clock and saw it wasn't as late as I had thought.

My sleep beginning to fade, I remembered the day's events and why I was here, though it still didn't answer what Michael was doing.

"Michael, slow down. I'm barely awake yet."

"We don't have time."

"Well, I'm not going anywhere until you tell me what's happening."

"Another body's turned up."

"Who?" I didn't think I had slept through another Amber Alert; at least I hoped not.

"I'll explain later. Move it. Let's go."

I dressed, clumsily and quickly, and followed Michael out the door. I assumed we were going to the crime scene, although he still wouldn't respond to my questions. When we pulled into the department lot, I was still mystified.

"I thought we'd be going to the crime scene?"

"We are—kind of. Just follow me."

It wasn't like Michael to keep me out of the loop, so his behavior was puzzling. Downstairs by the crime laboratory, the hallway outside was a circus. Everyone was there talking with—and over—one another, but the scene quieted down considerably when they saw me. Now I was beginning to get unnerved.

My first thought was that something bad happened in my family. I started picking up my pace, walking ahead of Michael, ignoring the other agents and detectives.

Once in front of the lab doors, I shoved them so hard, they slammed against the wall when they opened. I followed voices to one of the rooms on the far side, where I saw the sheriff first, outside the examination room door.

"Sheriff, what's going on?"

"CeeCee." He pointed into the room. "Take a look."

Inside, spread out and lying on a table, were bones; human bones. I learned that earlier, while Michael was leaving for the day, walking in the parking lot toward his car, a small boy, maybe nine or ten, was waiting for him holding a box. The boy said a man had paid him ten dollars to give the box to Michael. The man told the child which car to stand near, described Michael, and said to make sure not to leave until handing over the box.

Other agents had the boy and his parents upstairs, interviewing the child in hopes of getting a solid description of the suspect. The box contained a pile of bones, one red ribbon, and a dirty old My Size doll shoe.

I still wasn't catching on as to the urgency of my arrival, or why I needed to know about it right this minute. After all, it wasn't my show anymore. It was hard to get a grip as to who was in charge. I said this loudly and defiantly to Michael, and to the supervising agent standing next to him.

"CeeCee, he left *you* a note inside the box," Michael said quietly.

"Me?" Suddenly, I couldn't breathe.

Michael led me to the next room and closed the door behind us. Sitting on the table right in front of me, enclosed in a clear plastic evidence bag, was a large yellow piece of paper.

I walked over to the table and stared down on the note written in block letters in black ink. It said:

MY DEAREST CECELIA CATHERINE GALLAGHER,
PAY ATTENTION, CECELIA!
THE KING COMMANDED, AND THEY BROUGHT DANIEL AND CAST HIM INTO THE DEN OF LIONS, AND INTO THE DEN DID DANIEL FALL. AND THE KING SAID TO DANIEL: THY GOD, WHOM THOU ALWAYS SERVEST, HE WILL DELIVER THEE.
THAT IS THE ANSWER YOU SEEK, CECELIA.
BY THE KING'S COMMANDMENT, THOSE MEN WERE BROUGHT WHO HAD ACCUSED DANIEL: AND THEY WERE CAST INTO THE LIONS' DEN, THEY AND THEIR CHILDREN AND THEIR WIVES.
TELL ME, CECELIA, HAVE YOUR CHILDREN BEEN CAST YET?
TELL THE FBI THAT IF YOU ARE NOT NAMED IN CHARGE OF MY IMPENDING CAPTURE, ONE CHILD WILL BE TAKEN FOR EVERY DAY THEY DO NOT. I'LL BE WATCHING THE 6 O'CLOCK NEWS. AND SO IT BEGINS . . .

The letter wasn't signed. It didn't matter because I was already walking toward the door when Michael grabbed me.

"CeeCee, I already have the Cleveland PD standing outside your mom's door. The girls are okay and will remain safe. I promise you nothing will happen to them."

I jerked my arm away. "You waited *hours* before showing me this? What is the matter with you, Michael?"

Within minutes of reading the letter, I was in my car, Michael in the passenger seat insisting he make the fifty-minute drive with me. I'll be damned if my daughters will be threatened, and even though I knew Michael had ensured their safety, I had to see for myself.

To ease my mind, I had spoken to my mother just as I left the parking lot of the department. Initially, she was highly agitated, understandably, about the two uniformed officers planted outside her door. But having been the wife of a cop, she understood all too well why and what needed to be done to keep her and the girls safe.

I knew the letter would be examined by forensic scientists, handwriting experts, and agents who specialized in decoding messages. However, they would never figure out the full answer. I, unfortunately, understood some of it already.

"Daniel 6:16," I said softly.

"What?" Michael asked.

"The passage the killer referred to in the letter. It's Daniel 6:16, and part of Daniel 6:24, I think, in the Bible."

"How did you know that?" Michael sounded amazed.

"Twelve years of Catholic school. Anyway, if memory serves, there was a part in the letter that said something like 'into the den did Daniel fall.' That's not part of the scripture. The killer added that himself."

Our killer was more creative than any of us first thought. In the letter, he was implying that Albert Whitfield was Daniel, a man wrongfully accused.

But there was more to it, I was positive. The extra line the killer added meant something specific, but I just couldn't put my finger on it. The last biblical passage frightened me more than a little as well.

"Michael, where's Sean?" I asked, referring to his son.

"At home. Why?"

"The last passage refers to Daniel's accusers and their children being thrown into the lions' den. I'll get into the rest later, but consider yourself an accuser in the killer's eyes."

Michael didn't want to admit to the horror of that thought. The killer was angry that the FBI had fingered the wrong man. He wanted the limelight and didn't want to share it with anyone else. Therefore, the ones who had accused the wrong man would pay.

"That's taking it too far," Michael said, still not admitting to himself his son might be in danger. "He doesn't know anything about me."

I just glanced at Michael and kept driving. After a moment or two, he grabbed his cell phone and called his ex-wife's house to make certain the child was OK. Clearly and definitively, he told his ex-wife to take Sean to her brother's house until she heard back. Michael talked to his son for a while and hung up.

"Why did you tell her to go to her brother's house?"

"He's a Cleveland cop."

"Oh."

We made the rest of the trip in silence, except for the one call I made to Eric. I explained what was going on and said that I would be bringing the girls back. We agreed that he would take several days off and head with them to our condominium in North Carolina until he heard from me.

One thing I can say about Eric is that he would, without a doubt, protect our girls with his life. The call was quick and to the point, which was fine since I didn't need any more emotional drama right now.

It was late by the time we arrived, and I knew the girls would be in bed. My mother and stepfather lived on the seventeenth floor of a high-rise condominium on the coast of Lake Erie, just outside of downtown.

As I expected, the girls were asleep. I hated to wake them, but there was no other choice. Part of me didn't care since I was thrilled to see them and missed them horribly. As sleepy as they were, they were just as excited to see me, but exhaustion took them over again before they could ask about Michael, who had remained quiet. I merely waved my hand at my mother's impending inter-rogation about him. She got the hint.

While driving back, Michael told me that the next morning Earl Howard, supervising agent of the FBI, wanted to meet with me and the sheriff. Swell. He was the supervisor I had already butted heads with, and I wasn't exactly thrilled at the prospect of seeing him again. Michael was trying to prep me for the meeting, firm that I just hear Howard out and not argue. Naturally, I didn't want to listen to any of what he was saying either.

"That guy is a serious asshole and doesn't have a clue what he's doing."

"CeeCee, please."

I put my hand up to tell him to stop. We were arriving at the department, and Eric was standing by the front door waiting. Michael immediately headed for a side door, saying he'd see me inside. Apparently, he didn't want to go round two with Eric.

I woke the girls, and they were excited to see their fa-ther. Once they were settled in his car, he shut the door and turned to face me.

"You okay?"

"I'm fine. How are you?"

He leaned against the car. "I'll be honest with you, I'm having a hard time with this." He paused. "I told Jordan we needed to take a break until I get my head together."

"I'm sorry," not about the Jordan part, "but let's see

what happens, Eric. Please remember, don't say anything to the girls. You promised we would tell them together."

He simply nodded. Both of us hurt so much. As we said our good-byes I embraced the man I had called my husband for over eleven years. Eric didn't want to let go, so I allowed it to go on for another minute or so before taking his hands away gently. I told him I would be over in the morning to pack the girls' bags. I watched him drive away.

When I turned to go inside the department, I looked up to my office window and saw Michael standing there, looking down at me. By time I walked in, he was sitting down.

"Everything go okay, Cee?"

"We should go," I suggested, ignoring his question. "I have to get up early and go home and pack the girls' things before my meeting with your boss."

He nodded. We were quiet the entire ride back to the hotel, until we pulled in the parking lot when Michael couldn't take it anymore.

"I can't stand this, wondering what you're thinking all the time. Or feeling. It's driving me crazy."

"Eric broke up with Jordan today" was my only response.

"What? What does that have to do with anything? Unless . . . are you going back to him?" He was getting anxious.

I was not going back to Eric—there was too much damage done as far as I was concerned—but I also didn't feel like I needed to explain that to Michael.

When we got to the room, I went directly into the bathroom, slammed the door, and sat down on the floor with my head in my hands for what seemed like an hour.

When I finally felt like my head was no longer going to explode, I opened the door.

Michael was lying on the bed with his hands under his head, just looking up at the ceiling. He didn't acknowledge me, even when I sat next to him.

"Michael?"

"What." Terse and emotionless, to say the least.

I reached out and put my hand on his chest. "I am not going back to Eric. That is something you need to know, and to believe. But you also have to understand this is hard for me. I've been married to him for over eleven years and we have children. It's not all that simple."

It was at least a minute before he sat up and faced me, putting his hand on the small of my back.

"CeeCee, I'm the one who's sorry. I know this is hard for you. I've been through it myself. It's just that every time I see you and Eric put your hands on each other, it terrifies me. I ached for you for a year, and now when it looks like we might actually happen, it just seems surreal, and I keep waiting for something to get screwed up."

I put my hands on his face and started passionately kissing him. We fell back onto the bed, and made love. It was tender, and it was beautiful. I truly loved him. And I know for the right reasons.

We fell asleep in each other's arms and stayed that way all night. I set an early alarm so I could get over to the house and pack for the girls. I explained to them I was working all night so they didn't ask any questions. I let Michael sleep, but he must've gotten up shortly after I left, as he was in Coop's office when I arrived at work. Coop seemed a little brighter that morning than he had been in a while, and it reminded me that I never found out what had been going on to make him so distant and irritable. Some friend I am. I made a mental note to find time to talk with him privately. We chatted briefly before Michael and I went back to my office.

He closed the door behind us and grabbed me around the waist before kissing me long and warmly.

"I had to get that out of the way if I'm to function properly today, Detective."

"I hear you, Agent."

It was time for the meeting with Supervisory Agent Earl Howard. He, the sheriff, the chief, and two senior agents were waiting for us in the sheriff's conference room. We were just to the end of the hallway in the bureau when Kincaid poked her head out of her office.

"CeeCee, Michael! Wait! The sheriff just called. The meeting's postponed. They just arrested Albert Whitfield."

CHAPTER TWENTY

"They're on their way here with him now. CeeCee, the sheriff wants you to call him," Kincaid said.

Michael and I looked at each other before heading back to my office so I could call the sheriff. Michael got on his cell phone with Supervisory Agent Howard to get the details. After we had both finished, Michael told me he was ordered to oversee the interview. The sheriff ordered me to observe the interview.

It seems that Albert Whitfield turned himself in at the jail after seeing the news. This confirmed, to me, that he was not our killer. Our killer didn't go through the hype and creativity of the box of bones only to give himself up the next day. I couldn't believe the FBI's ignorance. I grabbed some coffee and walked into the observation room on the other side of the mirror that faced the interview room. Michael's boss, the sheriff, and others would be watching the interview on closed-circuit television.

Albert Whitfield, seated at the table, looked deeply frightened. He didn't have the confidence and arrogance shown by the killer. Two senior FBI agents entered the interview room and began.

Like everything else leading up to this point with the FBI, the interview was nothing but a low-grade comedy act. The agents' interview skills were some of the worst I've seen. I've actually witnessed first- or second-year uniform patrolmen do a better job of talking to a suspect. Michael knew this; he shook his head in disgust. The agent doing the primary interview was a tired-looking runt of a man who did nothing but yell in Albert's face, terrifying him even more.

While he did this, the other agent walked back and forth behind Albert, laughing. Albert kept saying repeatedly he didn't kill any children. This was his only response to the agent screaming "Whose bones are in the box?"

He was almost paralyzed and at the point of tears when I couldn't keep my mouth shut any longer. I was just about to tell Michael to do something when he beat me to it by leaving me and entering the interview room. He motioned for both agents to leave. They looked at each other in confusion before Michael raised his voice and ordered them out immediately.

It took Michael at least twenty minutes to establish a rapport with Albert and calm him down. Over the next two hours, Michael asked the right questions and received the appropriate answers.

When it was all said and done, Albert Whitfield had admitted to molesting five neighborhood boys and gave a written confession regarding the same. He vehemently denied any part in the murders of Hanna Parker, Ashley Sanders, and Emily Yoder. He came right out and said what I already knew: that he wasn't attracted to girls.

During Michael's interview, Albert insisted he was applying for unemployment at the time Ashley Sanders was taken. I confirmed that alibi myself. When the interview was officially completed, Albert Whitfield was taken to the county jail and charged with three counts of rape and two counts of gross sexual imposition, for starters.

As I watched the corrections officers lead Albert away, Michael came back into the observation room, looking exhausted. I know all too well from experience how mentally demanding an interview like that can be.

"Well? What do you think?"

"I think you saved the day, Agent. I was about to go in there myself after watching those two morons. We may not have our killer yet, but we got a child molester off the street. There's nothing wrong with that at all."

Michael sat down and let out a loud sigh, rubbing his eyes with one hand. I stood behind him and began massaging his shoulders when I heard the door open. I jumped back about four feet. The last thing I needed was someone to see me giving the FBI agent in charge a massage. It was Sheriff Stephens.

"Excellent job, Michael. Definitely a guy who needs to be off the streets."

"Thank you, Sheriff."

"Well, CeeCee, you know what's coming next. Agent Howard is upstairs waiting. Let's go get this over with."

The sheriff looked as thrilled as I was to be a part of this meeting. Agent Howard was seated at the conference table when we walked in. Idiot one and idiot two from the Albert Whitfield interview were on either side of him. I chose a seat on the far side of the table, and the sheriff and the chief sat next to me. Michael sat closer to his boss. Agent Howard opened the meeting.

"Well, it looks like Albert Whitfield isn't our killer after all."

"You don't say," I answered, garnering a horrific look from Michael. As well as one telling me to shut up and not say another word.

"Detective Gallagher, your reputation precedes you, I'm sure, but there's no need for rudeness in this room."

I didn't like being spoken to as a child, and if Michael

hadn't been there, I might not have been responsible for what would have come out of my mouth. "Agent Howard, you called this meeting. Why don't you get to your point?"

I was making him angry. It was very obvious. Michael leaned back and just stared at the wall, arms tightly crossed in front of him. I would hear it from him later, no doubt about it. Right now, I didn't care.

"My point is, Detective, we have a man killing children, and he seems to be fixated on you. I see that as a problem—a major problem—and I think you can enlighten me. Is there something you aren't telling us, Detective Gallagher, about this case? Possibly an old boyfriend of yours?" He hesitated. "Or girlfriend, maybe?"

I stood up ready to blast the agent with everything I had, but the sheriff beat me to it.

"That is quite enough, Agent Howard! I am still the county sheriff, and I will not allow you to talk to one of my officers like that! It seems to me that Detective Gallagher told you from the beginning you had the wrong guy, but none of you wanted to listen. Now, let's get to the point here. Are you going to name CeeCee as the lead on this or not?"

"No."

"Fine. The next child who dies will be on *your* hands, and I *will* let everyone in the media know."

The sheriff walked out of the room, though I wished he hadn't. Agent Howard sat in his chair smiling and began to talk again and, this time, much worse. The meeting was deteriorating rapidly.

"Detective, it seems you know something you're not telling us. Therefore, you are obstructing a federal investigation and could be criminally charged."

That was it. "Agent Howard, don't you *ever* threaten me, understand? If you would like to charge me with a crime, then arrest me now or sit there and shut the *fuck* up!"

I stormed out, knocking my chair down along the way. I was finished with this case. I was going to go home, pack my things, and go to North Carolina to be with my kids. My contempt for Agent Howard was such that I had nearly reached across the table to rip his eyes out. He was playing a deadly game with children's lives and didn't seem to care. All he cared about was being in charge and making the FBI look good. I wondered if he had children. I doubted it.

I went directly out to my car. After I pulled out of the parking lot, my cell phone started ringing like mad. I shut it off.

During the drive to my house I found myself fuming, thinking back to the meeting and how Michael just sat there and said nothing. Had the roles been reversed, I would've never allowed someone to talk to him like that. I don't care if it was my boss or not.

When I got home, I started tossing my beachwear into a suitcase: shorts, tank tops, and my bathing suit. When I was satisfied I had everything, I walked out the front door and ran smack into Michael.

He was out of breath, and I actually looked to see if his car was there of if he had just run the whole way.

"Where are you going?"

"To the beach with the girls." I stepped around him and headed for my personal SUV parked in the driveway.

"No, you're not." He tried to grab my suitcase, which I promptly yanked away from him and flung into the hatch of the SUV. Somehow, when I got into my car, he was already sitting in the passenger seat.

"Get out, Michael. You can't go to the beach with me," I said sarcastically.

"I'm not going," he said with a smile, "and neither are you."

I was getting angrier, if that was possible, and told him again to move his ass. It was five more minutes of us arguing like teenagers before I finally relented and told him to spit out what he had to say.

Turns out, when the sheriff left the meeting, it wasn't to abandon me. He called the governor's office. I knew the two men were good friends. The sheriff had been the county Republican representative during the election, and he played golf with the governor frequently. The governor's brother also happened to be a United States senator who had quite a bit of pull in Washington.

Then, when Michael left the room, the sheriff pulled him aside and told him he had called the governor, who was working to get things situated, including putting me in charge. It might take some time. Agent Howard was high on the FBI totem pole, so a lot of favors were getting called in.

I turned the car off. "Why didn't you say anything in there?"

"I did, after you left. I told him he was out of line and disrespectful. Then he accused me of protecting my 'bed partner.' He's heard the rumors. I'll be lucky if I have a job tomorrow. At this point, I don't care."

"It's my fault. I got you into this."

I didn't know what else to say. I should've acted more professional, there's no question there, but we were talking about children. And when it came to children, I had no patience for politics and games.

All this bullshit had taken away valuable time, and I

thought about the six o'clock deadline the killer had given us. I expressed my concerns to Michael.

"He just said he'll be watching the news, that's all," Michael said.

"No, he meant that if he doesn't hear what he wants to hear at six, he *will* take another child and I believe him wholeheartedly. We have to do something. We can't just sit here."

"I believe we should do the only thing we *can* do right now. We wait."

CHAPTER TWENTY-ONE

Michael and I went to lunch after leaving my house since I still needed to cool down a bit before heading back to work. The detectives from the other states had left the day before. They were tired of Agent Howard and the FBI, too.

When we walked into the detective bureau, Kincaid told us the bones from the box had been identified through dental records.

"Her name was Anna Kovinski. She was kidnapped in September of 1985 while walking her dog in Harrisburg, Pennsylvania. The FBI's in the process of getting the case file from them."

"1985!" I was incredulous. "I can't even begin to imagine what her parents have gone through for the last twenty-one years."

"Do you know if they told her parents yet?" Michael asked.

"From what I gathered, the father died several years ago of cancer. The mother never recovered from the kidnapping and has had severe mental health issues ever since."

I'll bet she has. I'd consider myself fortunate if I could continue breathing, let alone functioning, if something happened to one of my children. I couldn't imagine living for twenty-one years always wondering what had happened to my daughter. The thought sent a stampede of chills through my body. Kincaid and Michael sat quietly, probably thinking the same. Even though Kincaid didn't have children, anyone with a heart could imagine how awful it would be to lose one.

Michael excused himself, leaving Naomi and me alone. Technically, he was still in charge. He went into the hallway to call the agents who could fill him in on the identification. This was a wonderful opportunity to change the subject to lighter issues.

"You seem quite a bit better lately, Naomi. Things going good?"

She smiled and sat down. "Actually, they're not exactly *good* just yet, but definitely better. How about you?"

I told her about my impending divorce and even went so far as to tell her about Jordan. She looked at me with concern.

"I'd heard the rumors, but I figured if I mentioned something to you, you'd have bitten my head off."

I laughed and agreed. "I have no idea what's going to happen as far as Michael is concerned. I'm just taking it one day at a time."

"My ears are burning."

We both saw that Michael had returned. Naomi smiled as she left my office. Michael took the seat she had vacated.

"One day at a time, huh?"

I wadded a piece of paper and threw it at him, then opened my desk drawer and took out the item I'd been desperate to look at since I read the killer's letter. It was my Bible. I always kept one handy in case there was a day I needed divine intervention, which realistically was about 364 out of 365 days a year.

"Are we having a prayer meeting?"

"No, I want to look up that passage in the Book of Daniel, smartass. But if you want to, we can. I'm sure your soul needs a little saving, and I know damn well mine does." Michael merely laughed, and I lit a cigarette.

"You know those things will kill you, Cee."

"If they don't, this job will."

I found the appropriate section. I was right. There were no words in Daniel 6:16 that said "Daniel fell." I still didn't understand what he meant by that. Was it that Albert got caught anyway since, I assumed, the killer meant Albert Whitfield was Daniel? I wasn't supposed to do any investigation of this case anymore, according to Agent Howard and the FBI, but I knew I was on to something. Just what, it was too soon to say.

I wasn't sure what to tell Michael yet, because I hadn't fully checked into Jim Carlson. Then I remembered something. I had forgotten about the bag of garbage in the trunk of my car. Michael clued in.

"Uh-oh, I know that look. CeeCee got a brainstorm."

"I have to go." I stood, slammed the Bible shut, and grabbed my purse and keys.

"Whoa, wait just a minute. Where to now?"

"Just something I forgot to do." I was out the door before he could argue.

I needed to go somewhere by a Dumpster so I could toss out any unnecessary items. I also needed to be careful about anyone spotting me. I could just hear the calls going to the department about a woman digging through garbage.

I found an old abandoned warehouse near downtown and drove around to the back. There were two large, green Dumpsters in the lot. Whether anyone regularly checked them for garbage was anyone's guess, but I didn't plan on leaving anything consequential in them anyway.

I took the bag and a blanket out of my trunk. I laid the blanket out and set the bag on top of it. After putting on my latex gloves, I opened the bag. I wasn't overcome by any noxious odor, so I assumed there wasn't any food in there.

I tore the bag along one side to open it up and leave the garbage on the plastic. There wasn't much. It looked like someone was putting new wallpaper up. There were remnants of wallpaper, some that apparently didn't fit right after they were cut. The pattern was a gaudy, purple paisley design that I wouldn't even use in my attic. There was an old paintbrush hardened by wallpaper paste, rolled-up plastic, and newspapers.

Underneath the pile of wallpaper junk, I found an item that captured my interest, and I set it aside. I sorted through small pieces of carpet remnants and located another item. I placed that one with the other.

It was clear whoever lived there was remodeling. Maybe when Jim Carlson moved out, he'd left the place in a shambles and Carl Malone had to do some touch-ups.

I located several other interesting items before grabbing the corners of the bag, gathering the garbage, and throwing it in the Dumpster. Then I removed several evidence bags from my trunk and placed the intriguing items inside. I put all the bags at the bottom of a box, put the blanket on top, and shut the trunk.

Each of the items alone didn't prove much, but together they definitely said something. It was the totality of the evidence.

I was still debating whether to tell Michael about my private investigation when I pulled into the parking lot. Standing before me, next to Michael's car, were him and Jordan.

Michael was leaning back against his hood while Jordan

pranced around, flipped her hair and flashed her million-dollar smile. Every nerve ending in my body came alive, and I began to feel my blood boil.

I swung my car into the space next to Michael's and was almost out of the vehicle before it had stopped. Michael instantly saw the state I was in. It couldn't have been hard for him to guess why. Jordan followed Michael's eyes and stopped smiling.

I headed right for her, and Michael stepped in front of me. He must've thought I was going to smash her face in. Though I would've liked to, that wasn't my intention. At least for the moment.

"Move, Michael." I was seething.

"CeeCee, think before you do anything you'll regret."

I walked to his side and stepped in front of Jordan before she had a chance to leave. She tried walking around me, but I placed my hand on her chest, and pushed her back against the car, pinning her down. I didn't weigh much more than she did, but I was taller and stronger.

"All right, CeeCee, that's enough," Michael said sternly.

"I would like to talk only to Jordan, if you don't mind." I nodded for him to back away, then turned back to her.

"Now then." I was amazed at how calm my voice sounded. "I think you and I need to have a discussion. Did anyone ever tell you that fucking your training officer is a good way to get yourself fired?" I smiled.

She glared at me and started to say something, but chose to remain silent; a wise move on her part.

"Tell me, Jordan, how old are you?"

"Thirty."

I was taken aback. Sinclair had previously told me that she was twenty-four or twenty-five. She was only four years younger than I was, but didn't look a day over twenty-one. Regardless, she had been sleeping with my husband and now had the audacity to come on to Michael. Stupidly, she no longer remained quiet.

"Take your hand off me. I need to go." She fumed.

"You had the boldness to stand in that locker room the first day I met you and ramble on about me. All the while, you were sleeping with my husband." My voice was still calm.

She exploded, which I didn't expect. "That's right, CeeCee! I was sleeping with your husband! But it doesn't matter now, does it? He'll still chase you around even when he knows you don't want him, but that's what you want, right? You don't want him, but you don't want anyone else to have him either. When our child is born I fully intend to find a new job, you bitch!" She started to cry.

I felt the blood drain from my face and a punch hit me square in the gut at the same time.

"How far along?" I heard the quiet, scratchy words come out of my mouth, but didn't feel as if I were actually saying them.

"Eleven weeks."

Sucker punch number two. My mind was scrambling. Eric had only been training her a little over ten weeks. It finally hit me. Eric was an instructor at the police academy. He must have started seeing Jordan there. The academy lasts four months and if I did the math, they could've been seeing each other for as long as six months. When Eric referred to three months the night I overheard them talking, he was merely talking about how long it had been since she started in the department. Realizing she had me, Jordan laughed.

"What? You think it was an accident that Eric was training me? Wake up, CeeCee."

"Does Eric know?" There was the same scratchy, hoarse voice again.

"No, thanks to you! He left and said he needed time. Of course that could be since you guys slept together the other morning, too. I had planned on waiting until my first trimester was over, so I knew everything was okay before I told him, and get through my training. But then *he* came back"—she nodded at Michael—"and Eric became obsessed about it. I got scared about how he would take it." Her arrogant tone changed, and she began to beg. "Please, CeeCee! You don't want him! Quit being so goddamn selfish and just let him go. He's been miserable for the last year, and he deserves to be happy!"

She shoved my hand aside and took off, half running toward the department. I stood facing the car, absorbing the bombshell she just dropped. I wasn't taking it in all that well. I began to have a hard time catching my breath. My chest was heaving. I leaned on the hood for balance because I was getting rather dizzy. Michael was there instantly, but I pushed him away.

"I-I just need some air," I said breathlessly, and took in a deep lung full. It didn't seem to make a difference.

During incomprehensible situations, one's mind plays tricks. Now, for reasons unknown, I began to laugh. I laughed so hysterically, I was convinced I was having a good, old-fashioned nervous breakdown. Still not able to catch my breath, I squatted down and put my face between my knees. That didn't help. All it did was constrict my diaphragm even more.

She was pregnant. How would I explain that to my daughters? How could I tell them they would have a new brother or sister and that he or she had a different mother? I felt so betrayed to find out that all these months he was being unfaithful, and it was almost too much to bear. He could never, ever use Michael as an excuse. I never lied to Eric about Michael, and I hadn't slept with him when we first met.

I was shaking and sweating profusely. Michael picked me up off the ground.

"CeeCee, you need to calm down."

"I'm fine, Michael. Just let me walk." I headed for God knows where and he followed, looking like he wanted to take care of me, but also afraid of my increasingly irrational state.

Breathing was easier, but I didn't feel that much better. I walked toward a picnic table on the outer grassy area of the parking lot under a large maple tree. The closer I got, the more I felt myself begin to dissolve. Jordan's news was simply way too much to absorb on top of everything else.

I sat on the table, out of control yet numb, and just let Michael stand and hold me. I knew it was an unusual position for him to be in, but he handled it well. Eventually, I felt able to breathe and speak rationally. Now it was time to vent.

"I can't believe this lie after lie after lie from Eric. The day you two had your fight, he was begging me to go to North Carolina with him, alone, to work it out!"

"I'm sure he meant every word at the time, Cee."

"I'm so angry! I'm angry and hurt and confused. I mean, I remember three or four months ago when he would come home from work and everything seemed normal. Even the night I told him you were coming he seemed fine, for crying out loud. But now I find out it was all bullshit? And then, all the months I pushed you out of my head because I didn't want to dishonor and betray my husband? Ha! That's a laugh!" I started crying again.

Michael handed me a tissue (I have no idea where he

got it, but lately the need for tissues has been continual) and kissed the top of my head.

"You need to call him."

I had every intention of doing so when I got my act together. I'd call to congratulate him on his impending fatherhood. I'd let him figure out how to tell our daughters what was happening with their parents and why.

As angry as I was at Eric right then, there was a part of me that felt bad for Jordan. She obviously loved Eric, was looking ahead to, possibly, single motherhood, and it seemed to me she was all alone.

"She really loves him, doesn't she?" I whispered, the ill feeling coming back yet again.

"I'd say that's pretty obvious. She's right, you know." He was quiet.

"Right about what?"

"I know everything just happened, but no matter what you say, you can't seem to let go of Eric."

That was easier said than done. I also felt the need to apologize to Michael for continuing to put him in an awkward position of not fully knowing whether we were going forward or not. Each time I made a commitment to him, feelings rose up to loosen it. He said he wasn't uncomfortable with my behavior, that I needn't apologize, and he understood. How much longer would I continue doing this to him?

I looked at Michael. "I just realized, if you hadn't come back, we may have never seen each other again— ever. I mean, if Eric had left me for Jordan, I would've never gotten up the nerve to call you. I think I would've been too afraid you'd have already found someone else."

He responded by holding me tighter and quietly chuckling. "I'm sorry, I don't mean to laugh, but when I saw the look on your face I thought for sure you were going to knock her out right there in the parking lot."

I began to laugh just a little, too. Michael always tried to find the amusing aspect of everything, no matter how dire it appeared on the surface. We reluctantly agreed to go back to the office. While we walked, I asked Michael what he was doing in the parking lot and what Jordan was saying to him. Turns out, he had gone to get a file out of his car as she was pulling in. Just to be friendly, she walked over and started chatting away about nothing in particular.

"Why, CeeCee? Were you jealous?" He smiled.

"As a matter of fact, I was." I raised one eyebrow at him, and his smile grew bigger.

But we really needed to put the personal drama aside for more important efforts. Immediately, Michael started using my phone to contact other agents and direct them here and there. I still couldn't get myself back on track. All I could think of was that I couldn't call Eric yet. He probably still had five more hours of driving before he and the girls got to the condominium. I didn't want to shock him into a car accident by telling him about Jordan. He had said he would call me when they got there. There was nothing I could do till then.

CHAPTER TWENTY-TWO

Finally, I forced my mind back onto the job. There was more planning to be done. I needed to think about another surveillance, or possible break-in, tonight at Jim Carlson's house. Once again, I had to come up with something to tell Michael without revealing the sheriff's role. I also wanted to talk to Carlson's neighbors this afternoon.

Michael was gabbing away on the phone, so I motioned that I was going to get a cup of coffee. He gave a thumbs-up, and I quietly grabbed my keys from behind him. I passed the coffee machine and went straight to my car. I hated lying to Michael, but I was protecting him. What he didn't know couldn't get him in trouble.

As soon as I turned onto Jim Carlson's street, I spotted a woman with a small black terrier standing in the yard of her house, which sat directly to the east of his. I needed to be careful. She couldn't know I was a cop.

An idea came to me, and I pulled right into her driveway. I told her I was from a bank and that we were getting ready to foreclose on the residence next door. The payments hadn't been kept up and the house appeared to have been abandoned. I needed to make sure no one was living there before the foreclosure papers were filed. I said whatever I thought would make her comfortable with me.

"Carl fell behind in his payments? That's unusual."

She clearly knew Malone owned the house. "Unless the fellow who lives there fell behind in rent, and Carl just couldn't cover it." She looked down at the ground, thinking about what she had just said.

I told her I would appreciate it if she didn't say anything to Carl or anyone else right now. The foreclosure wasn't a done deal and if I could get a hold of the renter, I could see if he was planning on catching up the payments.

"He's not home much, ma'am. I just assumed he travels a lot."

I began to ask the woman, Ellen Powers, a series of questions. She said he was tall, wore glasses, had brown hair and a thick mustache. She had never spoken to him because he always seemed in a hurry. He had lived there alone for a little over ten months and drove a large black pickup truck.

It was him; it had to be. It was a dark pickup truck that tried to run me off the road. He traveled, which told me he was hiding the girls somewhere else. He'd only been here ten months, but that was just enough time to plan his kidnappings. I'd bet if I checked out his last state of residence, I'd find a couple of missing girls. If I knew his real name.

And lastly, I was sure his appearance was nothing but a disguise. I was itching to get inside that house, but I had to keep my wits about me. After I thanked Ellen and left, I drove past Carl Malone's house hoping to catch him and ask about his renter. No such luck because, again, he wasn't home. It was getting late. I had been gone over two hours and had turned my phone off. I turned it back on and called Michael, who, I was sure, was bouncing off the walls by then. Predictably, he answered on the first ring.

"I suppose it's pointless to even ask?"

"Pretty much, I'm headed back right now."

"Just go to the hotel and we'll go grab dinner."

He was irritated, which was hardly a surprise.

When I got to the hotel, he was sitting in a chair at the small table in the room, talking on his phone. I gave a playful wave and he only responded with a glare. He hung up and just as he began to badger me, my cell phone rang. Eric.

There were no lesser of two evils in this case. I didn't want to deal with either man right now. I pointed to my phone and mouthed *Eric* before stepping outside. He and the girls had arrived safe and sound, all three exhausted from the drive. For a moment I almost considered not raising the issue of Jordan at all, but I had to. It went worse than expected.

When I told Eric about Jordan being pregnant, I heard him gasp, and then he said nothing. I had to remind him several times that the girls were there and he needed to keep it together, though I hope he had the sense to leave the room they were in while we talked.

I told him how I discovered he had been seeing Jordan while she was in the academy, and I even went so far as to call him a bastard once or twice. I yelled that he deceived me, our daughters, and our marriage. He began to bring up Michael, but I cut him off immediately.

"Don't you dare! I made a choice a year ago, and that choice was you," I shouted. "I never lied to you, Eric. I told you everything about Michael. Had I known you'd make me pay for it every day since, I might've made a different decision and saved us both a lot of grief. If you didn't think you would get over it, why didn't you just walk away back then? Did I really deserve all of this?" Any attempt at composure was over. I was crying hard now.

He sighed. "I thought I would be able to get over it, CeeCee, but I couldn't. Now I see I never could. The minute I realized that, I should've walked but didn't. I kept thinking something would change."

"Do you love her, Eric?" I didn't know if I wanted the answer or not.

After a long moment of silence, he answered, "Yes, CeeCee, I do."

It was hard to hear, but at least I knew this time it was really the truth. At long last. He wasn't finished, but I already knew what he was going to say.

"But I still love you, and if I had the choice right now, I would give anything to work things out with you."

"I still love you, Eric, but you and I both know the damage is done and it's over. I could never look at you the same again, and you couldn't look at me. I've slept with Michael now and you know that and no matter what you might say or think, you'll never get past it. Not to mention the lack of communication we've had the last several years. After Murder Mountain you'd always say, 'I'm here if you need me,' but then would shut me out the minute I tried to talk. I felt very alone."

We remained quiet for a while. I saw I hadn't shut the hotel room door all the way. Michael could hear every word. It was just as well; I wouldn't have to explain everything later. I needed to hang up with Eric but had one more thing to say.

"Eric, you should call her. If you really do love her, call. She's carrying your child and she needs you right now." My stomach turned while I said this, but I knew it was right.

He admitted he had to. Then we said that the first moment it was safe, we would talk to the girls, agreeing not to throw Michael and Jordan in their faces. They would need a long transition, Selina especially. It would be a considerable amount of time before they learned about the baby. It was an hour and a half later by the time our conversation finally ended. I was drained.

Poor, poor CeeCee, he thought as he watched. So sad, so sad. If she only knew just how much sadder she was going to be. The thought made him want to clap his hands with joy, but he couldn't make a sound. She might hear him since she was still out on the balcony, crying like a small child. "If you weren't such a whore, my dear . . ." he whispered. It would be impossible for him to sleep tonight, feeling so anxious about the upcoming Grande Finale. He looked at his watch, a cheap silver knockoff that had somehow managed to keep time for the last twenty-five years. He refused to replace it, paying small amounts here and there to keep it running. It was a sentimental attachment. It had been with him during each and every one, just as it would be with him tonight, for the very last. The last guest was special, oh so special! She would ensure he would be remembered always, especially after tonight. With such an important father, his special guest would bring a reign of redemption from here to heaven. Along with the redemption would come the vengeance that he had waited for this very long time; vengeance against CeeCee Gallagher, a vengeance he had dreamed of for over two decades.

I stayed outside for another half hour, mindlessly gazing at the interstate. It had been another mentally exhausting day.

When I finally went back in the room, I leaned against the bathroom door and looked at Michael, who said nothing.

"You heard most of my conversation."

He nodded, but got up from his chair and came over. He pulled me into a comforting, forgiving embrace that seemed to last forever.

"The only thing I have to say or ask is, are you sure I'm

who you want? No matter how many times you said it, I'm still not convinced. I'm not going to lie to you, and as much as this might scare you right now, I want you to be my wife someday. Not tomorrow or next week, but when you're ready. *That's* how much I love you and can't live without you. But it's up to you to figure it out and keep to whatever decision you make. Most important, whatever decision you make has to be for the right reasons, and not out of fear of hurting me or Eric."

I pulled away. "I'm sure now, Michael. You're who I want, who I need, and who I belong with. Who I've always belonged with. I should've realized that when I thought you died on Murder Mountain. I didn't think I could go on."

We embraced again, completely silent. Too many words had been said too many times. Somehow I felt I may have been very near the end of all our problems. The tension released when we heard Michael's stomach growl and both of us laughed. It was an unusually warm night, so it was lovely to be able to walk to the nearest restaurant. Despite being a little more relaxed, I still didn't have much of an appetite. Today's events essentially still squashed it.

Michael expressed concern over my eating and sleeping habits, and promised that when the case was over, he was taking me away on a much needed vacation, anywhere I wanted to go.

The promise sounded wonderful, but a trip was a long way off. There were way too many things that needed to be taken care of before then, my planned stakeout that night being the first. I thought about waiting until Michael went to sleep and sneaking out, but after all the truth telling this afternoon, I didn't feel right about it. Back in

the room after dinner I took both of his hands in mine
and sat down with him on the bed.

"Michael, do you trust me?"

He looked baffled and a bit dismayed, worried there
was yet more to be hashed out. "Of course I do. Why?"

"I'm not talking personally, Michael. I mean professionally."

He looked even more confused. "CeeCee, get to your
point."

I told him. Not everything, but most of it. I told him
that I had been investigating the case behind the lines
and had found something, but I couldn't tell him what it
was right then. I wasn't sure about my find yet and the
less he knew, the better off he'd be. I told him I was close
to being sure who the killer was, but I needed a little
more time.

I told him I had to go out that night and he'd have to
take my word for everything and simply trust me.

"Trust you! You know who the killer is? Is that where
you've been? My God, CeeCee, what's the matter with
you! After Murder Mountain I thought you would have
learned!"

I had prepared myself for that reaction, but I wouldn't
budge about giving him any more information. He certainly wasn't finished.

"Where do you think you're going tonight?"

"I can't tell you."

He was floored. "You can't tell me?" Now he was getting angry.

"Michael," I said coolly, "you can't know. I have nothing on this guy yet. Think realistically. If I get caught
and the FBI finds out you knew about it, you'll lose your
job—if they don't throw you in jail first."

"Jesus! What the hell are you doing, burglarizing houses?" I felt my blood pressure rise a tad at his reference. He said it jokingly, but if he only knew. "I won't let you leave here tonight until you tell me. I picture you going out and getting yourself killed, or at least federally indicted. Prison or a graveyard are two places I really don't care to be visiting."

Before I could argue back, his cell phone rang. He looked like he didn't want to answer, but picked it up. "What is it!"

He laid the phone down. "Oh, fuck!"

"What?" I barked. Michael didn't curse very much, and it always scared me when he did.

"He took another one. Let's go."

CHAPTER TWENTY-THREE

I tried to get what I could while we half ran to the car, but Michael didn't know all that much. The agent had merely given him an address and told him another seven-year-old girl was taken. Curiosity got the better of me, so I called the communications center to find out who lived at that address. When I found out, there was nothing I could do but hold the phone and stare into it.

"Oh, no," I muttered.

"Who is it?"

"The Richland County commissioner's daughter, Brooklyn Phillips."

"A county commissioner's daughter? That's really pushing it. The killer definitely made a statement, didn't he?" Michael started to drive even faster.

"Yes, he did. I'd like to see Howard explain himself out of this one. The killer flat out told him he'd take another child unless I was put in charge."

As I'd expected, the Phillipses' house was complete chaos. Michael and I could barely get across the front yard. Neighbors and family members were screaming at the top of their lungs, and FBI agents and cops were swarming everywhere; there was no sense of order whatsoever. I assumed nothing vital to the crime had happened in the front yard since everyone was traipsing around so much.

Inside the house, the two idiots from the FBI were standing near Commissioner Alex Phillips and his wife, Jean. Some lady held a bucket in front of Jean, who was vomiting into it. The commissioner was rubbing her back and trying to soothe her, though he didn't look too good himself.

I'd always gotten along with him, and he maintained his position as one of the top supporters of our police department. This was a great benefit to us since he held the purse strings.

I saw good old Supervisory Agent Earl Howard come into the room from the kitchen. I just leaned back against the wall, crossed my arms, and said nothing. He went directly to Michael, glowering at me along the way. I happily returned the same. He spoke to Michael for about five minutes before returning to the kitchen.

Michael filled me in on some of the details. Brooklyn had gone through her nightly routine of taking a bath, eating a snack, and going to bed. Alex and Jean, after tucking Brooklyn in, stayed downstairs and watched television before they decided to turn in.

When Jean checked on Brooklyn later, her bedroom window was open, the screen had been cut, and Brooklyn was gone. The house only had one floor, and the couple had been in the family room about a good hour before checking on their only daughter. An entire hour for the killer to get away. They never heard a sound.

My attention was torn away from Michael by the shouts of Alex Phillips. Agent Howard had come back into the room.

"What are you going to do? You don't have a fucking thing, do you? So help me God, if something happens to her, I'll hold every one of you people responsible!"

Of course, Agent Howard gushed about how they

were doing everything they could and were following up on some good leads.

"That's a lie, and you know it," I said loudly. Gauntlet thrown down.

Both men turned to look at me. I stayed in position, straight-faced and staring down Agent Howard.

"Detective Gallagher? CeeCee." Alex stood up. "What's going on? What do you mean?"

"Commissioner, I'm so very sorry about Brooklyn. I strongly suggest you find Sheriff Stephens immediately to find out what the FBI is doing to find your daughter, and he'll tell you. Not a goddamn thing. And find out how much they've already botched this entire case."

Michael grabbed my arm. "CeeCee, don't," he whispered in my ear.

I jerked away to find Agent Howard less than an inch from my face. "Detective Gallagher," he said, his voice low and menacing, "you're treading on very dangerous ground here. At this rate, you'll be lucky if you're out of federal prison by the time you're eighty, if I have anything to say about it."

"Then I guess it's a good thing you don't have anything to say about it, Agent." The sheriff, who had come in and heard every word, stood behind Agent Howard.

"Sheriff, with all due respect, this is federal jurisdiction. . . ."

"Right, it is. Agent Hagerman is still the lead agent. However, as of right now, Detective Gallagher will be named before the media as the lead investigator. You, sir, are no longer needed, and if you call your boss—he's expecting your call, by the way—you'll find you're on the next plane out of here. Those orders are directly out of Washington."

I guess the governor and his brother came through. A

little late, but it was better than nothing. Agent Howard turned, saw the smile on my face, and looked back at the sheriff. As if the sheriff's word wasn't enough, Agent Howard called his boss in front of all of us.

Seeing his face pale told me the person on the other end wasn't too thrilled with him either. Agent Howard slammed his phone shut and walked out the front door without saying a word.

"Sorry it took so long, CeeCee. All of this could have been prevented."

Alex Phillips demanded to know what was going on, and the sheriff told him the truth. He told him about the letter, the threat the killer made, and how Agent Howard had ignored it. Alex looked devastated.

"CeeCee, you know I trust you. I can't take this. I really can't. Please, find my little girl." He began to cry.

I felt my own eyes well up. It was difficult to speak. "Alex, you know I'll do everything I can."

He nodded slightly, then went back to tend to his wife. It was a quiet few seconds before the sheriff took charge.

"CeeCee, it's your show now. You and Michael. Technically, it's still an FBI case, but I'm going out right now to announce to the media that you're in charge. Hopefully, our psychopath will see it soon and not take another child and, God willing, release Brooklyn Phillips."

It was evident Michael had relaxed considerably since the departure of Agent Earl Howard. He immediately took the reins, ordering agents to clear the front lawn and get everyone who didn't belong out of the house. Anyone without a specific job to do there was to be out looking for the child. Suddenly everything felt under control.

It was time for me to leave. All the bases were being

covered and I had to finally take care of the most important part of this case, finding out more about Jim Carlson. I motioned to Michael, letting him know I needed to leave.

"What do you mean you have to go? Oh no, if this is what you were telling me back at the room—forget it! You're not going anywhere until you tell me first."

"You said you trust me, now prove it. I'll be fine. This is extremely important and it can't be done any other way. We don't have time."

"You promise me that if something goes wrong, even in the slightest, you get your ass back here, or call me. And I want to hear from you in exactly one hour. If I don't, I'll assume something's wrong and act accordingly. Agreed?"

"I promise. One hour."

CHAPTER TWENTY-FOUR

I was out the door and heading to Jim Carlson's, making just a quick stop at my house to throw on my burglary gear. Chances were no one would be at the Carlson house, but I had to be extremely careful. I thought of something on the way home and drove back to the abandoned factory to check the Dumpster to make sure the garbage bag was still there. Luckily, it was. I grabbed it carefully, since I had torn it open, and dumped the contents inside a new garbage bag before throwing it in my trunk. I wished I hadn't promised Michael an hour; I was going to be pressed for time as it was.

To get a look at Jim Carlson's house, I had to drive around the block a few times. It was totally dark, and the black pickup truck his neighbor described wasn't in the driveway. I parked on the next street over and waited a few minutes to see if anyone turned on a porch light or was sitting outside. It was a warm night and people might stay up later. I also needed to listen for dogs, people sneezing, coughing, talking, chains rattling, anything that would indicate a witness could be around.

Once I was satisfied I was alone, I grabbed my bag of tools off the front seat and slowly got out of the car. I hadn't had time to get one out of the impound lot, but it didn't matter. All I had to do was say I was watching the house if anyone saw my car.

I put in the earpiece attached to the portable radio on my belt. I needed to hear if anyone called the police department about a suspicious person or car on this street. The radio was pretty quiet, so I felt safe to begin my adventure.

I darted through two backyards to get to the back of Jim Carlson's house. By this time, I was sweating and breathing hard, so I took a moment to settle down a little before entering the house. I approached the back door, took out my lock-picking set, and went to work. Surprisingly, the door was already unlocked. I took my bag and ran back to the first yard I crossed, the place where I had noticed an old wheelbarrow lying upside down behind a shed, alongside some other thrown-away gardening items.

I placed my bag underneath the wheelbarrow since it didn't look like an item the homeowner would check daily. I left the bag there in case I had to quickly get out of the house. If I had to move quickly, who knows if I would remember to grab it. This way, I could always come back later and retrieve it.

Now, with my radio, turned-off cell phone, gun on my belt, and flashlight in hand, I returned to Jim Carlson's back door.

The doorknob squeaked when I turned it. Noises always seemed to be magnified a thousand times when you're doing something illegal. I looked around yet again, then went in, quietly closing the door behind me. My eyes soon adjusted to the dark.

I was in the kitchen. There was an aluminum table and two folding chairs substituting as a dinette set. The countertops were bare; no toaster, microwave, or utensils. It was horribly hot, and my heart rate was raising my own body heat, making me utterly miserable. Plus, I was nervous. Something just didn't feel right.

I stood in the same spot in the kitchen for several minutes, listening to the crickets chirping outside along with the sound of my own labored breathing.

I finally mustered the courage to open the refrigerator. It was completely bare. Maybe Michael was right. Maybe I shouldn't have come here.

This was nothing like when I'd been in Carl Malone's house. I should've been more nervous there since I knew for a fact it was occupied. Here, it was anyone's guess whether someone lived in this house. The atmosphere seemed very wrong.

I waved my instincts off as overactive imagination and ventured through the kitchen doorway, slowly poking my head around the corner in the dimness. I was hesitant to use my flashlight in an open room with uncovered windows because someone outside might see me.

The room adjoining the kitchen was bare. It looked like it should've been a living room, but there was no furniture to indicate that. There was no wallpaper. When I ran my hand down the nearest wall, paint flakes began to chip off. I stood in that spot for several minutes listening like I did in the kitchen.

For some reason, the thought of walking across the dark open room terrified me. But thinking of Brooklyn Phillips, I grabbed my gun out of its holster and slowly began the trek across the room. I was heading for a staircase at the other end, and it seemed like hours before I got to it.

At the bottom of the staircase I leaned against the wall. I had to stop to breathe. This was ridiculous. I worked uniform patrol for seven years before going into the detective bureau. I always cleared houses, buildings, businesses, barns—any type of structure possible—even catching burglars inside, and I was never this tense and nervous. I honestly didn't think I would be able to bring myself to go upstairs. Now, on top of sweating and a heart that was beating like a newborn hummingbird, I was shaking like a leaf.

I felt nervous laughter begin to erupt, but did my best to quell it. This actually eased some of my nerves, so I was able to slowly start walking up the steps. My hand-gun pointed toward the top of the steps, and I was re-minded how much I hated climbing staircases. It was a bona fide kill zone. If someone were to peer around the top and fire at me, I would have nowhere to go.

The stairs squeaked, which made it worse, and when I got to the second-to-top step, I stopped. I didn't know the layout of the house from there and got to my knees before looking around the corner. This time, I quickly flashed my light twice. It felt safe to do so since there weren't any windows. When I decided all looked clear, I went forward.

There were three doors. Knowing I had to check every room, I moved to the first door. By now, I could see the tip of my gun bobbing up and down from the tremors in my hand. I wished Michael were there. I'd bet he did too. I hadn't bothered to look at my watch, but I knew I was well over an hour by now, probably going on two.

I got the first two, completely empty, rooms cleared without any restless souls jumping out at me or a barrage of gunfire erupting. Then I got to the third. There was a paint smell coming from this room. I looked in and didn't see any windows, so it was clear to use the flash-light. Shining the beam into the room, I sucked in my breath and stood still.

This room had a bed, a neatly made twin bed with a flowery blue comforter and white pillow at the head-board. It was at the farthest wall away from me and had a small nightstand next to it. On the nightstand was a white antique lamp. I took my chances and felt for a light switch next to me.

I flipped it on, and the room became illuminated in a dim, soft light. I was completely overcome. I could see the entire room as plain as day.

The room had windows, but they were covered with pictures, newspapers, and magazine pages. However, it wasn't just the windows that were covered. Every wall in the room was plastered with them, and half of the ceiling. There wasn't a centimeter of wall exposed.

It wasn't the wall being covered that disturbed me so much; it was what covered them that was so unspeakably macabre. Every newspaper, magazine page, and picture contained little girls. There were pictures of child actresses, sports stars, pages from children's clothing catalogs with girls who looked about five, and the newspapers all had pictures of little girls walking their dogs, playing in the park, or with their parents.

As I walked along each wall, scanning every horrific page, I realized I had walked into the room of our killer. It wasn't that each picture terrified me. It was everything put together and how neatly it was done. All the pages fit together, cut just right and glued onto the wall, one piece nestled against another.

My attention was drawn to a small box under the bed, a corner of its red lid sticking out. I didn't know if I was able to handle another surprise, but I grabbed the box anyway and opened the lid. It was full of news articles on the recent kidnappings.

The article on top was dated yesterday. The deeper I delved into the box, the worse it got.

At the very bottom was an entire stack of articles about me and the Murder Mountain case. My interviews, photos, personal information. Everything. There were photos of Michael and me as far back as last year at the trial. There were photos of us at the hotel, eating at the diner, walking out of the department, and standing at the crime scenes of the dead children. The killer had been watching us every minute from the very beginning.

My hands were shaking so badly I almost couldn't get everything back into the box the way I'd found it. Before I shoved it back under the bed, I took the lid off again, grabbed the picture of Michael and me at the hotel, and put it in my pocket.

Kneeling in the middle of floor, I looked around and above me at the crude shrine, then focused on the closet door. I hadn't noticed it before because it was covered with paper as well and blended in with the walls. I didn't know if I could open it without tearing the pictures until I saw the exposed seam running up the wall.

I opened the door and looked into the darkness of the closet, the dim light of the room too weak to do any good. I turned my flashlight on, but it was dead. I opened the door wider, hoping to catch some of the light from the lamp behind me.

When I looked back into the closet, I found myself screaming so loud it sounded like someone else. I flew backward, hitting the door, falling to my knees. My hands covered my mouth so tightly I thought I would suffocate.

There were children in there, at least fifteen of them. I could see them standing in rows, their eyes shining out at me in the light. I didn't think I would be able to compose myself, enough to get out of the house for help, until my eyes adjusted to the dark and I saw the children were actually My Size dolls.

There was no quelling the nervous laughter that erupted. I bent over and held my stomach. When I finally stood and walked back to the open door, I could see a white string hanging from the ceiling of the closet. I pulled the string, and the closet exploded in bright white light. There was no laughing now. I was horrified.

Each doll was different; its hair color, eyes, clothing, and shoes. They were meticulously lined up in four rows of four dolls each. The size of the closet was, at first glance, deceiving. In truth, it was absolutely enormous. The walls had been pushed back so they extended an extra six to seven feet, at least, in every direction. Most of the walls had been drywalled and wallpapered with the tacky purple paper I'd found in the garbage bag, but the wall in the back was not finished. Loose insulation hung from it; some pieces lay on the floor in front of it.

The first bedroom I came to in the hallway had to have been downsized to absorb this monstrosity. Probably a new wall had been built.

There were three dressers along the finished walls of the closet. Each one was four drawers high, finished in a deep, glossy stained wood. Above each of the dressers were clothing rods filled with girls' clothes. These were not doll clothes. They were very expensive clothes from high-end children's stores. There were dresses, frilly and casual; small pantsuits; skirts, silk tops; and jumpers all in various colors. The dolls themselves wore these clothes.

I opened the drawers and saw underwear neatly folded, socks sorted by colors, and T-shirts folded so neatly they looked like they had just come out of a package. Children's books were stacked on top of each dresser.

Then there were the ribbons and shoes. One dresser held two drawers full of red ribbons, and the other two drawers held My Size shoes in assorted colors. I grabbed a few ribbons and one shoe and stuffed them in my pocket, along with a piece of insulation.

I kept looking at one doll in the middle of the front row. It wasn't like the others. It was scary and disturbing. It was dressed in all black, with a long black wig, black fingernail polish, and dark makeup painted on its face. It was gothic. There was something else different about this doll, and I picked it up to examine it closer.

Feeling the objects under the doll's black shirt told me everything before I even pulled the shirt up and looked. The doll was modified with breasts. Crude circles of flesh-colored plastic had been glued onto the chest area. Pink cone-shaped pieces of plastic had been glued onto those, giving them the appearance of nipples. Not even able to imagine what was down below, I pulled the pants of the doll down. In the genital area, a yellow sponge cut into a triangle shape was glued to the doll. What looked like black hair netting was glued to the sponge to give the appearance of pubic hair.

I checked the other dolls. The gothic doll was the only one with modifications. There wasn't a doubt in my mind that this was his favorite doll, so I was going to take it.

Getting ready to leave—I had been gone well over three hours, so Michael probably had the National Guard out looking for me—I saw a small hole I hadn't noticed before back by the unfinished wall. As I bent over to peer inside, I heard the door slam downstairs. My nerves went into high alert.

I ran as quietly as I could back into the room and shut off the light. Someone was coming up the steps, so all I could do was go into the closet. I was shaking again and sweating. On the verge of hysterics, I pulled the string in the closet to turn off the light. I started to back up, but kept knocking over dolls, so I finally inched along the wall to the crawlspace I'd seen. I backed into it as far as I could go.

I put my hand down into something wet. I had taken my gloves off when I inspected the gruesome doll, an action I now regretted. By instinct, I raised my hand to my nose to smell it and started to gag. It was old urine. Through the crack in the door, I saw the light in the room go on. I used my clean hand to cover my mouth, trying to keep from breathing hard. When I tried to back up farther, my right hand brushed the cell phone attached to my belt.

I had to call Michael. By this time, I didn't care how I would explain being in here, but I needed help. When I opened my phone and turned it on, the light from the screen lit up the entire closet. My hands were shaking so hard I had a difficult time dialing. I could hear the person, who I assumed was Jim Carlson, our killer, moving around the room on the other side of the door.

When I finally was able to dial, Michael didn't let me down. He answered on the first ring. The time on the phone display showed I was almost four hours overdue.

"Michael!" I whispered loud enough for him to hear me.

"CeeCee, where the hell are you—"

"Michael, listen to me!" As much as I tried, it was impossible not to sound hysterical. "I'm in trouble and I need help, I'm at—"

The person in the room began to open the closet door. I had no choice but to close my phone, hanging up on Michael before I was able to give him the address. I could stand up and take Carlson at gunpoint, but I would probably go to jail, none of the evidence would be admissible, the killer would go free, and Brooklyn would die.

Light flooded the closet, and I crawled farther into my hole, praying he wouldn't find me.

"Oh, dear, how'd you fall down, darling?" The man

spoke in the familiar-sounding, gruff voice I'd heard on the phone.

At first I thought he was talking to me, but after hearing him set the gothic doll upright, I realized he was talking to it.

"My beautiful girl, I missed you. I know Daddy's been gone, but I'll make it up to you." He paused. "Oh, no, please don't cry. I promise I'll be back soon. It's almost over, my love, don't worry."

I wished I could get a look at his face, but if I tried, I risked getting caught.

"I have to go now, my love. I had to come back to see you, but I'll be back again soon. I love you now and forever."

I heard him kiss the doll, a loud exaggerated smack.

The man turned the light off and closed the door. I breathed an enormous sigh of relief. But he didn't leave right away. It was another half an hour before I heard the door shut and the truck start. I waited yet another fifteen minutes before I felt safe enough to leave the closet. Michael was probably beside himself.

I hoped I hadn't left too much evidence of myself in the closet. The clothes I had on were going to burn as soon as I got home, and I couldn't wait to scrub the urine from my hand. Urine from one of the recent victims, no doubt. The killer had kept them in the closet for a short time. Unfortunately, Brooklyn wasn't there, which wasn't a good sign.

Outside, the night air felt wonderful. I was literally soaked with sweat, my hair dripping. With the gothic doll tucked under one arm and my retrieved bag of tools in the other, I quickly made it back to my car.

I threw the doll and my bag in the trunk and took off. Just as I turned the corner to drive home, I was unnerved to see the black pickup truck pulling back into the driveway. My headlights were still off, so I drove away quickly.

The killer had come back for something. Whatever it was, he'd discover his favorite doll gone and it would push him over the edge. I hoped he'd be willing to make a trade.

CHAPTER TWENTY-FIVE

Once I was far enough away, I began to relax. I had found the killer, no doubts. But I wasn't going to call Michael until I had gotten rid of everything I needed to.

Back at my house, I took a long shower, feeling as if I could not get clean. Then I bagged up all my clothes, threw them into the backyard fire pit, and lit it. I had removed the photo, ribbons, insulation, and shoe.

These I placed in the bag of garbage I had taken earlier, crumpling up the photo before throwing it in. Then I put in the children's catalog photo and paper with fingernail polish on it that I had legitimately found in the bag earlier. I tied the bag again, shook it, and put it in my trunk. Now it was time to deal with Michael.

I assumed he wasn't at the hotel, so I called him first. As expected, he was extremely upset and worried.

"CeeCee, oh my God, are you OK? Where are you?"

"Michael, I'm fine, OK. I'm sorry I scared you earlier, my phone cut out and I didn't have any service."

"Scared me? We've got most of your department out looking for you! Where are you right now?"

"I'm headed toward the hotel."

"I'll let everyone know you're OK, and I'll be there in fifteen minutes. I'm glad you're OK, Cee. You scared the shit out of me."

When we hung up, I couldn't wait to see him. I had been terrified in that closet, and now all I wanted was to be safe in Michael's arms. I knew I would have to listen to a horrific verbal lashing from him, but I would sit through it patiently. I held my hand in front of me and saw it was still trembling. I shook it, as if that would make any difference at all.

I was sitting on the bed at the hotel when Michael came barreling through the door and grabbed me, almost lifting me off the floor.

"Cee, I can't tell you . . ." His head was buried in my shoulder, and it was hard to hear him. "I haven't been that worried since Murder Mountain. Where were you? You're shaking!" He pulled away and looked at me. "CeeCee, I keep begging you. Please tell me where you've been and what happened!"

He kept me close, his arm protectively around my waist. I told him the truth, at least up until the part where I broke into Jim Carlson's house. I also omitted the break-in at Carl Malone's house.

When I got to that part, I simply said I had been on surveillance, watching Jim Carlson's house, and I was so upset when I called because while I was taking the man's garbage, the truck came around the corner and I thought the driver saw me. Of course I doubted Michael would believe this story, but it was worth a shot.

Michael did look skeptical. "How did you know Carl Malone had rental properties?"

I anticipated this question. "When I looked into Carl Malone further, I checked with the auditor's office to see if he owned any properties. That's standard in investigations."

I told Michael about the neighbor's statements and the dark truck.

"It's him, Michael. I know it. I haven't had a chance to look through the garbage bag yet, since I had to get out of there, but there might be something. Believe me, he's our killer."

"You seem awfully confident." He eyed me even more suspiciously. "You don't have to lie to me, you know. If you think I would ever turn you in for something you did wrong—"

"I didn't do anything wrong, and I'm not lying."

I *wasn't* lying. What I did was illegal, but if you asked anyone whether it was *wrong*, you'd probably get differing answers. Wrong was only a matter of opinion.

By then, it was only a couple of hours until morning. I paged the crime lab and told them to be in first to open and process the garbage bag. Then I ran out to my car to grab the information I had put together on Jim Carlson. I handed Michael the thin file.

"You didn't find much on him, did you?" He flipped through the pages and looked at the photo I found from the Bureau of Motor Vehicles.

"Very inconspicuous. There's an Indiana driver's license, and, as you can see, it still has his old Indianapolis address. The photo matches the description his neighbor gave—tall, brown hair and a mustache, but that doesn't fit with other witness descriptions. This guy's very good at changing his appearance."

"There's also no pickup truck registered to him, Cee."

As Michael looked attentively through each page, I found myself in deep admiration of him as a professional. Of course, his stunningly handsome looks didn't hurt either. It took him a while to get through what little information there was, and I found my eyes getting heavy. The emotional letdown suddenly left me weak and exhausted.

The next thing I remember was waking up briefly to Michael covering me with a blanket, then lying down beside me, his arm tight around my waist. We had only slept a little over two hours before he was shaking me to wake up. I was drained, but knew it was vital we get to the garbage bag.

While driving to the department, I went back to thinking about the letter the killer had written to me. Under any circumstances, the letter was frightening, but there was one thing that stood out and bothered me most.

"Michael, did any of the agents come up with anything regarding the letter?"

"Not as far as I know, why?"

"We need to focus on the lions' den."

CHAPTER TWENTY-SIX

Michael looked at me as closely as he could without driving off the side of the road.

"What are you talking about?"

"The lions' den. The entire letter focuses on the lions' den." I rolled my window down to get some air. "When we get to the lab, call your agents and have them track down anything they can find with the word *lion* in it. I don't care if it's a street, building, candy store, porno shop, or bookstore. I even want them to check out the schedules of the lions at both the Cleveland and Columbus zoos. I know that sounds ridiculous, but have them do it anyway."

"Consider it done."

I carried the garbage bag down to the lab, the whole while trying to mentally sharpen my acting abilities to show complete and utter surprise about the items found inside.

In the lab, a technician took the bag and placed it on a table. There were evidence bags and tags next to it in case there was anything of importance. I counted the bags to make sure there were at least four. He began by carefully cutting a slit in the bag from bottom to top.

I didn't realize how fast my heart was beating, and I began to have serious doubts about my acting skills holding out much longer. The tech opened the bag and shook everything to the middle before laying it flat. The white My Size shoe sat on top of a piece of insulation.

"Oh, my God." Michael said each word slowly and distinctly.

I saw him look at me, so I made an exaggerated gasping sound, putting my hands over my mouth to look like I was shocked. It took all I had to restrain from cracking a smile.

"I apologize. You were right, Cee." He was shaking his head back and forth.

We watched as the tech placed the shoe and insulation into evidence bags. The process continued as he found the red ribbons, each of which were placed into a separate bag. When the tech got to the photo taken of Michael and me at the hotel, I knew I wouldn't be able to keep the charade going. Smoothing out the picture with his gloved hands, the tech stepped back so we could get a good look at it. Michael was outraged.

"That sick son of a bitch!"

I couldn't act anymore. The garbage bag had served its purpose.

"Michael, call everyone and get the search warrant ready."

He was already on the phone, rounding up the usual suspects. I told the sheriff we had our killer, without a doubt, but had to be very careful about nailing him if we hoped to find Brooklyn Phillips alive. I was hoping that taking his doll would buy Brooklyn some time. Of course there was always the possibility that it would backfire and he would kill her out of anger. I tried not to think about that.

It was going to take a little time to get the warrant ready and everyone together, so Michael and I headed up to my office. Passing Coop's office, we saw the sheriff there and he congratulated us. He said Alex Phillips had been told the news.

"I hope he's not getting his hopes up, Sheriff. You know the chances are slim his daughter is alive."

"I know, but he has to be informed about every break we get. There's still a way to go, but it's better than nothing. Anyway, there's a bit of brighter news, which is what I came up to tell you, CeeCee. The test scores are back. Congratulations, Sergeant."

What was he talking about? Suddenly, my memory kicked into overdrive. Four months ago, I had taken the sergeant's exam. I had put off trying to get promoted for years. Frankly I had no desire. But I got so sick of everyone badgering me, I caved and took the test. Then I forgot about it, until now.

I thought about it for a fleeting moment, though I know full well what my answer had to be.

"All right, I'll take the job."

They began clapping, which was embarrassing. When Michael and I got back to my office he shut the door and gave me a squeeze and a kiss.

"Congratulations, that's great. I always wondered why you were never a ranking officer. We need to celebrate."

I pulled away. "It's really not that big of a deal. A sergeant is nothing but a glorified patrolman or detective. They're the middleman, or as some like to say, the doormat between officer and lieutenant, a place to wipe your feet."

In truth, the primary reason I accepted the position was because of the substantial pay raise. With an upcoming divorce and raising two kids, the extra cash would be important. I had also given a lot of thought to making lieutenant, which you can't test for unless you're a sergeant first.

"Come on, CeeCee. Why can't you ever be happy for yourself once in a while? You're so busy looking out for everyone else, you forget about what's good for you."

He was right, to an extent, but I was wired that way and had accepted it years ago. When I walked back down the hallway to grab a strong cup of coffee out of the vending machine, I automatically glanced back into Coop's office. The sheriff was gone and Coop had his elbows on his desk, head propped up in his hands. I backed up and approached my old friend.

"Hey, you look like you've got a headache. I've got plenty of aspirin in my desk if you need it."

Coop shook his head, but didn't answer. This wasn't the man I had known so well for twelve years, the one who could make a person laugh on the day of their own funeral. He had been acting weird lately, and now I was now going to butt in and get to the bottom of it.

"Coop, look at me." He raised his head. "What in the hell has been wrong with you lately? Just so you know, I'm not leaving until you tell me." I got comfortable in the chair in front of his desk and gave him a large "gotcha" smile. Which quickly faded once he spoke.

"Okay, I might as well tell you. Everyone will know about it soon enough I guess. Cindy and I are splitting up."

I was more than shocked. Coop and Cindy had one of the best marriages I had ever seen. Of course, I thought Eric and I did too, but this information didn't make any sense at all. They had two children around the same age as my own, and our families often did things together. I thought I knew him so well. How could I miss what must have been going on for a while? However, on the flip side, when I had told Coop that Eric and I were getting divorced, he didn't seem surprised at all.

"Coop, what happened?" I was more than a little concerned. "Are you okay?"

He shook his head slightly. "There was a lot that happened. Something I couldn't control, and there was no other option. I couldn't hurt Cindy anymore."

What he was talking about? I thought maybe he was insinuating an alcohol or drug addiction, but that wasn't Coop.

"There must be something in the water around here lately," I said softly. "Just the other day, Naomi was . . ." I stopped.

Oh, no. As soon as I said it, I saw Coop's face. It was a split second of guilt that washed across his eyes, but I caught it instantly. And as I said the words everything clicked.

"Coop! Oh, my God. Naomi?"

He nodded and looked down. It all made sense now. I just never paid attention. I remember Naomi describing the "boyfriend" she was so broken up about and thinking briefly she was talking about Michael. That made sense because the two were pretty similar. Boy, was I wrong. Coop had been acting weird because he had tried to break it off with her, and that's why she'd been such a mess that day.

"How long?" I asked, after my shock had worn off.

"Since Murder Mountain."

My jaw dropped to the floor. That long? Despite my surprise, I also felt a little hurt. I honestly considered Coop one of the best friends I had. We told each other everything. The day I told him about Eric, I also told him about Michael, but he already knew. Why didn't he confide in me about Naomi?

"Coop, why didn't you ever tell me?"

He stood up and walked to his window. "Because I know how you feel about Naomi. I figured you'd tell me I must've snapped for being dumb enough to fall in love with her."

I thought of the million times over the last year I had badmouthed Naomi to Coop. I called her the only captain that climbed the ladder while lying on her back, just to name one of my very witty retorts. He must've wanted to clean my clock daily.

"You're right. There was a time I probably would've said that, but things have changed. Naomi and I have gotten along better. I'm getting to really like her."

"I know. She told me. That was one of the best things that ever happened to her, CeeCee. You know that? She's always admired you and wanted to be your friend. I know you never saw it, but she really is an amazing woman." He looked back out the window.

"Look. Maybe I wasn't that great of a friend to you, after all. You should've felt like you could tell me anything and I would've understood." I felt horrible.

I remember Naomi saying something similar about me biting her head off if she ever told me about the Eric and Jordan rumors. I know there are other people around here who think I'm an uncompassionate bitch. Now I was starting to believe it myself.

I walked over to Coop, gave him a large hug, and softly kissed his cheek.

"Just tell me. Does she make you happy, Coop?"

"Yes, CeeCee, she does, and I'm in love with her."

"Then that's all that matters. You'll get through this, and I'm here if you need me."

Coop seemed truly grateful for my good wishes and thanked me by hugging me back, but I still felt bad. I always seemed to be so consumed with my own life.

"What's going on here?"

Coop and I turned to see Michael standing in the doorway.

"I think I'm jealous," he joked.

Neither Coop nor I felt it right to continue talking about Naomi, so Michael's arrival was a good excuse to get back to business. Coop really did need to prepare for the search warrant, and he eagerly started shuffling papers. I think I had made him feel better. He was in higher spirits once he got he got the news about his new relationship out in the open.

There was a surprise waiting for me when I got back to my own office.

"What happened with Coop?" Michael asked curiously.

"His wife and he are splitting up."

"I'm assuming he told you about Naomi?"

I was floored. "You knew about it! How did you know?"

"CeeCee, it's been obvious since the day I came back, and I was always surprised you never picked up on it. Coop admitted it to me a couple of days ago since he figured I knew anyway."

How much did I hate feeling left out of things or not being smart enough to pick up on them on my own?

"Michael, can I ask you something?"

"Yes, I'll marry you."

"I'm serious."

"So am I."

I threw my pen at him. "Please, listen. Do you think I'm a *difficult* person to talk to or, let's say, reason with?"

He started laughing so hard and loud I thought he was going to fall over and hit the desk. I hadn't said that to be the day's comedy act, and his reaction had me a little miffed. When he saw the glowering look on my face, he tried to get serious.

"I'm sorry, it's just that, oh, how do I say this? As much as I love you with everything I have, you *do* have a very *strong* personality. What I mean is, you never think twice about telling someone *exactly* what you think. To some people, a person like that is scary. Others are put off by it. To me, of course, it is an extremely attractive and very sexy trait."

"Thanks a lot." Though he was smiling, I wasn't.

Michael made a few calls to make sure the search warrant and teams were ready to go. Again, we would be meeting at an undisclosed location to avoid media coverage until we were ready. We'd meet behind a family-owned grocery store a block away from Jim Carlson's house.

When Michael and I pulled around back at the meeting point, I saw we were the last ones there. Before we went over the game plan with everyone, it took a few minutes to get their attention. Most of the agents and police officers were rowdy, anxious to break down the door of a child killer. Agents and police officers would secure a perimeter around the house, while the SWAT team gained entry and cleared the place. An arrest warrant for Jim Carlson was also issued. If he was in there, we'd put him into custody immediately.

CHAPTER TWENTY-SEVEN

It only took one hit with the door ram to get inside, and I jumped at the sound of the flash bangs being thrown. Less than twenty minutes later, I was in the middle of Jim Carlson's kitchen.

The house wasn't very big, so the SWAT team didn't have much to clear. Some of us got antsy and went inside while they were still clearing the upstairs. However, when they yelled down to the rest of the agents that they had found the closet, I did my best to act surprised. At the same time, my stomach lurched.

Two agents had already cordoned off the room. All I could do was pretend to be shocked at what they found. The crime lab was already inside, processing everything, and until they were done, we would have to wait.

Worried that I had left evidence of my visit behind, I tried not to dwell on it too much and had gone back outside when Michael yelled out for me to get back inside quickly. I followed him upstairs, already knowing he intended to show me the small box they located under the bed. By this time, the crime lab had finished and all the photographs and newspaper articles were separated in clear plastic bags. One by one, Michael held them up for me to see.

"He's been fixated on you for a long time, CeeCee. Just look. These articles go all the way back to Murder Mountain."

"I wonder why. I mean, I've never heard of the guy before."

Michael stopped talking and looked at me, making me feel like a child caught with her hand in the cookie jar. His eyes narrowed to slits as he put the bags down and crossed his arms, all the while staring me down. I tried to look innocent, but he knew me too well. He yanked me into the second bedroom and shut the door.

"You've been here already, haven't you?"

"I have no idea what you're talking about." Now I really was surprised.

"Knock off the bullshit, CeeCee. I told you, you don't have to lie to me. Besides, your face said it all. You weren't surprised by those pictures because you've already seen them before. I was a little suspicious when they opened the garbage bag, but I gave you the benefit of the doubt. Now I know. You put those things in that bag! Jesus! Do you know how long you could go to jail for?"

"I thought you said you'd never turn me in." I looked at him defiantly.

He took a step back and looked at me like I told him I had two weeks to live.

"You did do it!" He turned and started to pace, putting his hands on top of his head, taking deep breaths. "Last night you weren't in trouble while you were taking the garbage—you were inside this house and he came home, didn't he? Answer me!" I didn't answer, but he kept going anyway. "Do you have any idea what could've happened to you, or how much you could've fucked this case up if you got caught? The killer could've walked free, CeeCee!"

"Could've. But he won't. I didn't get caught, and I'm not going to. Evidence was found in the bag legitimately. That's what all the paperwork says, and that's what the evidence says. No one has any reason to believe otherwise."

"You're a cop. How could you do this!"

"He's a child killer. I'm sure the parents of the dead children wouldn't complain. Quite frankly, I don't think anyone else would either. Who knows how many other children might've died? There was no other way. Laws get put into place that end up protecting monsters like Carlson and sometimes we have to bend the rules a little."

He just stared. I didn't feel bad or guilty in the least. I would do it all again if I had to. Calling Michael's bluff, I opened the door.

"Go right ahead. Turn me in. Who do you think they'll be more pissed at? Me or *you*? And if memory serves, did you not illegally enter a witness' house on Murder Mountain and stick a gun in her mouth to make her talk? Are you going to stand there and tell me what I did was any worse?"

He glared for a few more seconds before walking right past me and out of the room. He wasn't going to say a word. I knew there were two reasons why. One, ultimately he knew I was right. There was no other way. Two, he loved me and would never let me go to prison.

Michael was gone when I went out into the hallway. Most likely, he had gone outside for some air and to calm down, which sounded like a good idea to me, but I looked around and didn't see him anywhere.

Maybe he was calling my bluff and turning me in. But in a moment I saw him come from around the side of the house. We both stood watching as the lab technicians carried the dolls out, one by one.

All the dolls were confiscated, but only I was aware that Jim Carlson would know I had taken his favorite. When he came back to the house last night, he saw immediately there was one doll gone.

Kincaid pulling up to the house distracted me. I went

over to talk to her. Michael still seemed a little agitated.
It was best I left him alone for a while to cool down, so I
took the time to fill Naomi in on what was going on. I
also caught myself looking around for Coop. It didn't
take long for her to bring up the subject first.

"CeeCee, Jeff told me you know. I hope you don't
think I'm horrible."

For a second I didn't know who she was talking about.
I hadn't called Coop "Jeff" in years.

"There isn't one of us carrying a badge who has the
right to point a finger at anyone else. Admittedly, I was
caught off guard, but he clearly loves you."

Her face brightened, and she let down her guard. "You
really think so? I mean, he says he does, but you think it's
for real?"

"Yes, I do. You're getting one hell of a guy."

"I know."

*He had to suppress the urge to get out of his car and kill CeeCee
Gallagher with his bare hands. He knew he couldn't because she
was standing around too many officers and it would ruin everything anyway. She took her! That sleazy, incompetent, repre-
hensible cunt took her! Oh, he wanted her dead! As enraged as
he was at her, he was more enraged at himself. He knew he
should've watched her, but he was too busy with his guest. He
had no idea she would actually take one of them. And his favorite! She was going to pay; she was going to pay dearly. He then
decided to change his plans and up the ante of the game. Picking
up his stolen cell phone, he dialed her number. . . .*

My cell phone rang, and I excused myself to take the call.
The number on caller ID showed "unavailable."

"Gallagher."

"I want her back, you bitch! You give her back to me,

or this little girl will suffer the worst death you could ever imagine!"

I began furiously looking around to get someone's attention. No need to guess whether Jim Carlson knew I took the doll.

"Don't bother drawing attention to yourself, Cecelia! I want my fucking doll!"

He was watching us. He was watching me right now on the phone. I saw Michael look at me strangely, and he started to walk toward me. I jumped into his car and locked all the doors.

"You get nothing until I know Brooklyn Phillips is okay."

He started to laugh. "You're not in a position, Cecelia, to demand anything!"

"Actually, yes, I am. Unless you want to watch me dump lighter fluid all over your little whore doll and set her on fire."

Michael was banging on the window. I, of course, ignored him. I was waiting on a response from our killer, who was completely enraged by now.

"Don't you dare! If you touch her I will kill you, your family, and every child in this county! Do you hear me, you cunt!"

"Yes, I hear you." I was calm. "There's no need to yell. I suppose you could do all of those things, but you still won't have your little freak doll, now will you?"

If Brooklyn was alive, I was buying her time by threatening his doll. I knew he couldn't bear the thought of something happening to it and he would do whatever it took to save it. Including keeping Brooklyn alive. Michael had stopped banging and began to fumble around in his pockets for his keys. I shook them at him before starting the car and driving away from the house.

"What do you want?" he asked. My gamble had paid off. Jim Carlson had calmed down and spoke quite meekly.

"I want a trade. If you want your doll back, I get Brooklyn Phillips, unharmed and returned to her family."

"And now for what I want. You haven't solved the letter yet, have you, Detective? I'll give you ten days to figure it out. If you do, you'll find us and you will bring the doll with you. If you don't, then the girl and everyone with me will die. In the meantime, you keep my doll safe and I'll consider a trade."

"Why wait ten days? Unless you prove to me that Brooklyn is alive right now, I'll be roasting marshmallows over your little vampire bitch within five minutes."

"You'll have it before the day is over." He hung up before I could question him further.

I pulled the car over and took a deep breath. I hoped I had bought Brooklyn Phillips some time, though I would have a hard time explaining to anyone how I got ahold of the creepy doll. And Jim Carlson knew it. I turned the car around and drove back to the house. Michael was standing in the driveway fuming. I didn't even have the car in park before he opened the door and jumped into the passenger seat.

"Drive!"

I didn't argue. I didn't know where he wanted to go, but when we passed a small park and tennis court area, he pointed to it.

"Pull over there and park."

When I get nervous, sometimes a tight smile automatically appears on my face. Unfortunately, it happened once again.

"You think this is funny, CeeCee?"

I pursed my lips and said nothing, turning my head to look out the window so he couldn't see my face.

"Who was on the phone? Tell me. And tell me now."

"Jim Carlson."

"Uh-huh. And this was something you didn't think needed anyone else's attention?"

I didn't answer and got out of the car. In seconds, he was right behind me, slamming his door in the process. I walked over to a purple, bouncing dinosaur and sat on it.

"I'll tell you what happened, Michael, if you calm down."

"*You* want *me* to calm down?" He pointed at my chest and then at his own. "Let's cover today's events, shall we? You've admitted to committing burglary, you've planted evidence, and now you've just spoken to the nation's most sought-after child killer and didn't feel the need to tell anyone. That's for starters. And you are asking me to calm down? Perfect."

He sat down on the bouncing dinosaur next to mine. This one was red with green polka dots. I was looking at the ground, drawing a circle in the mulch with my foot.

It was time I told Michael about the goth doll, how I assumed and confirmed it was Jim Carlson's favorite. I told him it was my plan to make a trade. I knew Michael would be disappointed in me, but I felt secure in my decision and with no regrets.

"How do you know it's going to work, CeeCee? Maybe all you did was piss him off and Brooklyn is dead right now?"

"It worked, Michael. When I told him what I would do to his doll, he freaked. I'm telling you, that guy is not going to so much as put a scratch on that little girl until he gets that *thing* back. That buys us and Brooklyn time."

"I doubt it. Chances aren't good. How is he supposed to let you know?"

"I have no idea. He said by the end of the day, somehow.

I have to figure out that letter, Michael. Don't you realize he's been watching us? He's probably watching us right now."

Michael looked around before rubbing both of his temples. He stood up and walked over to me, holding my head against his stomach in a tight embrace.

"I'm sorry. At times, I don't know what to do with you."

I stood up and kissed the tip of his nose before walking back to the car. "I'm sure you'll get over it."

What I hadn't told Michael was that Jim Carlson had threatened me, my family, and every child in the county. As far as I was concerned, that was irrelevant. If he had the chance to kill me before I took the doll, he probably would have. He was a murderer.

We stayed at the house for about another hour, then followed the crime lab vans back to the department. It took a few hours to catch up on paperwork before we were able to head out and grab dinner. It must be something with us and food, because we weren't even halfway across the parking lot before Michael's cell phone rang. It was the sheriff. A videotape had been delivered to the jail with my name on it.

"I'm on my way to the jail now," he said. "I'll meet you and Michael there."

"Now what?" I said under my breath. "I think I'm a little scared to see what's on that video."

"I believe all of us should be."

Once we arrived, I grabbed a couple of corrections officers to try to locate a television with a VCR, while Michael called the senior agents to come watch the tape. One of the corrections officers, on his way into work, had found the tape wrapped in brown packing paper lying in front of the employee entrance. Convenient, since there are no security cameras by that door. I doubt Carlson walked in front of any other security cameras near the building, but we had all the tapes pulled from those cameras as well. There was always hope. It was another twenty minutes before everyone was present. Michael, wearing gloves, inserted the killer's tape.

It was awful. We watched in horror as Brooklyn Phillips appeared on tape, crying and wearing only a dirty white T-shirt. She was seated in a wooded area with trees and brush all around, holding up a copy of *The Mansfield News Journal*. The camera zoomed in on the newspaper, showing today's date and headline. The voice from behind the camera spoke, first reading the Bible passage from Daniel. The familiar low, gruff voice addressed me.

"There's your proof, Cecelia. Don't you hurt her! You have the time I gave you. Now you can show the world just how smart you are. Remember, I made you a promise of consequence if you hurt her in any way. I'll be in touch, if I don't see you first!"

The screen slowly faded, before blacking out completely. Brooklyn, as you'd expect, looked terrified beyond imagination, but she was still alive and that was most important. The room remained silent, and I wondered if everyone was as sickened as I was by what we had just witnessed. I hoped the sheriff didn't plan on showing the commissioner and his wife the tape. It would send them both over the edge in a heartbeat.

Michael was eyeballing me, which he had started doing when the tape made mention of a "promise of consequence" if I didn't do what I was supposed to.

The sheriff exhaled a slow, deep breath. "That has to be one of the worst things I've ever seen."

Everyone grumbled in agreement, and the lab tech immediately went to make a copy of the tape so we could study it. We needed to tear the tape apart frame by frame, checking the landscape, dimming the voices for any familiar noises, identifying the types of trees and plants and where they grow, and anything else we could come up with. We had to locate this child.

"CeeCee, what the hell did he mean by 'don't hurt her'? I assume he meant that if you don't figure out the Bible passage he's going to kill Brooklyn?" the sheriff asked. Michael glared at me sharply.

"Most likely. As we all know, the guy doesn't necessarily make much sense, and his grasp of reality and its consequences is limited at best. Sheriff, are you going to give him to the media?"

"We have to. I know the guy changes his appearance, but we have a suspect that people, especially parents, need to know about."

I nodded, then stepped out into the hallway with Michael.

"What was the whole 'promise of consequence' thing, CeeCee?"

"Simply that he would kill me and my family if I didn't figure the letter out within ten days."

"How very nice. Thank you for sharing this with me earlier." His attitude was still hostile.

"I'm not worried about it, and you shouldn't be either."

We decided to take the copy of the tape and the Bible passage back to the hotel to go over it all night if necessary. The FBI was preparing a statement for the media in cooperation with Richland Metropolitan Police. Chief Raines and a senior agent would be reading the statement. Now it was time for everyone to hold their breath and pray.

CHAPTER TWENTY-EIGHT

Back in our room, I ordered take-out food and began to spread out the entire file on the floor. It was going to be a long night. Michael hooked up the VCR he'd borrowed from the department, then came over and picked me up off the floor, and carried me over to the bed. Apparently, he had gotten over being angry with me. Or he was just plain tired of arguing.

"It's time to play nice." He began taking off my shirt and pants.

I laughed. "I surrender. . . . Don't forget we have food coming, though."

"Trust me, this won't take that long."

Every time we made love, I fell deeper and deeper in love with him. I thought about my life without him and didn't think I would ever be able to cope. As we lay breathless and naked in each other's arms, he read my thoughts.

"What happens from here, Cee?" He was drawing one of his fingers along the contours of my body.

"What do you mean?"

"I mean, we can't stay in this hotel forever. This case will end eventually, then what? I think we should start planning what comes next."

"I know, and I have thought about it, trust me. Right now, I just don't know where to begin. Eric said I can keep the house, but I simply can't move you right in with the girls. You know this. You're a parent. And what about Sean? We can't figure it all out in a conversation or two. It's going to be slower than that. Please understand. I love you. I know that for sure. Let's just take it one day at a time, and it will play out."

"I understand and accept that, but your one-day-at-a-time scenario will only keep for so long. Eventually, after this case is over, we need to sit down and take concrete action. You promise me that, and I'll say no more, my dear."

"Promise."

Though nothing had been solved, we both felt better knowing we were committed to moving forward. We eventually got up and dressed, just in time for our Chinese food to arrive. After dinner, it was all business.

Over and over we replayed the tape and scoured every inch of the Bible passage. At one point, I saw Michael stick his ear against the television and write something in his notebook.

"What's going on?"

"I can't tell, but I think I hear water running. I'm going to have the technicians enhance it in the morning."

The more I read and reread the passage, the more confused I got. I even took the first words from every line to see if they spelled out something. When I got nothing there, I took the first letter from every word, then the last. I wrote it backward, upside down, sideways; I skipped every other word, and still I came up with nothing. The only thought I had seemed a little ridiculous. But sometimes, those were the things that made the most sense.

"Michael? Have you ever been to the Cleveland Metroparks Zoo?"

"I took Sean there once. Why? The zoos have been checked out. Remember?"

"I don't know. It's all forest, and if memory serves, there's a small river through the lions attraction. What exactly did the agents check out?"

"I think just the den area plus all the employees. If I know what you're thinking, Jim Carlson couldn't have driven to Cleveland, taken the video, and driven back to deliver it in time after you talked to him."

"How do you know the tape wasn't made prior? Earlier in the day? How do you know he didn't stash her around here somewhere before going back up?"

"Could be. I just don't understand why he would make the tape earlier. He didn't know you wanted proof then unless, and this isn't off the mark, he did it just to fuck with us."

"He could've *anticipated* it. Don't forget, we're playing with a smart man who's predicted—or watched—every move we've made so far. He knew I took his doll for a reason."

Michael thought about this, while I called the girls. I hadn't spoken to them yet that day. Talking to them was always the bright spot in my day, and it kept me going no matter what else was happening. They were having a great time, but missed me. I promised I would come down once I caught my bad guy. Before Eric got on the phone, they talked my ear off about watching a man on the fishing pier catch a baby shark, which they got to pet.

"You let them touch that thing?" I asked Eric.

"Don't worry. It was only about a foot long and they thought it was great. We had gone down to the pier to get ice cream and there it was. Selina ran over before I had a chance to say anything."

These few minutes, painfully, brought back our routine in North Carolina on the Cape Fear coast. After spending the day at the beach, we would go out to dinner and then take the girls for ice cream at the Kure Beach Pier. It was so very sad realizing those days were long over for us, at least as a family. Eric, knowing just how to kick me when I was down, broke our silence.

"I spoke with Jordan today."

"Fabulous." I wasn't in the mood to get into that.

"CeeCee, she's due in January. We're going to have to figure out what to tell the girls."

"*We* don't have to figure out anything, Eric. This was your bed, you can lie in it—no pun intended, of course. All I agreed is that we tell them together."

"Please, CeeCee."

"Are you going to marry her?"

"God, I was hoping there was a chance, though I know it's a long shot, that you and I could try to work this out. I'm not going to push off my responsibilities as the baby's father, and I can't undo my affair with Jordan, but I think with counseling we might be able to work through this."

"There have been too many lies, Eric. It took a while, but deep down I believe we can't go back." Michael had stopped the videotape and was looking at me, with no pretense about trying to avoid listening to the conversation.

"Just promise me you'll continue to think about it. That's all I'm asking—especially for the girls. Please."

"Yes, I'll still think about it."

I hung up. Michael was sitting on the floor, quiet, putting the videotape back in its box.

Tentatively, he asked, "What are you supposed to think about?"

"He wants me to think about counseling to save our marriage. I only said I would think about it. Right now is not the time for an argument. Of course, he reminded me to consider the girls, as if that wasn't primary in my mind.

Essentially, yet again, he laid the guilt trip. Michael, I love you, and I am *not* raising a child my husband had with his mistress. I want you, and I can't ever be without you again. It's just sad. When I was talking to the girls about their day, it hit me very hard that we would never be in North Carolina as a family again. I've been trying to back away from that thought for a while, but it keeps coming up and I have to deal with it."

He nodded, and I knelt on the floor beside him, gathering him in my arms. I inhaled the smell of his cologne and knew there would be no thinking about counseling for Eric and me. We were finished, but since we both loved the girls deeply, we would find some way to make their lives secure. For that, I would always love Eric.

There wasn't much more to do that night, and as we were gathering all the files, I broached what I wanted to do the next day.

"I want to go to the Cleveland Metroparks Zoo and look around."

"Okay, if you think it's necessary. I'll have an agent call up there and make sure someone is waiting for us. The lion exhibit, of course?"

"Of course. The entire exhibit, not just the den."

We decided to get a good night's sleep so we could start our day early. That night, for the first time in months, I dreamt of Murder Mountain. The nightmares had been horrific, and I'd had to take medication for a quite some time afterward because of them.

I had thought the dreams long gone, but apparently they weren't. My latest dream was one of the worst ever.

In my dream I was on the edge of the well filled with rats again, this time alone. No one was anywhere nearby. Not the corrupt cops or their sidekicks, not Michael, Eric, Naomi, or Coop. Although I was alone, something from behind pushed me into the well. I kept falling until I felt the mushy thud of hitting all the rats. They were climbing all over me, biting me, and shrieking their high-pitched squeals. I tried to swat at them, but my hands were tied.

I woke up covered in sweat and screaming. Michael was shaking me. When I was fully awake and realized it was a dream, I began to sob uncontrollably. Michael took me in his arms.

"Shh, it's going to be OK. I'm here. You're safe. My God, what happened?"

When I was able to speak, I told him. Michael had been there when all of it happened originally, so he understood about the nightmares. "I thought you said you were all done with the dreams, Cee." He was gently stroking my hair.

"I thought so, but I guess not. I quit taking medicine months ago and haven't had a nightmare since. I wonder if you being back and this whole case didn't trigger them again."

Michael held me for the rest of the night, not that I was able to go back to sleep. I was too keyed up and terrified that the dream would return. It felt better simply to get up early and go to work, though it was still dark when we got to the department. The night shift was just coming in, ending their day. Jordan and her new training officer, who was filling in for Eric, were standing by the door.

I had every intention of ignoring her, but she waved me over to one of the patrol cars. Michael stopped, anticipating a problem, but I told him to go ahead. I'd deal with her alone.

"CeeCee, I just wanted to tell you that Eric called. He

told me you said he should. I just wanted to say thank you, and I'm sorry for what I've put you through."

"Do you have any idea how Eric and I are supposed to tell our daughters they're going to have another brother or sister, Jordan? I don't. And secondly, what do you think is going to come out of all this?" Right then and there I knew I didn't want her to have Eric. Maybe it was a pride thing, and I was being catty and selfish, but I couldn't help it. Not that I wanted him . . .

She shrugged. "I don't know."

"You realize Eric wants to work out our marriage, don't you? We spoke last night and he wants us to go to counseling. I haven't decided yet, but that's a scenario you might want to start considering. Your baby will be taken care of no matter what. Eric would never abandon you there, but start allowing for all possibilities."

She began to cry while I just stood there. A slight part of me felt bad, but the rest of me didn't.

"Jordan, if you don't need anything else, I'm going in now."

I left her there crying. By the time I got upstairs to my office, I was entirely riddled with guilt. Although I had nothing but contempt for her, her baby was Eric's, and our daughters' sibling. Jordan was obviously under a great deal of stress, and I certainly hadn't helped her situation. But I didn't want her to do anything outrageous.

Acceptance breeds action. The first thing I did was leave a message for an attorney friend of mine to discuss filing for divorce. Michael was around for that call. There was no turning back.

"Your conversation with Jordan went well, I see."

Michael never wanted to say much when it came to Eric and Jordan, and this time was no different. All he cared about was that I had taken the first concrete step to legally end my marriage.

I wanted a respite from thinking about all of this mess and to get going. It was time to drive to Cleveland.

Less than an hour later, we were pulling into the entrance of the zoo. The zoo wasn't open yet, but we had arrangements to see the lions exhibit first thing. The zoo's director had the trainer in charge waiting for us at the gate in a golf cart gassed and ready to drive us back to the lion exhibit.

It was a large area of forest, and it was going to take us a while to walk the whole thing. But walk it we did, with the temperatures soaring into the mid-nineties by the time we were done. We found nothing. Not a footprint, piece of paper, or a chewed piece of gum. I was so hot and sweaty by the time we were done I gave serious thought to jumping into the river. However, the idea that every animal in the zoo used it as a bathroom dissuaded me.

"If I'd known we were taking an African safari nature walk today, I would've worn shorts," Michael grumbled.

"Sorry, I didn't know we were supposed to have Congo-like temperatures."

On the ride back to the hotel to clean up, we reviewed our little adventure, both of us acknowledging that no one, let alone a man holding a little girl hostage, had been anywhere near those woods.

"At least we know for sure now. Damn," I said.

After a long shower, which we took together, we grabbed lunch and headed back to the office. Coop's door was open, but I didn't see him. A couple of the other detectives were in their offices working away on other cases. It was business as usual.

It was back to the Bible passage for me. I hoped the

time away might have brought some fresh insight. Again, I looked at the passages before and after the one given by Jim Carlson.

"Michael, do you know why Daniel was cast into the lions' den?"

"He prayed to God." I didn't know Michael knew that.

"Right, but because praying to God was 'breaking the law,' or 'breaking the rules.' Daniel was thrown into the lions' den for breaking the rules."

"Where are you going with this, CeeCee?"

I wasn't sure. What initially came to mind didn't make sense, but then again, nothing in this case did.

"Michael, I think *I* might be Daniel."

"Now, how do you figure that?"

"Jim Carlson has predicted every step we've taken in this case. He's done homework on me and knew I would eventually find him. Knowing I wouldn't have enough for a search warrant, he predicted I would go in his house anyway. What he hadn't anticipated was me taking his doll. Regardless, I had become unethical and broken the law, therefore deserving some type of punishment. Plus, this being a game to him, I had broken the rules. Jim Carlson considers himself king and would not be outwitted."

"That's really stretching it, Cee."

"Agreed, which is why I think I might be right. It's too simple to believe. Again, the question we need answered most is what the hell, or where the hell, is the lions' den?"

"Wait, back up. You think Carlson considers himself the king, accusing *you* of a crime or breaking the rules of his game, for which he will punish you by throwing you into a den of lions. Nope, I don't buy it, sorry. It has absolutely nothing to do with these murdered children."

Now I was feeling angry. Michael simply did not understand what I was trying to get across. "It has everything to do with these children, Michael! I think he chose me, and Richland County, ahead of time. He wanted to see just how smart he really was. And who should he test that theory against but the high-profile, newsworthy CeeCee Gallagher? Except he knew I would cheat, hence the Bible passage, and I did; I didn't play fair. Now, he's not either, but I need a penalty for my foul—catch me? This is one big fucking game of cat and mouse, and his only goal is to see if I'm smarter. Period."

Michael sat quietly, mulling over everything I had said, but I knew he wasn't convinced. I wasn't so sure I was either, but it sounded good. Yet the more I thought about it, the more I thought I might just be right after all.

"CeeCee, do you know why he uses the dolls?"

"I have a fairly good idea."

"No, I don't mean just for sex. He knows he's sick, and I think he has remorse. I'll bet years ago he got the doll idea to suppress his urges so he wouldn't hurt a child. When those weren't good enough anymore and he started with real little girls, painting them up like the dolls made them seem a lot less human to him. Therefore, easing his guilt. You might be right. He wants to get caught."

CHAPTER TWENTY-NINE

As I was figuring it out, Michael left to get coffee for us. He hadn't been gone for more than thirty seconds when my cell phone rang.

"CeeCee!" Naomi yelled into the phone, making me jump right out of my skin. She was sobbing.

"Naomi? What the hell's the matter?"

"Pl-Please, Jeff broke up with me again and I . . ." She was unable to compose herself. "I can't take it again. I don't know what I might do."

"What do you mean you don't know what you might do? Naomi, where are you?"

"I-I'm at a pay phone by the Falls. I'm going to the Falls, CeeCee. I really need help."

"I'm on my way. Don't do anything! Do you hear me?"

She sobbed again into the phone, and then it went dead. I was staggered as I ran into Coop's office to see if he was there. He was going to get a piece of my mind later, no doubt about it, but first he was going to help me with Naomi. He wasn't there, so I tried his cell—no answer. I left quite a nasty message saying that I was going to get Naomi at the Falls as she was "quite a mess," thanks to him, even threatening to harm herself.

I couldn't believe what was happening. And now I couldn't find Michael either. Where the hell did he go to get coffee? I left a quick note telling him I was going to the Falls, why I was going, and that I would be back shortly.

The Falls was a hiking trail in the Mohican State Forest in the southern part of the county. The trail ran along the bottom of the Clearfork Gorge, which was a thousand feet across and three hundred feet down.

I don't know if classifying it as a waterfall quite works, since every time I've been there the water trickling from the top has been as wide as a faucet, with no water at the bottom. At its highest point, it was about a hundred feet. Whatever. It was very dangerous no matter what.

I wasn't thrilled about the drive down. The state forest was made up of the Appalachian foothills and reminded me entirely too much of West Virginia and what happened at Murder Mountain. Eric and I had built a home in the hills several years before, but sold it last year and moved back to the city. I couldn't live in the woods anymore.

On the way, I tried calling Michael but was surrounded by small mountains and couldn't get a signal. Why was Naomi down here? The obvious answer was that she was going to jump off the falls, which I prayed wasn't the case. What a horrible way to die.

However, if she was as upset as she sounded, she may very well want to die horribly. I was furious at Coop, who got her hopes up and then stepped all over them. Again. I knew Naomi must really love him, but I never took her for being suicidal, no matter the circumstances.

After entering the state forest, I forgot how to get to the beginning of the trail. It took twenty minutes of turning around and getting lost before I finally found a ranger and flagged him down for directions.

"The trail's closed, ma'am."

"Why?"

"They're going to start digging out all the ruts and rocks. Every day someone was breaking an ankle, and emergency personnel couldn't get to them quickly enough, so the state finally decided to get it cleaned up."

I told him I wanted to get to the covered bridge instead, which was right by the trail to the falls, and he gave me directions. I was glad I'd dressed casually, and I was hoping Naomi would be out by the entrance. If not, the forty-five-minute hike on the trail was a treacherous one. I had almost broken my own ankle hiking it several times over the years.

As I neared the covered bridge, I saw Naomi's SUV parked on the other side, near the entrance to the falls. I parked next to her and started yelling her name as I got out, hearing nothing back but the echo of my own voice. There was no one around.

It took a few minutes to find the sturdiest walking stick I could; I would need it. The trail sometimes leaned at an angle and if you didn't hold on well enough or secure your footing, you were apt to tumble down through a hundred feet of rock and trees into the river.

Twice the walking stick broke and I lost valuable time finding another. At one point, I thought I twisted my ankle hard enough so that I wouldn't be able to continue, but after a short rest, it was fine.

It was when I had to go to the bathroom and couldn't hold it any longer that I stopped. Something bit my leg and caused me to cry out in pain. I hoped it wasn't a spider bite. I didn't need to get sick over halfway down the trail and not be able to make it back. I stopped to see if any poison would kick in and silently admonished myself for being such a city girl.

The entire time I was walking, no matter what minor "catastrophe" took place, I continued calling Naomi's name. I was almost near the falls when I thought I heard something behind me. I looked about and there didn't seem to be anything, so I wrote it off as a deer.

Yelling as loud as I was, Naomi should have heard me. If she was still alive, that is. But I refused to let myself think the worst. It was impossible to believe that Naomi would truly harm herself. Maybe it was all a ploy to get Coop's attention. That sounded like Naomi, but I didn't think she would put her job in jeopardy by faking a stunt that would end up with her on the psychiatric ward of the hospital.

I was almost at the point where the trail turned into pure sand, leading back to the falls. I saw signs that pointed in the direction of the cliffs and to the smaller falls farther down the trail.

I stopped in my tracks, and my blood went cold. I looked at the signs again, my mind reeling as the magnitude of what I was looking at finally hit me. I had forgotten that, being locals, we all referred to the falls as just that, the Falls.

Only when I saw the sign did I remember the Falls' true name: *Lyon's Falls*.

CHAPTER THIRTY

There it was, right in front of me. Lyon's Falls. The falls had been named after the reclusive pioneer Paul Lyon, who moved his family into the forest to get away from civilization. He'd died one night trying to find his cow in a rainstorm. He and the cow went over the falls, dropping eighty feet to the jutting rocks below. Legend said his family buried him between two of the falls.

I had known about Lyon's Falls my entire life and never gave a thought to them during this entire investigation. But here I was, standing before the sign, knowing now that Naomi wasn't suicidal. Jim Carlson had her, and she would be extremely lucky to still be alive.

I was about to run the trail back to my car and call for help, but it was too late. Just then, I heard a small child screaming. The cries came from the falls area. Jim Carlson was waiting for me.

I continued down the sandy path, around the bend into the opening of the falls. Their majestic presence stood high in the forest with the deep cavern below.

The falls themselves were almost in the shape of a horseshoe. I walked into the middle, stopped at the mass of rocks before me, and looked up.

The screams had diminished to low sobs but were echoing throughout the cavern, so it was hard to pinpoint their origin.

"It's nice to see you, Cecelia!" A voice rang out from the top of the falls. "You were not smart enough to figure it out on your own, so I enlisted the aid of Naomi, your friend and captain."

I kept looking around and hoping the forest ranger I had spoken to had seen our cars and assumed I went on the trail anyway. With luck, he would see that I wasn't on the covered bridge and was heading my way to arrest me for trespassing.

"No one's coming, Cecelia. Now, take off your gun and throw it into the rocks, or the child dies."

Normally, we're taught never to give up our gun no matter the circumstances. However, this time I had no choice. I took my .45-caliber handgun and threw it as hard as I could into the cluster of rocks, hearing it bang around before stopping.

"I want to see Naomi!" I yelled out, looking above me.

"Here she comes!" he yelled back.

Naomi Kincaid came sailing over the side of the falls to my right. I began screaming until, instead of falling into the rocks below, she stopped halfway down. Her hands were tied with a long rope that went up to the top and over the edge. He must've secured it to one of the trees lining the edge.

Regardless, the fall she took surely would've pulled both arms out of their sockets. I don't know if she even noticed since she was covered in blood, beaten beyond recognition.

I was pretty sure at that point she was dead. I began to cry at the sight of her, hanging there with her hands above her head, swaying back and forth. I fell to my knees.

"Get up!" yelled the voice. "You have exactly one hour and ten minutes to go back to your car and get my doll—I know you have it! If you are one minute late, you'll find little Brooklyn lying down below in the rocks! If you try to call for help, and believe me I'll know if you do, she dies!"

"The hike is forty-five minutes one way!" I was screaming hysterically by this point.

"The clock has already started, Cecelia. Bye-bye!"

I turned and started running down the trail as fast as I could go. It was hard to run and cry at the same time, so it was vital to get myself together. Tearing down the trail, I twisted my ankle more times than I could count. I also fell more times than I could count, one time hitting my face on a large tree root smack in the middle of the trail. Even as blood ran down the side of my face, I felt no pain. I kept running until I thought my lungs would explode. If this did not make me stop smoking, nothing would. That is, if I survived.

At last the end of the trail was in sight, and I ran full speed toward my car, fumbling for the keys in my pocket. Sweat and blood poured into my eyes, but all I could think about was getting back in enough time to save Brooklyn.

I didn't bother closing the trunk after I grabbed the doll. My watch said I had only thirty-five minutes to get back. There was no way I was going to make it. Out of breath, tired, and cramping, I kept dropping the doll because my hands were so sweaty. I finally looped my hand through the belt around its waist to keep ahold.

Getting closer to the falls again, I felt myself near the brink of full-blown hysterics. I had to get the thought of Naomi out of my head or I would fall apart and not be able to continue.

When I ran back into the middle of the falls I looked at my watch and saw I was five minutes late. Heaving and trying to catch my breath, I dropped the doll on the ground and looked around the rocks for Brooklyn's body.

I didn't see it, but now I began to vomit from my run, falling back down on my knees and arms. I was dizzy and couldn't catch my breath no matter what.

"Very good, Cecelia!" the voice yelled while I was still throwing up. "Did I say an hour and ten minutes? I'm sorry, I meant an hour and a half!" His unsettling laughter started again loudly.

I began taking deep breaths and tried to focus on something, anything except the situation at hand. My chest felt like someone had driven a pickax right through it, and God only knew the ass-kicking my heart had taken.

Still on my knees, I leaned back and looked up, crossing my arms above my head while taking deep breaths.

"Not in good shape for a police officer, are you, Cecelia! I'll let you rest. We've got all day and night!"

How I prayed Coop got my message in time. Every time I looked up and saw Naomi hanging there, I thought I might be sick. I couldn't believe she might be dead. I started to sob again, thinking how young she was and how we had just patched things up. Coop would be devastated. My thoughts were interrupted by the sounds of Brooklyn Phillips crying.

"Jim! Let me see Brooklyn, please!" I yelled.

I waited for almost ten minutes and listened to the child's racking cries before I caught just the glimpse of her head peering down at me from the top of the falls where Naomi was hanging. I looked up at her and yelled.

"Brooklyn! I'm going to help you, okay? Can you be a big girl for me? Please!"

She just cried harder; that was one of my less brilliant moves. She knew I couldn't help her. She saw me dirty, bloody, and crying on the ground below. She also knew what was waiting for me on the top. I sat there waiting for my next instructions.

Brooklyn's sobs dissipated, and Naomi still hung from the cliff. I tried hard to see if there was anything that indicated she was still alive, but she was too high. She had been thrown from the highest ridge of the falls, well over one hundred feet up. That was where Jim Carlson and Brooklyn Phillips were located.

At that point, I couldn't believe Coop hadn't gotten his message yet. I knew once he did he would, hopefully, figure it out. He would know he and Naomi hadn't broken up and that she wasn't suicidal. He would have to know it was all a setup involving Carlson and he'd tell Michael. I imagined them charging down the trail any minute. But that still had not happened. And I was afraid it never would.

It was quiet. I heard crickets, birds, and the slight trickle of water running over the falls. Usually, these were some of the most soothing sounds of the forest. They weren't soothing now. The quiet was terrifying. My biggest fear was that Jim Carlson had a gun and had me in his sights, ready to shoot any minute. I had no idea where he was, but he knew exactly where I was. The doll lay next to me about three feet away. Carlson eventually broke the silence.

"Okay, CeeCee," he called down. "I think I've given you enough time to catch your breath. Now, grab Elsa and climb the ridge to your left. When you get to the top, wait."

I looked at the ridge to my left. It would be a hell of a climb, and I didn't know if I was in the shape to do it, especially lugging the doll named Elsa. Making it more problematic was my paralyzing fear of heights. I suffered from severe vertigo when I got more than ten feet above the ground. Plus, the ridge itself wasn't more than a couple feet wide on that side, and I could easily fall off under the best of circumstances.

Frighteningly, finding myself once more with no option, I grabbed the doll and began to climb.

On the other side, where Jim and Brooklyn were located, there were crude steps cut into the rock that made it easier to climb. On this side, it was nothing but rock and tree roots. I had taken the doll's shoelaces and tied the doll to the back of my belt so I could use both my hands. Elsa was now bouncing back and forth behind me, a grisly reminder of what was ahead.

I started climbing, grabbing each root and rock along the way for support. If I looked down, I was done for. Though my clothing was comfortable, the chunky heels on my boots were making it difficult to get my footing, and I was certain I would plummet to my death on the rocks below. When I got to the last root and began to pull myself up, I couldn't believe I'd actually made it.

I faced the rock and the woods, with my back toward the ridge. If I turned around I would instantly get dizzy and start to lose my balance. As it was, my legs were already shaky from the run and the climb.

"Turn around, CeeCee!"

I couldn't do it. Just thinking about it made the vertigo creep in, and I remained as I was.

"I said, turn around!" Carlson yelled. I heard Brooklyn cry out in pain.

I managed to turn and saw Jim Carlson and Brooklyn Phillips across the falls. In a small clearing next to a large rock, Brooklyn was on her knees. She was still wearing the white T-shirt she'd had on when she disappeared, and she had not stopped crying. Carlson had the back of her hair and was pulling it to make her scream. The rope holding Naomi was tied to a large pine directly behind the rock. Jim started to pull Brooklyn toward the edge of the falls.

"No! Okay! I'm turned around!" I screamed.

He stopped. My mistake was to look down. The only thing that prevented me from falling over the side was dropping to my knees and grabbing the ground. My vision seemed to turn upside down, along with my stomach. I closed my eyes.

"Stand up and look at me, goddamn it! Do it or she dies!"

I bit into my lip so hard I tasted blood. This was enough to allow me to stand back up, but not enough to take the dizziness away. I leaned back against the rock, focusing across the falls at him and Brooklyn instead of looking down.

"Now, walk around the edge of the ridge to me."

He could have easily had me climb up on his side, but no, he wanted to play games. Every obscenity in the English language went through my head right then. I swore if I got the chance, I would make Jim Carlson suffer the most painful death imaginable.

Looking across, I could see a smirk on his face. He knew this was difficult for me, but how in the world did he know I was scared of heights? I tried to remember any interviews I'd given about the Murder Mountain case, but couldn't recall the subject of heights ever coming up. But he knew just the same.

I started to sidestep, slowly, along the ridge. The doll kept dragging and bouncing behind me. With each step, I took a deep breath and continued to look at Jim Carlson, my anger forcing me along one step at a time.

I was halfway around when my foot slipped. A loose rock had given way, causing me to skid forward to the edge of the falls. At the last moment, I grabbed a tree root that kept me from plunging over completely. My legs and the doll dangling over the side, I hoisted myself back up. I curled up into a ball and held on to the root with everything I had, near total panic. I heard Jim Carlson laughing.

"Whoops! Almost gotcha, didn't it? Get moving!"

I stood again, trying to regain my balance and composure before moving once more. Now he upped the ante. He had a bucket in front of him. He pulled something out of it and threw it at me.

It took a couple of more throws before I realized he was throwing mice. Jim Carlson had uncovered my fear of all fears. Mice weren't rats, but they damn sure were close enough. Jim Carlson knew all about the rats. It was not hard to do since it was in every single article written about the happenings on Murder Mountain. I remember articles where I was quoted saying I could never look at a rat or a mouse again without becoming hysterical.

But I was managing quite nicely, considering the circumstances, even able to use my foot to push the mice off the ledge, whenever one landed on it.

But it was the one that hit me on top of the head, before climbing down to my back and getting caught in my hair, that almost made me lose my life. The familiar squirm and squeal of a rodent flying about my head did it. I bit my lip again, tears uncontrollably running down my face, and slowly reached behind my head to grab the mouse. I used every ounce of will to keep from going into total, blind panic. When I was able to grab the mouse, it began biting me while I pulled it from my hair. I opened my hand and let it fall to its death.

I stood still, beginning to cry again while more mice pelted me. If one more got stuck in my hair, I honestly didn't think I would have the strength to keep myself from becoming totally unglued. I wanted Michael desperately. If he saw what Jim Carlson was doing to me, Naomi, and Brooklyn right now, he would kill him with his bare hands.

"Keep going!"

How many mice are in that bucket? I thought. He had thrown at least thirty so far. As if someone from above were graciously looking down on me, the mice quit coming. I breathed a loud sigh of relief, but I couldn't imagine what he had for me next.

As I got closer to his side, and Naomi, I heard her moan. She was alive. Barely, I'm sure, but the fact was she was breathing. I didn't say anything to her. I didn't want any attention drawn to her. I hoped he thought she was dead. If he did, I wanted to keep it that way. With any luck, she wouldn't make any more sounds.

I came around the curve of the ledge and saw Naomi tilting her head, looking up at me, breathing hard and moaning softly. I tried to give her a look that would make her keep quiet but, as usual, Jim beat me to the punch.

"Don't bother. I know she's alive, and there's a reason for that, Cecelia. A reason you'll soon find out. Keep going!"

I tried to give Naomi a reassuring smile, but it was impossible. The look of terror on my face wasn't going away anytime soon. Likely, it would get worse, especially, when I came to the break in the ridge. There was an approximate two-foot gap along the lip of the ridge. Not a large one, but I would have to make a small jump. If I didn't land right, down I'd go. Way down. I didn't know how I would manage to do it with that damn doll hanging behind me. It would be easier if I could face the rock, but Carlson wouldn't let that happen. Every time I tried to turn around, he'd scream at me.

Brooklyn looked terrified. She'd quit crying when the mice throwing started. The look on her face told me she didn't think I was going to make it. I have to admit, my own outlook on the situation didn't appear very bright either.

My knuckles were bloody from digging into the rock behind me to keep my balance. When I got to the gap I didn't stop, because if I did, I wouldn't have had the guts to continue. I took a small hop sideways and made the gap, saying a silent thank you before moving on.

I thought about the situation. It was my choice to be here. I could've walked away, saved myself, and let Naomi and Brooklyn die. However, I never could've lived with that. I was here to help them, and that was exactly what I would do. Thinking about this gave me the courage to make the final thirty or so feet of the ledge.

I was about fifteen feet away from Carlson and Brooklyn when he told me to stop, which I did with no problem. The clearing was nearby now and the ledge had widened considerably. There was room enough to do a cartwheel if I wanted.

This was the first time I had seen Jim Carlson in person. As I stood looking closely at him, I noticed his face was very odd. It looked slightly deformed, or crooked. I remembered his driver's license photo, but didn't recall noticing the oddness of his face the way I did now.

"Congratulations, Cecelia. You made it. Now sit down." I sat, and he smiled. "Tell me who I am."

"James Carlson," I answered.

He began to howl with that disturbing laughter of his. In fact, he actually bent over, slapping a knee before falling to the ground on both of them, all the while clutching his stomach. After he calmed down, he stood and pointed at me, snickering.

"I beat you! I did it! I beat Detective Cecelia Catherine Gallagher! Whooee!" He started jumping around. "I knew I was smarter than all of you, and I've just proved it. You ignorant bitch! I gave you every opportunity under the sun to catch me and you didn't! How does that make you feel, Cecelia? Incompetent? Worthless? It should! Oh, you made me want to kill you with my bare hands and now you're here. You just needed a little coaxing, is all."

He stopped dancing and turned around. Now his look was serious. No laughing. Not even the hint of a smile.

Jim reached up to his face, and began to peel off the latex nose that covered his own. Then he took off his wig, revealing the thinning gray hair underneath. Next were the mustache and the glasses. He must have been wearing brown contact lenses, but he left them in.

Standing before me was none other than Carl James Malone. Still reeling from shock, I began to put the pieces together. I cursed myself and every other investigator who'd worked the case. It was the obvious answer, and we had overlooked it. The simplest part of the investigation is always connected with its outcome. That was the standard. What a bunch of buffoons we were.

Carl Malone had every right to be proud. He *had* beaten us. The name alone was cause enough for me to turn my badge in. If I made it out of there alive, that was. *James Carlson. Carl James* Malone. How could I have missed it?

I thought back to the first time I ever talked to Carl. He said he had retired a little less than a year before. Obviously, he could no longer choose his victims while traveling. Knowing his time was nearing an end and knowing he could never suppress his urges and rage, he planned carefully, very carefully. He chose me (I still didn't know why, and now I probably never would), did

research and had the entire case mapped out minute by
minute. All the while he strung us along, laughed at us,
and brought us here to this very moment, at this very
place. He was right; he had won.

I think, in time, I would've figured out that the Bible
passage meant Lyon's Falls. *And into the den did Daniel fall;*
the one part of the passage that was made up lurched out
and slapped me in the face, and I had ignored it.

Carl Malone knew I would've figured it out, too. He
just didn't have the patience to wait. He saw his victory
in dreams and was beginning to taste it. That was where
Naomi came in.

Carl Malone planned on dying today. I also knew he
planned on taking me, Brooklyn, and Naomi with him.
He would go down in a blaze of glory, taking the
gun-totin' CeeCee Gallagher with him. I had been right
about one thing: I *was* Daniel.

I thought back to when I had broken into his house.
There was always something that bothered me a little, and
now I knew why. Carl had said his wife died recently, but
there was not one picture of her in the house. I chalked it
up to a grieving widow at the time and never gave it much
thought after that. Another admonishment to myself.

"You were never married, were you, Carl?"

He laughed again. "Only to Elsa, my dear. Only Elsa."
His smile faded. "Give her to me now."

I untied the doll from behind me. When Carl got a
full view of it, he began to shake, and his eyes welled up.
He ripped the doll from my hands, crouching over with
it wrapped in his arms.

"Oh my baby! Did she hurt you? Daddy missed you.
I'll never let this happen again!"

I thought now was a good a time as any to make a move.
The best course of action would be to grab Brooklyn and

run. Cautiously and quietly, I took one step to his side before he stood up straight, gun in hand and pointed it at me. The gun must've been tucked in his pants. I knew I hadn't see it earlier.

"Don't even think about it, Detective! We're not done yet. Now sit down! I've waited twenty-six years for this. I won't let it happen again!"

I hadn't a clue what he was talking about, but there had to be a way out of this. Outside of a miracle or the spot Carl was standing on crumbling away, I couldn't see one.

"Why the kids, Carl? How many children are there?" I wanted to keep him talking.

"Why? You know why! You all say I'm sick, that's why!" He walked over to Brooklyn and I honest to God thought he was going to shoot her. He only patted her hair. "I lost count around twenty-five or thirty. I had hoped that you would've been smart enough to stop me, Cecelia, but you weren't! You stupid, wretched bitch."

He was losing it totally now, walking in a circle and reciting nursery rhymes. Brooklyn started to cry again, and I shook my head at her to stop.

"Shut up! Shut up, you little bitch!" he screamed in Brooklyn's face. It worked; she was too startled to cry. "The dolls, oh my precious dolls. They were so good for me for such a long time, but the feelings came back and I couldn't be completely satisfied. My father"—he started swinging at the air—"my father should've had dolls. He liked little boys, though, little boys like me!" By now he was no longer in touch with reality.

I had to do something, and the only thing I could do was to grab Carl Malone's doll.

"What are you doing? Put her down!" He looked ill.

I threw the doll as hard as I could over the edge of the

falls. Carl started screaming at the top of his lungs before he stopped and smiled again. He was uncomfortably, then frighteningly, calm.

"It doesn't matter now, does it? We'll be together in the end, and that's what's most important. Come over here, Cecelia, and kneel down."

He pointed with his gun at a spot about three feet away from Brooklyn and about two feet away from the rope holding Naomi.

"Face the edge."

Carl walked behind me, and I braced myself to get shot execution style in the back of the head. I closed my eyes as I felt the blow hit me, knocking me forward onto the ground. I lay there for a few seconds, feeling the warm blood run down my face, and I realized I was still alive.

I began to sit up, instinctively putting my hand to my head to feel the large welt from where Carl had smashed me with a rock. He'd hit me high on the head, and the blood was pouring down my face and into my eyes. The wound didn't hurt all that much, but when I looked down at myself, I was covered with blood.

"That's for Elsa, you little whore!"

I tried to wipe the blood out of my eyes, but it seemed to keep coming. I tilted my head up, which helped considerably. It didn't last long.

Carl grabbed me by my hair and dragged me to the falls' edge, forcing me to look way down at the ground below. The blood started to pour down my face again. I lost it and began to scream, thinking he was going to throw me off.

"Understand? Any more pranks and down you go!"

I saw Naomi looking up at me, struggling. If she was smart she'd stay still. The rope holding her didn't look too sturdy and she'd never survive the fall if it broke. She quit moving and her head bobbed forward. I thought she passed out again, which was probably for the best.

Carl pulled me backward, dragging me to the spot where he had hit me. Brooklyn started crying again. I needed to calm down for her sake as much as my own.

"What do you want, Carl? Me? I'll stay. Just, please, let Brooklyn and Naomi go."

He squatted down, getting an inch away from my face. The stench of his breath made me lean back before he jerked my head and brought me forward again.

"No, Cecelia, we're going to finish this. All of us. Just like I planned. Now, I want you to scoot forward to right here. Stay kneeling. Do it."

Using his gun again, he pointed to a spot about three feet from the edge. Obeying, I moved and found I could see over the edge, just slightly.

However, it was just enough that I had a full view of Michael climbing up the large sandstone rock that was the core of the formation at the bottom. My heart went into a spasm. I tried to look away quickly before Carl saw my face, but he put his gun to my temple immediately.

"Stop where you are, Agent! I'm so glad you could be here for the finale, but unfortunately, you only get to sit back and watch."

At that point, Michael had a clear view of what was happening and a look of horror flew across his face. I actually wasn't in much pain, but with the amount of blood all over me, I knew I looked terrible.

"Motherfucker, when I get my hands on you—and I will, I promise—you will suffer!" Michael called up to him.

Carl merely laughed at Michael's threats. Then I glimpsed Coop standing at the bottom of the sand rock where Michael had been. He was looking up at Naomi. There were only two other agents with them, and they stood at the end of the trail, guns drawn.

"You're in no position to threaten me, Agent! Tell your other goons to toss their guns. You and your sidekick do the same. Do it. I said, do it."

Michael nodded toward the other agents and watched as they all threw their guns into the woods or onto the rocks. However, I knew Michael and Coop carried back-up weapons.

"Cee, you okay, baby?" Michael called up to me.

I nodded. Carl positioned himself next to the rock where Brooklyn was sitting, out of Michael's view or anyone else that might be nearby. He sat quietly, humming to himself, before starting to belt out a series of nursery rhymes. His voice went from barely audible to loud and raucous in seconds.

I kept looking at Michael, wanting more than anything to hold him and find myself out of this mess. I desperately wanted to be with my girls, but had to drive the thought out of my head so I wouldn't break down completely.

My mind was spinning. There had to be some way out. Snipers would work, but unless they were already on their way, it would be all over before they arrived. There was also no way a sniper could get into position without being seen by Carl. The only way would be to climb down the Clearfork Gorge about three hundred feet, and that would only be if they didn't break their necks first. The killer definitely had all this planned down to the last detail way ahead of time.

I hadn't realized Carl had stopped with his nursery rhymes until he was standing right in front of me. What was he going to do next?

Carl deliberately stood at an angle by the rock so Michael and Coop wouldn't have a clear shot. He also had his gun six inches from my forehead.

"It's time. Yes, now it's time. It's going to be you who will choose, Cecelia. You get to choose who dies first."

I looked back down at Michael. He needed to do something fast. But what?

"Pay attention, Cecelia. This is how it works. I can either shoot you first, or Brooklyn, or the rope that holds the captain. You pick the order. Any order you wish."

Brooklyn was howling now, her screams echoing throughout the falls. I looked at the rope that held Naomi and then at the little girl. I looked at Michael, then back at the rope.

"Make your choice now, Cecelia, or I will make it for you."

I thought about when Carl had my face over the edge of the cliff earlier. Knowing it was my only chance, I did the only thing I could do.

I looked at Michael and mouthed *I love you*. I watched as he grew deathly pale, the blood draining from his face. He knew exactly what I was going to do.

"Well, Cecelia? Who's first?"

"Shoot the rope."

In the split second that Carl shifted the gun from my forehead to the direction of the rope, I moved.

"CeeCee! No!" I heard Michael scream.

Then the king commanded, and they brought Daniel and cast him into the den of lions; and into the den did Daniel fall.

Grabbing the barrel of the gun with one hand, I pushed it to the side. Then, with all the strength I had, I stood up and grabbed Carl tightly, and pushed us both over the edge of Lyon's Falls.

CHAPTER THIRTY-ONE

I figured I only had a slim chance of surviving the fall, though when Carl held my face over the side, I had seen the pool of water below. Was it deep enough?

Normally there was no water at the base of the falls, but we'd had a large amount of rain this year, so there was a small basin that had filled, the middle darker than the edges. At its deepest point, I estimated the water to be seven to eight feet at the most, if I was lucky. If I landed in the water at all.

There was no way to push Carl over the side without going over myself. The amount of strength I had to use made my own momentum impossible to stop. What I needed to do was fall as far to the right as I could.

When I grabbed Carl, I shoved him to the left, toward the rocks, before I let go. If I landed in the deepest part of the water, I would most likely break every bone in my body, but the possibility of survival was still there; a very slight possibility. This was the only way. Otherwise we would've all died.

From Michael's vantage point, he couldn't see the pool or even assume one was there. As I soared over the edge, I could hear him screaming. My arms were flailing in the air, and I was trying to turn myself. As I fell closer to the deepest part of the pool, I flipped over at the last minute, my body hitting the water in a v-shape, left hip first.

The water was ice cold, and it shocked me as I went in, knocking the wind out of me. But luck happened to be on my side, because the water was closer to nine or ten feet deep. It wasn't deep enough to prevent me from slamming onto the bottom, but it *was* deep enough to keep me from dying, and that was all that mattered.

I hit the bottom with my left hip, shattering it instantly. The searing pain caused me to scream out all my air, which resulted in me sucking in water.

With my right leg, I pushed off the bottom as hard as could, driving my head directly into the bottom of the sand rock that jutted out underneath the water. Woozy, now I was taking in too much water and getting disoriented, not knowing up from down.

I was panicking and started to black out before I felt a pair of arms around my waist, pulling me to the surface. Thinking it might be Carl Malone, I began to fight with what little consciousness I had left. The arms wouldn't let go and when we broke the surface I heard Michael yelling next to me.

"CeeCee! It's me! Stop!"

Once I hit the air, I was desperate for breath and began spewing out water. I continued gagging while Michael pulled me up to the shallow part of the pool. He turned me over immediately, so I could get all the water out of my lungs.

My hip was in horrific pain, which made my gasping worse. I cried out. The blood continued to pour from the place on my head where Carl had hit me, and now from the new wound I received when I hit the sand rock.

Michael took his shirt off and wrapped it around my head. I grabbed on to him as tight as I could, my face resting on his lap. He held me. I don't know which one of us was shaking more.

"Oh my God, baby! You're okay, you're okay, and I'm here."

I was still having a hard time catching my breath, but somehow managed to get out the most important question.

"Michael! Where is he? Where's Carl!"

"Dead, Cee. Shh. He hit the rocks." He was gently rocking me back and forth.

As my head cleared a bit, my next thoughts were about Naomi and Brooklyn. I tried my best to sit up and had to lean on my right side to keep my left hip from paralyzing me with pain. I held Michael's shirt, which was now completely red, to my head before looking up and seeing Naomi still hanging.

"Help Naomi, she's not dead! I'm okay, but please get her and Brooklyn down from there!"

"All right, you sure you're okay?" He was shirtless, covered in my blood, soaking wet, and had nothing but concern for me on his face.

"Yes, go!"

Michael ran over to the bottom of the falls that led up to Brooklyn and Naomi. Coop was already halfway up. I started looking around to find where Carl had fallen, but didn't see any sign of him nearby. When I looked up toward the large sand rock that Michael had been standing on, I saw the blood dripping over the side. Carl and I had fallen perfectly; me into the pool and him to his death on the rocks.

Michael and Coop were at the top now and out of my sight, but when I heard Brooklyn start to cry, I knew she was okay. She would have to stay put a few minutes more until they pulled Naomi up.

Then I saw Coop's head and shoulders appear over the edge of the falls, and he called down to Naomi. She didn't move. Coop yelled back to Michael to start pulling before getting up off the ground and helping. They did it slowly, obviously taking into account the condition of the rope. As soon as Naomi's hands were within six inches from the top, Coop reached down and grabbed them both, leaning backward to pull her up over the cliff.

Naomi came to again, screaming in pain. With both arms dislocated from her shoulders, having them pulled on even more would be unbearable.

Michael appeared at the edge, helping Coop. They were both making me nervous standing at the brink of the falls like that. I hadn't realized I had been holding my breath until I saw Naomi's feet disappear over the top. Only then did I let out a long, deep breath. All I could hear was Coop yelling after seeing the condition Naomi was in.

Once again, Michael appeared at the edge, calling to the other agents to get up there and get Brooklyn down. I watched as they made the climb and then as they helped the child down to safety.

"Bring her over here!" I called to them.

They walked Brooklyn over, and she promptly sat down on the rock next to me, still crying. I reached out, took her hand, and squeezed.

"Honey, my name is CeeCee. I'm a police officer and a friend of your parents. We're going to get you home soon. I promise, okay?"

She was frantically looking around, and I realized she was looking for Carl. Since I was alive after going over the falls, she must've assumed that he was too.

"He's not going to hurt you anymore, honey. He's dead. You're safe."

She looked at me with wide eyes and disbelief before she clung to me for dear life. I held her tight while she cried into my shoulder. She eventually quit crying, but she never let go of her grip. This was fine by me because I had no intention of letting her go of her either, unless it was to her parents.

Michael and Coop were still on top of the falls performing, I assumed, some basic first aid on Naomi before carrying her down. I heard her cry out a couple of times, but it was music to my ears. We had all survived except Carl. I wouldn't have settled for any other outcome.

When I took the shirt away from my head, I saw the bleeding had started to slow considerably. One less thing to worry about. My attention was focused on Michael and Coop carrying Naomi. Coop had his shirt off, too, and I saw pieces of it holding her arms down as well as wrapped around her head. Coop's hands were under her back while Michael was supporting her legs. They were side stepping toward the crude stone steps that would take them down. I didn't think it was possible for them to carry her back that way, so I was in utter amazement when they reached the bottom. They laid her down right there, and Coop cradled her in his arms.

The severity of it all kicked in now that she was safe, and Coop leaned over her and sobbed. I'd known him for thirteen years and had never seen him break down like that. I was so absorbed watching them that I didn't notice when Michael arrived at my side. Seeing Brooklyn in my arms, he bent down and smiled.

"She okay?" he asked quietly.

"She'll be fine. As you can imagine, she's terrified. How's Naomi?"

His smile faded. "She's not good, Cee. He beat the hell out of her. The biggest problem is it looks like he smashed the entire right side of her head in. It could be her hair is just matted with blood, but I can't tell right now. I don't know how she's alive, let alone half conscious. She doesn't know where she is or even who she is right now."

Please, let her look worse than she is, I thought.

"Coop isn't doing so well, either," I said.

"No, he's not. When we pulled her up, you should've seen his face." He sighed. "Your bleeding looks like it's slowing down."

"There's a positive sign. . . . The bleeding may have stopped, but my head and hip are absolutely killing me." My voice was scratchy.

The other agents came over and said help would be there within half an hour. They would be sending ten emergency medical technicians in, with backboards, to carry me, Naomi, and Brooklyn out. Two ambulances would be waiting at the entrance to the trail for me and Brooklyn, and a Life Flight emergency helicopter was going to land right in the parking area to fly Naomi to Cleveland. I hoped she lasted another half hour. I felt Brooklyn lift her head from my shoulder and saw she was looking at me.

"When do I get to see my mommy and daddy?"

"Soon, honey, very soon."

She laid her head back down and closed her eyes. It was when she fell into a light sleep, exhausted from her ordeal, that Michael had a chance to find out all that happened.

"CeeCee, honey, I'm sorry, and I know you're in a lot of pain, but I need to know, what in the world were you thinking when you did that?" he said, referring to my nosedive over the side of the falls.

"That was the only choice. He was about to kill all of us. We'd be dead right now if I hadn't." In her drowsy state, I felt Brooklyn shudder and I held her tighter.

"I honestly believed I would never see you again. I've never been so scared in my entire life. Ever."

I reached out and put my hand to his cheek. He grabbed it tightly, holding it there, before putting it to his lips.

"Michael, how did you guys figure this out? I'm assuming the messages I left you and Coop had something to do with it."

It did. Michael said he found my note and didn't quite have it figured out, until Coop came looking for him. At first, Coop didn't pick up on it either. He was explaining to Michael my message about the Falls when Michael asked what that was.

As soon as Coop told Michael the real name of the place, it all came together. Michael was running out the door as he was explaining it to Coop.

Two other agents just happened to be standing in the parking lot when Michael and Coop were leaving. Michael yelled for them to follow him.

On the way, Michael called for more help until his cell went out of service. The help had yet to arrive. He said they literally sprinted down the trail and just got to the opening of the falls when Michael heard me screaming. He didn't see Carl Malone push my face over the edge, but heard the terror in my voice.

"CeeCee, when I heard you scream like that, I thought for sure we were all too late, especially when I saw Naomi hanging there."

Michael had tried to climb the sand rock to get off a good shot at Carl, but he couldn't. Carl spied him. I knew the rest.

"CeeCee, who the hell was that? That wasn't Jim Carlson, was it?"

"It was Carl Malone, the owner of the stolen van and

the rented houses. He also went by the name Jim Carlson."

I saw Michael silently curse himself, just as I had done, when he found out the large mistake we had made. I then began telling Michael my own story, of how I got here and everything that had happened.

"Is that why your knuckles are all cut up and your face scratched?"

I nodded. I omitted the part about Carl throwing the mice at me. I knew Michael would get even more upset than he was now.

"You forgot the part about the mice," Brooklyn lifted her head and exclaimed. Ah, children. You gotta love 'em.

"What's she talking about?"

I told him, matter of factly, and went on to add that maybe it was the best therapy ever. It was the ultimate test in facing my fears. Michael knew that was nothing but pure bullshit. Predictably, I felt him get angrier and angrier.

"There's nothing you can do about it now, Michael. He's dead."

"Not at first he wasn't," Michael mumbled, turning to look at the blood starting to coagulate on the sand rock.

"What did you say?"

"Nothing, except that I made Carl Malone a promise and kept it—that's all." His face showed no expression.

I didn't ask what he meant. I already knew. When Carl hit the sand rock he was still alive. Barely, I'm sure, but he was breathing. Michael was in the water within seconds pulling me out, so whatever he did to Carl was quick. I'm going to go out on a limb and say he snapped his neck, but I don't, nor will I ever, know for sure.

We heard voices coming down the trail at long last and prayed it was the medical personnel. Ten to fifteen cops ran out of the trail. I'd say they were a little late. There was a lot of yelling, mostly by the cops, and stern voices from the agents before things started to quiet down. I felt a hand on my shoulder and looked up to see the sheriff.

"Please, tell me you're okay."

"I'm fine, Sheriff."

He actually trembled when he saw Brooklyn in my arms, and he gently patted her back.

"I called your dad, CeeCee. He's on his way. Alex and Jean Phillips should be here any minute, as well. When we called them we didn't know what was going on down here yet, so we had to be somewhat vague. They're certainly going to be two happy people. As usual, a job well done, Sergeant."

I'd have to get used to my new title, which still sounded strange. I pointed toward Coop and Naomi.

"Sheriff, Naomi isn't doing too good. When are the medical personnel going to be here?"

"Should be soon. Let me get over there."

He half jogged over to Coop and Naomi. I saw him hold her hand and lean over and talk to her, then he yelled to a group of the uniform officers to get on their radios and tell the ambulances to hurry.

Fortunately, this wasn't needed as the first team of medical technicians raced in. Everyone was silent as we watched them work on Naomi, getting her stabilized and onto the backboard. It troubled me that a couple of the medics' faces indicated they weren't very hopeful. It was only a matter of minutes before four medics and Coop picked up the backboard and started quickly walking toward the Life Flight helicopter, which was already waiting at the trail entrance.

The sheriff signaled to me that he was going with Naomi, and I gave him a thumbs-up. A captain of the police department might die. The sheriff needed to be there.

They weren't gone for more than five minutes when I heard Alex Phillips's voice. Brooklyn heard it, too, because her head popped up. She started looking around frantically, before finding her father and mother standing by the uniformed officers who were trying to figure out exactly where she was.

"Daddy! Daddy! Mommy!" She jumped off me and started running to her parents.

They ran to her. Both grabbed her at the same time and fell to their knees, crying and kissing her. I was overcome watching the reunion. This sight was worth everything to all of us. It was the scene I had hoped to watch; a happy ending.

Michael had gotten a blanket from one of the medics and brought it over to me. By now, the effects of the cold water and loss of blood had me shivering and I wrapped the blanket tightly around my body, covering the top of my head like a hood. Alex Phillips came over and crouched down in front of me.

"Detective, I don't know how I'll ever thank you enough. I hope you aren't hurt too badly. What can I do for you?" His eyes were still watery.

"Nothing . . . really, Commissioner, I'll be fine."

He patted my shoulder and walked back to his daughter so they could wait for the other team of medics. They would take Brooklyn first. She was alive, but I'd make a bet that when the hospital examine her they'd find that she had been sexually assaulted. Brave little Brooklyn Phillips would have years of therapy ahead of her.

The rest of the medical personnel arrived at the same time. I wasn't very happy about being put on a backboard. I would've much rather just hopped out on one leg, with Michael for support, but he wouldn't hear any of my complaints. (It sounded good when I suggested it, but as much pain as I was in, I knew I couldn't possibly make it out of there standing upright.) I kept myself propped up on my elbows so I could watch where we were going the whole time.

The uniformed officers stayed behind to protect the scene while the crime lab and the coroner's office made their way back. They were waiting when I was brought off the trail to the ambulance in the parking area. Michael told them that all the injured parties were out and they could go back. My dad was there, looking nervous.

"Dad, you could've met me at the hospital instead of driving all the way down here. I'm fine."

He merely raised his eyebrow at me before noticing Michael. He'd heard the rumors; we all worked at the same department. He gave him a slight nod.

"Dad, I need you to call Eric in North Carolina. Tell him what happened and that's it's safe to bring the girls back."

"I'll take care of it. Me and Carly will follow the ambulance and meet you at the hospital. I hear Captain Kincaid isn't doing too well."

I shook my head. I was worried about Naomi, more so than anything right now. My dad leaned over and kissed my forehead, which was covered with drying blood, before heading back to his car.

CHAPTER THIRTY-TWO

Michael rode with me in the ambulance. While I was in one of the rooms waiting for the doctor, my dad snuck his cell phone in and handed it to me.

My girls were on the other end and they were wonderful. I only said I had fallen down at work and got a bump on my head and hip. Not that they weren't used to seeing me in the hospital, but the less they knew the better. They were excited to come home. We missed each other so much. When I talked to Eric, he was very concerned and worried, but I reassured him I'd be fine. I hung up with a heavy heart. I knew when they got home we would have to tell the girls that we were divorcing, and I knew how devastated they would be.

Meantime, within fifteen minutes of our arrival at the hospital, Michael had over forty FBI agents going to search Carl Malone's house and other rentals, while others were checking deep into his personal background.

I waited for over an hour before seeing a doctor and getting taken for x-rays, which not only irritated me, but which made me a less-than-pleasant patient. Two hours later the doctor came back and told me that my left hipbone had been completely shattered and that I would need it replaced entirely.

"What exactly does that mean? How long am I going to be off my feet?" I was entirely too impatient to be laid up for a long period of time; I thought I would go crazy last year when I was in the hospital for three weeks. The doctor said he would schedule me for surgery in the morning and that they would have me up trying to use a walker the next day. He predicted I would be out of the hospital in three days and off work, if all went well, for six to eight weeks. I closed my eyes and groaned.

When he came back in later to stitch up my head I argued with him about that too. He wanted to shave the entire top, but I forbid it. I was still a woman and my hair was most precious to me. Michael stood there and shook his head while my dad yelled at me. I was stubborn and the doctor finally relented. He let me hold a mirror so I could watch him shave a very small area around each head wound.

The cut where Carl smashed me was the worst. It took seventy-two total stitches. It was deep, so they put thirty-six stitches inside the cut and thirty-six out. The other wound required thirty-four stitches on the outside only. A grand total of 106 stitches in my head. Fantastic.

I kept asking Michael to call Cleveland Metro and get an update on Naomi. She was still in surgery, so we didn't know anything yet. It was about two hours later that Coop finally called. It was rough, but she was going to make it. I breathed a loud sigh of relief.

The right side of her skull had been crushed with a blunt object, a rock probably. The doctors said that none of her brain shifted during the blow, so most likely she wouldn't suffer any brain damage. Nine of her ribs had been fractured, but none managed to puncture either of her lungs. And lastly, both shoulders were dislocated.

When they arrived at the hospital, her pulse was good and she was breathing on her own, so they didn't put her on a ventilator. She was only intubated during surgery while they placed a small metal plate in the right side of her head and put her shoulders back into place. The ribs would have to heal on their own. She would be in the intensive care unit for at least two weeks, healing and receiving frequent neurological checks.

The doctors anticipated her being awake and coherent in the morning, but doubted she would remember much, and they estimated she would be off work for three to four months. That is, if she wanted to go back at all. I wouldn't blame her if she didn't.

After being shot last year, this might well be the last straw for Naomi Kincaid. Regardless, it was all wonderful news. Michael said Coop sounded thrilled on the phone.

"I've known Coop for many years, and I've never seen him as upset as he was today," I remarked.

"I know how he feels," Michael said softly.

He was sitting next to me and holding my hand when my dad walked back into the room. Michael dropped my hand instantly. My dad wasn't stupid, and I got one of his "looks." When I was feeling better and all was well with the world, he would have one of his talks with me. No doubt about it. Until then, no use getting aggravated.

The next afternoon, after my morning surgery, which resulted in staples going up the entire left side of my hip, Michael came in my room looking grim.

"I've got bad news."

"Is it Naomi?" I hoped she hadn't taken a turn for the worse.

"No." He pulled a chair next to my bed. "They found where Anna Kovinski's bones were buried."

"Where?"

"In Carl Malone's backyard. There was a hole dug back there, and one of the bones was left in it."

I thought about the first time I met Carl. He had come from his backyard, dirty and wearing gloves; doing some landscaping. I shuddered.

"That's not all."

I didn't know if I wanted to hear any more. The anesthesia still in my system left me sleepy and with an upset stomach. Each word out of Michael's mouth made me feel worse.

"I told them to get the cadaver dogs back there, just to be on the safe side, and," he paused, "they're digging out the fourth set of bones right now."

"In the backyard?" I was astonished, and mortified.

"CeeCee, we need to prepare ourselves for a high number of bodies buried in Carl Malone's backyard. He kept two separate identities for over twenty-five years."

I shut my eyes tightly. I thought of the countless number of parents who would be getting phone calls over the next several months telling them that the child they'd longed for and prayed for had finally been found. Dead.

Carl Malone was the devil himself with a closet full of sins; sins that we would be digging up and identifying for weeks, if not months. I almost wished he weren't dead. I would've liked to have seen each parent face the man who killed their child, and witness his execution.

"You said he kept those two identities for twenty-five years?"

"At least." Michael nodded.

Michael went on to tell me the check into Malone's background was mystifying. It seemed that Carl Malone was an upstanding citizen, salesman of restaurant supplies for the entire Midwest, and one of the best neighbors a person could have.

Jim Carlson, on the other hand, was a vagrant and a drifter with a fascination for children. Carl Malone would go on business trips and prove to be a top salesman, but when the trips ended, he would stay in that city for a week or so disguised as Jim Carlson, letting out his inner demons.

"He was raised in foster homes after his father was arrested for raping him and his younger brother, who subsequently committed suicide fifteen years ago."

"Where's the father?"

"Don't know. When he was released from prison, he disappeared. The mother took off when the boys were little."

"I'll bet we find dad buried in the backyard with the others."

Even though he was dead, I could almost hear Malone laughing and screaming *I beat you all*, exactly like he had at the falls. He had accomplished what he'd set out to do, with the exception of killing the three of us. But I don't really think he would've cared all that much. It was the entire game that got him off, not just me, Naomi and, even, Brooklyn.

"How's Brooklyn Phillips?"

"Physically she'll be okay and she'll be able to have kids when she grows up. The bad news is that he raped her repeatedly, so, emotionally, she's got a long road ahead of her."

I was beyond sickened by the innocence that was lost. All of these beautiful little girls had to face the devil. Thinking about it could drive someone crazy. Alex and Jean were just happy their daughter was alive right now, but the repercussions would be lifelong for all of them.

CHAPTER THIRTY-THREE

I'd been thinking of my own daughters when I heard a familiar giggle in the hallway. Selina and Isabelle ran into my room to the edge of my bed, their tan, beautiful faces smiling ear to ear. I sat up and leaned over, gathering both of them in a tight squeeze. I don't know which one of us was happiest.

I saw Michael smiling but noticed the look faded quickly as his eyes went toward the doorway. Eric was standing there. Michael quietly excused himself and left the room, he and Eric saying nothing to each other. Eric, like the girls, had a dark, healthy-looking tan. He looked great.

"How are you feeling, CeeCee?" He stood behind our daughters.

"I'll be fine. Thanks so much for bringing them. You have no idea how much I missed them both." I was still holding both children, and Isabelle had crawled up onto the bed with me.

"Did you miss *me*?" Eric asked.

I shot him a hard look. I didn't want him to start anything in front of the girls.

"Mommy, tell Daddy you missed him, too!" Selina pleaded.

"Daddy knows how I feel, honey. It's so good to see you guys!"

They were with me for about half an hour, Eric remaining quiet, when my dad came back into my room. He had gone home last night and this was the first time he'd been back. The girls, elated to see their beloved grandpa, ran and jumped on him.

"Dad, would you do me a favor and take them down to the cafeteria to get some ice cream?" I asked. He saw Eric looking gloomy and got the hint.

"I guess now's the time we have to talk, Eric. I'm being released in two days, and we need to figure out some arrangements. I don't think it's a good idea that we're both staying at the house."

He nodded and rubbed his eyes. "Did you give any thought to counseling?"

I sighed. "No. I don't think it will work, Eric. I have already called an attorney to get the paperwork going."

"That was quick. Can't get to your precious lover fast enough, can you?"

"Don't start. I'm trying to deal with this calmly and constructively. Listen, I'm not the one who got knocked up."

He stood up and walked over to the window. This wasn't going well, and I didn't know how to make it any better. My throat was tight. My cheeks were soon wet when I thought again about everything we had gone through in the last year. And what was about to happen to us as a family.

"When you come home, I'll go stay at my parents'." He still faced the window, his back to me. "For the first couple of days, we'll just tell the girls I have to work early every night and that's why I'm not there in the evening. Since I'm on nights and sleep all day, hopefully they won't notice. When you're feeling better, we'll tell them and figure it out from there."

"That's fine." I was quiet, still teary. "Eric, I'm sorry for everything. I'm sorry it came to this, I really, truly am."

"Yeah," he whispered, "me, too."

He turned around and walked out of the room. My heart sank and broke at the same time. It was truly over.

I was wiping my eyes with a tissue when my dad brought the girls back in to say good-bye. He didn't say anything. He knew. I told the girls the bump on my head hurt and it made me cry, but the nurse gave me medicine and I felt better. It was shortly after they all left that Michael came back. He saw my red, puffy eyes and let out a loud sigh.

"Are you going to be okay, Cee?" His face showed concern as he held my hand.

"I will be . . . eventually."

Michael had been in the cafeteria having coffee when my dad and girls entered. Isabelle remembered him and told him she was getting ice cream. They all began to chat about who liked what flavor. I smiled.

He thought my dad might confront him about our relationship when the girls were running around the cafeteria out of earshot.

"Do you know what he said to me, CeeCee?"

"I can only imagine."

"He only said one thing to me. He said, 'I hope you realize what you're getting is beautiful, wonderful, and most important, never dull.'"

I laughed. It sounded just like my dad. But it also confirmed my suspicions that he was well aware of the seriousness of our relationship. I asked Michael how he responded.

"Just asked him to tell me something I didn't already

know." He kissed my cheek and cupped my face in both of his hands.

"Tell me, CeeCee, where do we go from here?"

"We go the only way we can, Michael. We go forward."

CHAPTER THIRTY-FOUR

In the days following the incident at Lyon's Falls, I went through rigorous physical therapy and was released with a walker to go sit at home until I was strong enough to return to work.

The media had a field day with the case. Front-page headlines screamed that Carl James Malone was the most notorious child murderer in history.

However, on the positive side, the country had been released from Carl's grip of terror, and parents across the nation breathed a sigh of relief.

A total of eleven sets of bones were found buried in Malone's backyard. Some of the items and clothing found with the bones indicated that several of them were more than twenty years old. All the sets of bones were found with red ribbons on them or nearby.

Each week, a new identification came back, putting a face and name to the bones. There was even a family I remembered hearing about when I was young.

In 1984 in the small town of Holland, Michigan, nine-year-old Bethany Simpson was playing kickball with a group of neighborhood kids about a hundred feet from her house. Bethany stayed behind to the kick the ball around after her friends left and was never seen again. She would've been close to my age by now. Her parents were still alive, having raised Bethany's two younger sisters.

Over twenty years later, the news was devastating. Bethany's bones, like all the others, were found with the distinctive red ribbon.

In 1992, six-year-old Darcy Fulmer had been trying out her new roller skates on the driveway of her home in Olive Hill, Kentucky. Her mother went inside to get a sweater and found Darcy gone when she returned. The roller skates were buried with Darcy. Her mother, who was raising her alone, had died several years before of ovarian cancer. Relatives told of how Darcy's mother had prayed for death so she could see her daughter again.

One of the missing children I remember most was eight-year-old Carla Dumont. Her father was the mayor of the town of London, Ohio. Carla had been taken right out of her bed while she slept at night, just like Brooklyn Phillips. It became statewide news. It happened in 1982, and I was the same age as Carla at the time. I remembered being scared by it and my older brother Tony teasing me that the man was going to come get me. Carla's mother was sent to a mental hospital a year later, spending five years there until she committed suicide in 1988. Carla's father remained in London. They had no other children.

The rest were the same, different names, different cities, but all little girls whose lives ended, destroying the lives of their surviving family members and friends. The FBI estimated that Carl had possibly killed up to forty children. They had to go back and track his whereabouts from the time he became an adult, and they compared all abductions to the area he was staying in at the time. We knew most of those bodies would never be found. But we would try. Every family of a missing child deserved some kind of answer. It would take a long time to close out this case.

I found myself in the media spotlight. I had job offers from major television networks to be their crime consultant. I had teaching offers and radio offers. I turned them all down with the exception of one, a publisher who asked me to write my story. I haven't said yes yet, but I thought it was something that could be therapeutic while I still kept my job.

Once I could walk on my own, I had Michael take me to see Naomi, who was still in intensive care but doing much better. Coop hadn't left her side for a minute. It had been only two weeks, but her appearance had improved drastically, with the exception of her eyes. They were still swollen and black from the blow to her head.

With the aid of a cane, I hobbled into the room, carrying a bouquet of flowers and some magazines for her. She was thrilled to see me and started to sit up until Coop gently but firmly told her to lie back down. She could talk just fine from that position.

I had called every day to talk to her and Coop, but seeing her in person was different. Coop and Michael left to go for coffee while Naomi thanked me for the flowers. I pulled a chair over and put it next to her bed so we could be closer.

"It's good to see you finally. You look much, much better."

I saw the tears well up in her black, puffy eyes. "CeeCee, I wanted to tell you this in person." She started to cry. "I'm so sorry. It was all my fault. I'm so sorry I called you down there like that. You must know he made me do it!"

I was surprised she even remembered. "Naomi, don't you ever apologize for that, understand? You didn't have a choice. None of us did. He had it all planned out, and you did what you had to. I'm just glad you're alive."

"Something else, CeeCee. Thank you. You saved my life."

"I owed you one. Remember the bullet you took for me on Murder Mountain? Speaking of which, exactly how much do you remember about Carl Malone?"

She remembered most of it, up until when Carl hit her at the Falls. So much for the doctor's predictions. She'd been leaving her apartment for work that morning when she was hit in the back of the head and knocked out cold. It wasn't the blow that crushed her skull, though.

She woke up in the trunk of a car and it was a few minutes after she felt the car stop that Carl, or at that time Jim Carlson, opened the trunk. Brooklyn was standing with him, and he had a gun to her head. They were by a pay phone. Carl told Naomi to do whatever she could to make me go down there. Or else she and Brooklyn would die immediately.

"He said you got away, and it wasn't going to happen again," Naomi said.

"I don't understand."

"Neither did I."

Naomi had hoped that if she told me the story about Coop, I would give him a piece of my mind before I left, and that's when I'd find out it wasn't true. She knew me well, and what she'd done was smart.

"I figured as soon as you got off the phone with me, you'd at least get him and make him come down with you. That's why I threw in the part about harming myself. It just so happens my timing was perfect and Coop was out eating breakfast," she said sarcastically.

After she made the call, Carl put her back in the trunk. She wasn't released again until they got to the falls. He walked behind her and Brooklyn with the gun on them both, all the way on the trail and during the climb to the top. He had taken her gun away after hitting her at her apartment.

She didn't think the beating was part of his plan, but when she found the right moment, she tried to push him off the side. He overpowered her. He started kicking her in the face, and that was the last thing she remembered.

"I kind of remember seeing you standing on the edge of the falls, but at the time I was so out of it I had no idea what was going on or where I was," she said. "Did all that really happen?"

I nodded.

"I can't say I really remember much of anything after he beat the life out of me on that godforsaken cliff."

"Which is probably for the best." She obviously hadn't seen us fall over the edge or Michael snap Carl's neck.

With the promise of visiting within the next week or so, Michael and I left. He was going to drop me off at home before going back to his hotel. He had packed the few things I had left in his room before I was released from the hospital. My mother was staying with me and the girls for a while, helping out while I recuperated. Eric was at his parents'.

The day we told the girls about our divorce was one of the worst days of my life. Isabelle, at her innocent four years, was watching cartoons and within twenty minutes of being told, babbled on about how much fun it would be to have two bedrooms. Selina, on the other hand, didn't take the news well at all. She broke down, sobbed, screamed, and begged for it not to happen.

First she yelled at Eric that it was his fault, and then she yelled it was mine. Then she didn't want to live with either one of us and, finally she calmed down enough to throw herself into Eric's arms, still crying.

I tried to hold it together for her sake, but watching her made me break down. I wished at that point that I would've been able to deal with Jordan being pregnant and their relationship so we wouldn't have to get divorced and hurt our children, but I couldn't.

Watching Selina so devastated, I even thought I'd be able to put Michael on hold for a while if I had to, but I couldn't get over the impending baby. I could only imagine how she was going to react to the news of Jordan's pregnancy.

Ultimately, like most children, Selina was resilient and accepted it. She pouted and was very quiet for a few days before telling me that she was okay with everything and that "we'll all be fine, Mom." Her maturity at ten years old never ceased to amaze me.

Michael was concerned about the girls and how they took it. I think he knew I was taking it hard and tried not to push anything. When I first got home from the hospital, we went almost a week without seeing each other, a period he called "excruciatingly painful."

It was almost a month after the incident that Michael came to my house with my dad, which greatly surprised me. They both looked grim. There was something I needed to see. We were sitting in my living room when Michael handed me a large yellow envelope.

"What's this?"

"Just open it."

I pulled out a large, old-looking photo of a little girl walking with a policeman. They looked like they were in a field by some woods. The little girl was holding the policeman's hand, and they were walking away from the camera. The little girl had turned her head, looking back, when the photo was taken, giving a clear view of her face. A face I recognized instantly.

"Selina?" I flipped the photo over, looking for a date, since I had never seen the photo before. A growing sense of dread and remembrance of the face told me it wasn't Selina. "Where'd you get this?"

Michael spoke; my dad was pale. "We got it at Carl Malone's the day they searched his house. CeeCee, it's not Selina." He paused. "It's you."

I flipped the photo back over and looked at it, my heart racing. He was right: it was me, and I was about eight years old. The policeman I was walking with was my father.

"I don't understand." I looked back and forth between Michael and my father. "I don't remember this picture. You say Carl Malone had it? How the hell did he get ahold of it?"

"He took the picture, CeeCee."

"Would one of you two please explain to me what this is all about?" I stood up from the couch. "You're scaring me."

"CeeCee, when we found that picture, we thought it was of one of the victims. It took us a while to enhance the photo enough to see the police patch on your dad's arm since his back was to the camera and we couldn't identify him visually. But at the department, your uncle Mitch identified you immediately. That's when I called your dad. I'll let him take it from here." Michael looked over at my father.

My dad stood and came over to the couch and sat me down next to him.

"Honey, you don't remember anything about that day, do you?"

"No."

"I do, every detail. It's haunted me for years, ever since it happened." And then my dad told me the story of the picture.

It was summer, about six months before Carla Dumont

disappeared. My brother, Tony, and I were playing in a creek that was on the far side of a field across the street from our house. A fairly busy road ran along the creek. My father, who had just gotten home from work and was still in uniform, looked out across the field, trying to see me and Tony. He was always worried we would get too close to the road.

Not being able to spot us, he was on his way inside to change clothes when he heard Tony screaming. He saw Tony screaming and running across the field toward the house.

"Every nerve in my body lit up, CeeCee. I didn't see you, so I knew something was wrong. Tony had a look on his face like I'd never seen before."

My dad said he started sprinting toward Tony, and met him halfway in the field. Tony, out of breath and terrified, told him what was happening.

Tony and I had been collecting rocks out of the creek bed when he had to use the bathroom. According to him, every time he would go behind a tree, I would yell, "I see you!" So he went farther back into the woods that ran along the other side of the field.

It was when he came out of the woods that he saw the man pulling me up the small hill by my arm to a waiting car on the side of the road. I was screaming bloody murder. I was a cop's kid and had been taught all about stranger danger. Not only was I screaming, I was trying to bite the man's arm. By the time my dad got there, other cars were stopping on the road, seeing and hearing the commotion, so the man let go, jumped in his car, and drove away.

They only got a description of a blue car and a white man wearing sunglasses and a red baseball cap.

"I looked for him for years after that, CeeCee."

The on-duty police officers were called and an extensive search of the area began, but they found nothing. My dad said I was hysterical by the time he got to me, and I couldn't tell him much more than what Tony said. We stayed by the creek for a good half an hour, speaking to the officers who were trying to get a description from me. Then we walked across the field toward home, my dad holding my hand.

"He had to have driven around, parked somewhere, then hid in the woods. That picture was taken from the woods." He rubbed his temples. "I remember that day as if it were yesterday. I've never been that scared in my life. When Michael brought this picture to me and told me where he got it, I thought my heart was gonna stop."

"You're the only one who got away from him, Cee-Cee, and it angered him in a way none of us would ever be able to understand," Michael said softly. "For the last twenty-six years he's looked forward to this. I didn't tell you this earlier, but your high school yearbook and a cell phone bill that he apparently took from your mailbox were found with the photo. That's how he got your number."

My senior year, my friends and I had all taken a day off to go hiking and drink beer at Hemlock Falls. Similar to Lyon's Falls but not as high, it was also in the state forest area. I was the only one who didn't go up to the top. There was a large photo taken of everyone standing on top, with me at the bottom. The photo wound up in the yearbook with a caption underneath. I don't remember exactly what it said, but it poked fun at me for being scared of heights and staying grounded. That's how he knew my fears.

"After that day, CeeCee, you were scared to leave the yard for a while, but you got over it. You never mentioned it again, so I thought you had forgotten. Even when the little girl was taken from down in London later that year, you never brought it up."

I was almost one of Carl Malone's victims as a child. Even as I sat and listened to them both say it, I didn't believe. Without saying a word to either of them, I walked over to the phone and called my brother in Columbus.

He remembered the day well and told it to me exactly like my father had. He, like my father, thought I had forgotten it, so he never brought up the subject. As I hung up the phone, I felt quite ill. I remembered, now, Carl Malone saying something while we were on the cliff about how I wasn't getting away again. He'd said it to Naomi, too. I just never understood until now.

Waiting for twenty-six years to punish someone the way he wanted to punish me added "pathological narcissism" to the top character traits of Carl Malone. Talk about not taking rejection well. All of this was way too much for me to handle, and I felt myself starting to sweat, as if I was running a fever. I was still by the phone.

"Honey, you should sit down. You don't look very well. Actually, you're green," my father said.

Feeling my lips tingling and fogginess enter my head, I knew what was about to happen. Apparently, Michael did too, because he jumped out of his chair and caught me before I went completely down on my face.

I didn't go out totally, but I wasn't able to sit up, even after a couple of minutes. My dad got a cold washcloth to put over my face and forehead. When I felt able to get up, I crawled over to the couch and pulled myself up on it so I could lie down in comfort.

"What happened? Are you sick?" my dad asked, clearly concerned.

"No. I don't think so. I'll be fine. It's just after talking to Tony I started feeling a little dizzy."

I'm sure the wooziness came from the fact I was realizing that a child murderer tried to make me one of his victims when I was little and had been watching me for most of my life. It was a hard pill to swallow.

I looked at the photograph again. It was like looking at a picture of all the other little girls, the ones who had died. I felt a chill run through my entire body while I stared at my own face. It was a photograph I would never look at again, ever. I put it back in its envelope and handed it to Michael.

"Get this out of here, please. I don't ever want to see it again."

Michael nodded. "You okay?"

"I will be," I said, then added, "someday."

He went out to the car, giving my dad and me the chance to be alone and talk.

When he was satisfied I could hold up my own head and that I would be able to process what almost happened to me so many years ago, my dad brought up the subject of Michael and of my marriage. I came clean and told him everything, making an honest effort to not place all of the blame on Eric.

"Maybe it was my fault, Dad. I had feelings for another man. How is a husband supposed to deal with that? I mean, I tried to deny that I cared for Michael, but the feelings were there, and Eric saw it. He certainly didn't deal with it in the best way since he got Jordan pregnant, but really we're both at fault."

My father has always been close to Eric and treated him like a son. I told him that didn't need to change. Eric would always be the father of his grandchildren and a loving parent to the girls. No matter what else might come between us, that is one area Eric and I will always agree on.

"Are you in love with him?" My dad nodded toward the driveway where Michael was.

"More than I could ever explain, Dad. It's something I've never been able to put my finger on, but it's there. It was different with Eric. I mean, this may sound silly, but with Michael I get butterflies in my stomach. And he knows and accepts me no matter what." I giggled like a schoolgirl.

"I understand completely." He smiled.

Dad came over and enfolded me in his arms, giving me a kiss on the forehead.

We walked outside so I could say good-bye to Michael. He still had his hotel room, but would be leaving soon. His transfer to the Cleveland office hadn't come in yet, so he would have to go back to Virginia. We didn't know how much longer it would be until we were together again. It was something I didn't care to think about right then. Nor did he. I kissed his cheek in front of my dad and watched them pull out of my driveway and head down the road.

CHAPTER THIRTY-FIVE

It took eight months for the FBI to officially close the Carl Malone case and for the rest of us to get acclimated to our new lives.

In the meantime, after Michael went back to Virginia, I bought a massive, brand-new home a block away from the old one, which Eric decided to keep. Michael kept telling me not to buy it, that it was entirely too big. Money wasn't an issue; I had more than enough. I took the book deal, which included a very handsome advance, to write a book about the case. And when Eric and I split, we sold our jointly owned stocks and I got half the proceeds. In my mind, the house was not too big. I just wanted plenty of room for all three children, including Sean, to romp around.

Our divorce finalized, we had agreed to share custody, with each of us keeping the girls three to four days a week. It's a fairly loose arrangement that's been working out very well. All of us have adapted nicely. The girls eventually learned Jordan was pregnant, something Eric and I told them together. They were actually excited and looking forward to having a baby brother. Eric and Jordan had found out the sex a week earlier. Jordan moved in with Eric.

I took things a little slower with Michael. His transfer came in for Cleveland, and he kept an apartment there.

He usually stayed there the days I had the girls and was able to visit with his son, Sean. On the days I was alone, Michael stayed with me and commuted. About twice a month, we would get the girls and Sean together. They all got along well, and Sean took to me surprisingly quickly, as did I to him.

I was off work for only seven weeks, and the sheriff appointed me acting captain until Naomi returned. That was about four months ago. To everybody's relief, she was as good as new. In fact, she was doing so well, she and Coop exchanged vows. I had graciously accepted Naomi's invitation to be her maid of honor, and Coop asked Michael to be his best man.

The ceremony took place at her parents' house, a very large and beautiful home on Pleasant Hill Lake. They had an arched bridge going out to a private dock that was covered with a gazebo. This was where they exchanged their vows. They were lucky; it was early spring and the weather turned out warm and sunny. What a lovely way to start a new life.

I spent most of the day helping Naomi get ready. She was breathtakingly beautiful. Her dress was a light tan formal with spaghetti straps, accented by her blonde hair cascading down onto her shoulders. I told her Coop might fall off the bridge into the water when he saw how incredible she looked.

"You don't look too shabby yourself, CeeCee. Michael may push us off the side and force you to marry him right then and there."

I wore a formal peach-colored strapless gown that clung to my body. It set off my deep tan. (Michael had kept his promise and took me on a dream vacation to Jamaica.) My hair was pulled up with loose strands framing my face.

Standing outside and waiting for the music to begin, I saw that most of the department was there, Eric and Jordan included. I couldn't see Michael or Coop yet, since I was behind a fence that blocked the gazebo. Michael and I were the only members of the wedding party and the ceremony was a civil one, so it wouldn't take too long.

When the music began, I grabbed my bouquet of flowers for my walk down the aisle, Naomi and her father behind me. When I first looked into the gazebo and saw Michael, it took my breath away. He was wearing his black tuxedo and looked stunning. Coop looked good, too, but I couldn't keep my eyes off Michael.

He had the same look on his face when he saw me and I think we both had the same thoughts. And I'd been right about one thing. Coop almost fell over when he saw Naomi walk down the aisle. Michael and I could not stop looking at each other throughout the entire ceremony.

All in all, it was a perfect day for Naomi and Coop, and I was thrilled. Toward the end of the evening, I had walked away from everyone and was standing on the dock looking at the full moon shining on the water. I had only been there for a few minutes when I felt Michael put his arms around my waist.

"I was looking for you, gorgeous. What are you doing down here?"

"Thinking."

"May I ask about what?"

"Yes, you may. I was just thinking about how the name CeeCee Hagerman sounds. I'm not sure, what do you think?"

"Do you mean that, CeeCee? You'll marry me?" he said quietly.

"I do."

He pulled me into a kiss that would win awards. When we stopped we just looked at each other.

"Michael, you realize, don't you, that a life with me is never a boring one?"

He laughed and picked me up off the ground. "That it isn't, Sergeant. That it isn't."

AUTHOR'S NOTE

Although fictional, *The Devil's Closet* was inspired by an actual case that I investigated during the course of my law-enforcement career. It is said that all law-enforcement officers have that one particular case that becomes permanently embedded in their memories—and souls. The case that I refer to here is that "one" for me.

The inspiration for the book is a man or monster (take your pick), that I investigated for child pornography after the case was passed along to me by the FBI. Unfortunately, the case became much more than that. As a parent and human being, it's frightening for me to realize that a man such as this, a man I'll call the Doll Man, has been functioning in our society for the fifty-plus years of his life.

Take a minute and look out your window across the street to your neighbor's house: the quiet, private neighbor with the well-manicured lawn who has been in the neighborhood for over twenty-five years. Most consider him harmless, right? I'm sure the Doll Man's neighbors were just as naïve until I found his personal chamber of horrors. Little did the parents know that on the days their small children were playing outside in the sprinkler, the kids were being photographed by a dark shadow that loomed in the attic of a house down the street. In reality, to comprehend another human being as sadistic and ill as the Doll Man is sometimes too much for the average citizen to bear.

Only a few significant scenes and characteristics of *The Devil's Closet* are actual accounts of situations I encountered during the investigation. The scene when CeeCee describes the contents of the closet, I can assure you, is true. The fictional killer's modified doll, as disturbing as it seems, is also true. I couldn't help incorporating the Doll Man's utter hatred for me into the fictional killer's feelings of CeeCee. The numerous death threats made during the investigation led me to believe that the Doll Man knew that I saw him for what he was. Of course, like CeeCee does in the novel, I took his favorite doll, which further infuriated him. He didn't fixate on the FBI agents, the other detectives, or anyone else—only me. Of course, these threats ultimately added several months to his sentence. He was convicted of child pornography and aggravated menacing. Frightening is the fact that this man is now out among us again, with no supervision or sex-offender label. He's out to do what he pleases.

If you wonder how this is possible, understand it is not a crime in the state of Ohio (or any state I'm aware of) to pretend that a harem of dolls are little girls. To sexually molest life-sized dolls while pretending they're little girls is quite legal. Disturbing, isn't it? But the question remains: Where does it end? There was no concrete evidence that this man had ever touched or harmed a child, and the investigation was not authorized to go forward. Like most writers, my imagination went into overdrive at that point. What is he doing? What *has* he done in the past? What *will* he do in the future? How long will he be satisfied with only dolls? My concerns fell on deaf ears.

Some of you may remember the case of Amy Mihaljevic,

the ten-year-old girl abducted from a Cleveland suburb and brutally murdered in 1989. Her killer was never found, and although there has been much speculation from the experts, no arrest has been made. Chillingly, her body was found in a cornfield less than fifteen miles from the Doll Man's house. Coincidence? Could be, but, again, there's always the possibility. This is a possibility I have considered since the day I opened his closet doors.

It's an unsettling story, one I felt could be told through CeeCee and her coworkers. Although CeeCee's family and friends strongly resemble my own, they are not my family and friends. With such a disconcerting subject, I added more of CeeCee's ongoing romance with Michael to lighten it a bit. The reality of it is that marriages in law enforcement make Hollywood marriages look like those in the Bible belt. Sad, but true.

Every time we turn the news on it seems that another child has been abducted or, worse, murdered. The unfortunate reality is that there are many child predators, like the fictional killer in *The Devil's Closet*, who exist in society without our knowledge. They could be your quiet neighbor next door, the retired fellow who bags your groceries, or even your child's Little League coach. Be diligent and aware.

I hope you'll walk away from *The Devil's Closet* with not only an enjoyable read, but also a clear message. The message isn't that you should spend your life looking over your shoulder.

But the next time you're walking with your child at the park on a warm summer day, you may want to hold his or her hand just a little tighter. I know I will.

—Stacy Dittrich

Turn the page for an advance look at Stacy Dittrich's next thrilling novel.

CEECEE GALLAGHER WILL RETURN IN . . .

MARY JANE'S GRAVE

COMING IN MAY 2009

PROLOGUE

March 3, 1898

She had been unconscious only for a few moments, but that brief reprieve had been more than welcome. Now, as she opened her eyes and saw the men peering down at her, she prayed for the blackness to envelop her once again.

Her legs were broken, and she was unable to move away. The runt of the bunch and the one with the terrible skin had been responsible, their leader standing apart watching it all, laughing. Now, the brightness of their torches was an assault upon her sight, and she closed her eyes to restore the bleak comfort of the dark, cold night.

She opened her swollen eyes and tried to focus on the small lifeless shape that lay ten feet away; it had once been her baby son, Ezra. They had killed him, just as they intended to kill her, and had forced her to watch. Never had she known such anguish, and a part of her had died along with the child. Only her body continued to endure, but for how long? And did it really matter?

She pulled herself up by her arms, feeling the blood run into her eyes, blinding her. A sharp pain in her left side forced her to lie down on the ground again. Their kicking had finally begun to taper off. Could they be getting tired? She lay motionless, praying that Madeline had gotten away, if only to be spared witnessing the horrific acts taking place here in front of their home.

She knew the men blamed her for something she'd had no part in, and she rued the day the girl had pulled up in her horse and buggy asking her for the medicine. If she'd only known then, she would have sent her away and told her never to return. But now it was too late. There was no escaping her nightmare. There was only "the blessing."

Ever since she was a small child, her mother had taught her that the blessing was only to be used for the good of others, not for their downfall. Her mother had had the blessing, as had her sister and her grandmother, and she suspected that Madeline had it, too, although they'd never discussed it. She had wanted to wait until Madeline was eighteen and a grown woman before telling her of the special gift God had blessed her with. But from this day forward, if Madeline escaped from these men, she would be on her own and would have to discover it for herself.

She smelled the sour alcohol on their breath as the men's rough hands reached out to grab her arms and drag her toward the large pine tree that dominated the land in front of her house. She suddenly flashed on an image of her husband, Joseph, who had died two months after Ezra was born. How proud he had been of his son! She hoped they were together now, and she told herself she would be seeing them soon, very soon. She stared at baby Ezra's body for one last time as they pulled the rope around her neck, and as it tightened, finally a new emotion rose within her. Rage.

"Die, witch!" the men shouted in unison.

It was then that she made the decision. Putting aside all she had been taught, she vowed that these men would pay dearly for what they had done.

"Do it!" the leader yelled. And as she felt the rope be-gin to pull her upward, she used every ounce of her last breath to finish what she had begun. *"Ego vomica quisque vestrum, Ego vomica vos totus!"* she managed to croak as the noose grew tighter.

And then the darkness she had prayed for finally came.

CHAPTER ONE

Present Day

The healing rays of the sun shone down on me as I dug my toes into the warm, crystal white sand. Closing my eyes, I listened to the tranquil sound of the waves breaking ten feet away. Michael's hands lovingly caressed my shoulders, and I knew I was about as close as I could get to heaven on earth . . .

And then the phone rang, and I was no longer on my fantasy beach, but here in bed, my body screaming that I had been asleep for only five minutes. After painfully forcing my eyes open, I focused on the clock next to me.

Wrong! I had been asleep for five hours. I closed my eyes again as Michael sleepily groped toward the phone, picked it up, and mumbled, "Hello?"

I prayed that the call was for him, not me, but I expected the worst. Michael was a supervising agent with the FBI, but rarely got phone calls in the middle of the night. I, on the other hand, received them at least once a week. Because I worked in the major crimes division for the Mansfield, Ohio, Richland Metropolitan Police Department, most calls came straight to me. Still, I prayed the call was for Michael. God, I needed more sleep.

"It's for you, Cee," he mumbled, handing me the phone and snuggling deeper beneath the covers.

Damn! As my dream of suntan lotion and a fabulous

massage ebbed away, I switched on the bedside lamp. "Detective Sergeant Gallagher," I said, trying to sound official.

"Sergeant Gallagher, it's Jan at the Communications Center. There's been a homicide at Mt. Olive Cemetery at the end of Tucker Road, and we need you there as soon as possible."

"Are you talking about Mary Jane's Grave? Seriously?"

"Yes, ma'am, we were all talking about that, too. Captain Cooper is already on her way and told us to call you."

"All right, give me half an hour." I cradled the phone, threw on some clothes, and gulped down some O.J. There was no way that I wanted to leave my fiancé and my warm bed to examine a dead body at this ungodly hour. But Mary Jane's Grave added a new level of urgency to this summons.

As if he could read my thoughts, Michael asked, "What was that all about? Who's Mary Jane?"

"It's been a local haunt for as long as I can remember. Legend has it a witch, Mary Jane, was hanged from a pine tree in the middle of this old cemetery. Supposedly, a burnt cross formed in the tree because she was buried underneath it.

"People tell stories about weird things that happened to them at the gravesite. My friends and I would go there when I was in high school, daring each other to stay there for a while."

"Are the stories true?" Michael asked.

"Nope. Obviously, local historians have looked into it. Mary Jane was nothing but a herbalist who cleaned houses, died of cancer, and was buried in a normal grave. There's a campground nearby, so the legend probably got started to scare campers. The cemetery *is* pretty creepy, though."

"Sounds like it. I'll go make you some coffee," Michael offered, now awake. What a guy, I marveled. But then I reminded myself that he'd probably jump back into bed the minute I kissed him good-bye and shut the door. Life wasn't fair.

If someone had told me two years ago that I'd be engaged to Michael Hagerman, I wouldn't have believed it. Two years ago, I'd said good-bye to him for what I thought would be the last time.

My divorce from Eric had been finalized six months ago, and his son with second wife, Jordan, was now five months old, so everything had worked out just fine. Even Michael's six-year-old son, Sean, got tossed into the mix, staying with us every other weekend. His ex-wife, Vanessa, now lives in Cleveland.

Michael makes the hour commute to the Cleveland FBI office every day and has never complained. It meant the world to him for us to be together; we'd been through a lot. I wore my engagement ring faithfully, but continued putting off a wedding date. I tried to not let my ten-year, failed marriage to Eric make me bitter, but sometimes it got the better of me.

Looking into the mirror for a final inspection before I left, I paused. Appearing in a pane of mirrored glass, I saw what everyone else did. CeeCee Gallagher: long blonde hair, piercing green eyes, and a face that, for a brief time, graced the covers of newsmagazines.

On the outside, I was an attractive thirty-four-year-old woman admired by her coworkers, with a reputation for toughness beyond her years. But deep down, I heard the occasional whisper of insecurity as I found myself questioning my ability to continue pulling off law-enforcement miracles. The curse of high expectations—my own as well as those of my community—was a shadow that followed me everywhere. Sure, it made me a better cop, but I often wondered, at what expense?

I sighed. It was time to get my butt out of here and find out why this latest victim was lying dead at Mary Jane's Grave.

Michael handed me my coffee as I was walking out the door.

"Do you want some garlic or something to take with you? I can't have my gorgeous, soon-to-be-wife getting hurt."

"Very cute. There's supposedly a witch buried there, not a vampire," I reminded him.

He grinned impishly as I gulped down my first coffee of the day, welcoming the warm burst of caffeine. "Sorry, I'll be home today brushing up on my creatures of the night facts," he said.

"You'd better," I murmured, kissing him good-bye. "There'll be a quiz when I get home."

On my way to the homicide scene, I turned up the SUV's heater and admonished myself for not grabbing a jacket. Although the days were still warm, the fall nights could be bitter cold.

This murderer had a sick sense of humor. With Halloween just weeks away, the perp evidently thought law enforcement would get turned on by the location. But I was not amused. Although the grave is nothing but a myth, the childhood stories I'd heard about my clairvoyant relatives and bona fide exorcisms were enough to make me fear anything that lacked a pulse. Raised as a good Catholic girl, I don't believe in ghosts, but I do believe in something; I just don't know what that is—yet. Let's just say I respect the dead.

Turning onto Tucker Road brought back a flood of memories. The foothills of the Appalachian Mountains were beautiful terrain by daylight, but very different at night. I hadn't been on Tucker Road since high school. Even after I began working for the force, I wouldn't drive back here; there was no reason to do so, I told myself.

As the asphalt narrowed into a dirt road and then into something that resembled a hiking trail, I was careful to maneuver my SUV around the deep ruts in the ground. I parked behind the last car in a line of police vehicles, their lights spinning in the darkness like a Friday night disco.

As I walked between the line of cars, I passed two uniformed officers talking to four teenagers seated on the ground. All the youths looked pale and grief stricken. One of the girls was crying hysterically, and I assumed they were the ones who had found the body.

"Excuse me, Officer, are they witnesses?" I asked Jack, the taller of the two men.

"They found the body, Sergeant. You need to talk to them, right?" he asked, though he knew the answer.

"Of course. Have their parents been notified?"

"They're on the way."

"Just have them all go downtown and wait for me. There's no sense in them standing out here freezing. I'll probably be a while."

I continued toward the bright floodlights illuminating the cemetery. I felt bad for those kids. Unfortunately, what they had seen tonight was something they would never forget as long as they lived.

The crime laboratory had managed to get its vans back into the cemetery so they could collect all the evidence and process the entire scene. Until they finished, no one could do a thing. I saw Captain Naomi Cooper and her husband, Jeff, standing by the entrance to the cemetery.

With all of the crime lab equipment and vans, I couldn't see the body and since I knew nothing about the murder, I promptly asked Naomi to fill me in. "What happened?"

"Spooky, isn't it, CeeCee?" Coop whispered.

"Not hardly. Prank gone bad or what?"

"I don't think so." Naomi continued to look out over the vans. "It's not pretty. She was strangled, and apparently parts of her body were burned. Someone also cut her wrist."

Not your ordinary recitation of physical abuses. "I wonder why?" I asked her.

"Probably to paint the big bloody *M* that's on the tree above her," offered Naomi.

"You mean she's actually at *the* tree?"

"Yes, and wait until you hear what the kids who found her are saying."

"Was there any sexual assault?"

"We don't know yet," Coop put in. "As remote as this place is, no one would hear anything if there had been."

I looked over at the vans and saw one of the crime lab technicians wave us over. They had finally completed the scene, and we were now free to poke about.

As I came around the side of the van to face the actual site where the body lay, I felt myself suck in a massive amount of air. The victim, a pretty young blonde, was sitting upright with her back against the tree. Her eyes were open and speckled with broken blood vessels from the strangulation. She was shirtless and braless, exposing the odd triangular burn marks that went across her chest just below her neck.

Her arms were down at her sides with the palms facing upward; a large cut across her left wrist had poured blood into her palm. It was this blood that had likely been used to paint a large *M* on the tree directly above her. Like most homicide scenes, it was not for the faint of heart.

One disturbing reaction I tend to have at homicides that involve young girls is superimposing the image of my daughters' faces onto that of the victim. I wonder what it would be like to be a parent and have your child brutalized to the point of death. While just a split-second reaction, the idea always makes me feel momentarily light-headed.

"Good Lord," I muttered under my breath. I began to slowly walk around the body, observing all of it from a closer point of view. One of the crime lab technicians was standing a few feet away and sauntered over to compare notes.

"What do you make of this, Bob?" I asked. I was pleased to see him here—Bob was one of our better lab techs, and I respected his opinion.

Rubbing his chin thoughtfully, he offered: "Other than the fact that murderer was a very disturbed individual, I haven't made much, CeeCee. I took blood samples and photographed the burns. I couldn't find any shoe prints other than hers and that of the kid who walked up here. No trace of any weapon that could have cut her wrist. Her shirt and bra are nowhere to be found. I photographed the kids' shoe treads and took dirt samples from the area and from inside their car."

"What about the strangulation? If it was done manually, you should be able to swab her neck for DNA, no?"

"I don't see any ligature marks, so a manual strangulation would be my first guess, too. The coroner should be here any minute," Bob said, looking toward the road.

"Why don't you go ahead and swab her neck anyway, just in case," I suggested.

"No problem," he agreed. "Nothing else to do while we wait."

I watched as Bob took out a long cotton swab from the back of the van and put a couple of drops of sterile water on it. Wearing latex gloves, he carefully took the swab and rubbed it over the entire neck area of the victim. Our best-case scenario would be that we'd find the killer's DNA and run it through a statewide database known as C.O.D.I.S, which holds the DNA of anyone ever incarcerated in a state prison. Even if the killer hadn't been in prison before, we could still use the DNA as a match when we found a suspect.

The worst-case scenario would be that no DNA would be found, but I wasn't ready to entertain that scenario.

"What was she doing here?" I asked Coop, who was standing nearby.

"According to the kids who found her, they were all here together," he answered.

"How is that possible unless they're responsible?" I asked. "And why didn't you tell me this in the first place?"

"Hey, take it easy," Coop said soothingly. "You'll have to talk to them. Allegedly, they dared the girl to walk back here by herself, and she took the bait." He walked over and stood next to me, looking down at the body. "When she didn't come back, they walked down here to find her, and voilà! They claim that no cars passed them on the way in, and there weren't any down here when they found her. They're all pretty torn up. I don't get the feeling that they're lying."

"That's a little strange, though, Coop, don't you think? Is anybody out talking to the nearest residents and farmers?"

"The uniforms are on it."

"Had I known this earlier, I would've blocked off the road from the asphalt on down," I murmured, irritated. "We may have been able to get tire tracks. Now that every cop car in the county is parked down here, it's pretty pointless."

"Don't look at me," Coop said defensively. "Naomi and I got here right before you did."

I was interrupted by the arrival of the Richland County Coroner and his assistant, J. P. Sanders, who, regardless of the circumstances, would have every officer at a crime scene laughing hysterically within minutes. In his late fifties, with gray hair and Coke-bottle glasses, J.P. has an unusual talent for lightening the most intense situation. To his credit, however, he will maintain the utmost professionalism when in the presence of family members. He has never disrespected the dead; he merely tries to make it easier for us to cope.

J.P. is also the person you'd most want to consult with at a homicide scene. He could look at any evidence and tell you just about everything you'd want to know. Even though the county coroner is an elected position, everyone for the last thirty years has kept J.P. as the assistant—a smart move, since he knew more than all of them combined.

"J.P., long time no see," welcomed Coop. "How's business?"

"Dead."

I smiled as I watched J.P. eye Bob, who was fairly new to the crime lab and had yet to experience a crime scene with J.P. He was fresh, juicy bait. Coop winked at me. We all waited to see what J.P. would do next. He carried his suitcase-sized bag and set it down next to the van.

He started fumbling around in it as if looking for the most important of all tools, and I couldn't stop myself from bursting out laughing as he pulled out a large-brimmed black witch's hat and put it on top of his head. The hat was so large it fell over his eyes.

"That's just wrong." Coop laughed, wiping tears from his eyes.

J.P. had more gadgets and one-liners than anyone I'd ever known. I didn't doubt for a minute that when he was called here, he'd known exactly where to find the witch's hat—probably in his bedroom closet. But he wasn't finished with us yet.

Bob's mouth had already dropped to the ground when J.P. produced the hat. Now, he was watching intently as J.P. leaned over the body, still wearing the hat, scanning it up and down before stopping in the area of the victim's legs.

"Well. I'll be damned. Did anyone photograph this?"

Bob, who prided himself on covering every aspect of a crime scene, darted over to J.P. and put his hands on his hips. "What? I photographed everything!"

"You didn't photograph this, kiddo. Haven't seen one in a while, but this victim has a cheek-for."

"What the hell is a cheek-for?" Bob took the bait hook, line, and sinker.

J.P. stood and kissed Bob's right cheek, sending Bob into a tailspin. He violently wiped his hand across his face.

"What's wrong with you? Are you crazy!"

Our laughter prompted Bob to stop and realize the joke he'd just missed. When he caught on, he was quite embarrassed.

"Oh, I get it. Very funny."

"You're lucky he didn't do the butt-for joke, Bob," Naomi laughed.

Once everyone regained their composure, J.P. removed the hat, put the jokes aside, and got down to business. He wouldn't do much here; right now, he was just looking over the body before they bagged it and took it away for more extensive tests. I saw him scrunch up his face and rub his chin as he looked at the marks on the victim's chest.

"What is it, J.P.?" I asked, realizing that he'd seen something.

"These burns," he said, pointing to the marks. "I would bet my wife's fat fanny they came from a fireplace poker. The point is a dead giveaway, no pun intended."

"How would someone keep it hot if there wasn't a fire nearby?" Coop asked. "With a blowtorch?"

"We'll know more by the end of the week. CeeCee, can you forward all your paperwork to me when you're done?"

"Of course," I told him. "I'll work up the case as fast as I can. How's a two-day turnaround?"

There wasn't much more for me to do here; the next step was to read all the reports on the incident and then get my input over to J.P. It was near daybreak, and I was sure the distraught teens were ready to go home. They'd been waiting at headquarters with their parents for almost two hours now, and their imaginations must be working overtime.

Sighing, I pulled open my car door and climbed in. I felt tired and cranky; it had been another long night, and I didn't do well with interrupted sleep—an unavoidable aspect of this crazy job. Now I had to deal with an unhappy group of people who wanted nothing more than to go home and forget what had happened that night at Mary Jane's Grave.

But it was my job to find out.

SANDRA RUTTAN

The police get the call: A four-year-old boy has been found beaten to death in the park. And almost as soon as Hart and Tain arrive at the scene, the case takes a strange turn.

They find the victim's brother hiding in the woods nearby. He says he saw the whole thing and claims his older sister is the killer. And she's missing....

When the boy's father is notified that his son is dead, his first response is to hire a high-powered attorney, who seems determined to create every legal roadblock he can for Hart and Tain. The search is on for the missing girl, and the case is about to get even stranger.

THE
FRAILTY
OF FLESH

ISBN 13: 978-0-8439-6075-4

**HOW MUCH DO YOU OWE
A FORMER LOVE?**

WINDY CITY
KNIGHTS

Against his better judgment, private detective
Ron Shade let Paula back into his life, but then
she left again, without so much as a good-bye
kiss. Now she's turned up dead. Paula's cousin
doesn't think her death was an accident, and she
wants Shade to find out the truth. But the truth
is hard to find, and every time he gets close to it,
someone gets killed.

MICHAEL A. BLACK

ISBN 13: 978-0-8439-6162-1

LEE JACKSON

REDEMPTION

Even though he never had a trial, Homeland Security has labeled Ben Trinity a terrorist. Guilty or innocent, it doesn't matter. He's been forever marked. Free on parole, Trinity just wants to start over. And since it appears he'll be stuck there for a while, Redemption, Montana, seems as good a place as any. But everyone knows it's impossible to keep a big secret in a small town. And once the residents of Redemption get wind of Trinity's past, they have no intention of letting him have a future....

ISBN 13: 978-0-8439-6158-4

✂ ❑ **YES!**

Sign me up for the Leisure Thriller Book Club and send my FREE BOOKS! If I choose to stay in the club, I will pay only $8.50* each month, a savings of $7.48!

NAME: _____

ADDRESS: _____

TELEPHONE: _____

EMAIL: _____

❑ I want to pay by credit card.

❑ **VISA**   ❑ **MasterCard.**   ❑ **DISCOVER**

ACCOUNT #: _____

EXPIRATION DATE: _____

SIGNATURE: _____

Mail this page along with $2.00 shipping and handling to:
Leisure Thriller Book Club
PO Box 6640
Wayne, PA 19087
Or fax (must include credit card information) to:
610-995-9274
You can also sign up online at **www.dorchesterpub.com**.

*Plus $2.00 for shipping. Offer open to residents of the U.S. and Canada only. Canadian residents please call 1-800-481-9191 for pricing information.

If under 18, a parent or guardian must sign. Terms, prices and conditions subject to change. Subscription subject to acceptance. Dorchester Publishing reserves the right to reject any order or cancel any subscription.